D0042273

Hi, I'm JIMMY!

Like me, you probably noticed the world is run by adults.
But ask yourself: Who would do the best job
of making books that *kids* will love?
Yeah. **Kids!**

So that's how the idea of JIMMY books came to life.
We want every JIMMY book to be so good
that when you're finished, you'll say,
"PLEASE GIVE ME ANOTHER BOOK!"

Give this one a try and see if you agree.
(If not, you're probably an adult!)

JIMMY PATTERSON BOOKS FOR YOUNG READERS

For exclusives, trailers, and other information,
visit jimmypatterson.org.

ERNESTINE
Catastrophe Queen

MERRILL WYATT

JIMMY Patterson Books
Little, Brown and Company
New York Boston London

Text copyright © 2018 by Merrill Wyatt
Illustrations copyright © 2018 by Joey Chou

JIMMY Patterson Books / Little, Brown and Company
Hachette Book Group
1290 Avenue of the Americas, New York, NY 10104
JimmyPatterson.org

First Edition: August 2018

JIMMY Patterson Books is an imprint of Little, Brown and Company, a division of Hachette Book Group, Inc. The Little, Brown name and logo are trademarks of Hachette Book Group, Inc. The JIMMY Patterson Books® name and logo are trademarks of JBP Business, LLC.

The publisher is not responsible for websites (or their content) that are not owned by the publisher.

The Hachette Speakers Bureau provides a wide range of authors for speaking events. To find out more, go to hachettespeakersbureau.com or call (866) 376-6591.

Library of Congress Cataloging-in-Publication Data

Names: Wyatt, Merrill, author.
Title: Ernestine, catastrophe queen / Merrill Wyatt.
Description: First edition. | New York ; Boston : Jimmy Patterson Books, Little, Brown and Company, 2018. | Summary: While trying to jumpstart the zombie apocalypse, twelve-year-old Ernestine Montgomery and her new stepbrother, Charleston, stumble upon a murder mystery in the retirement apartments where their parents do maintenance.
Identifiers: LCCN 2017036919| ISBN 9780316471589 (hardcover) | ISBN 0316471585 (hardcover)
Subjects: | CYAC: Eccentrics and eccentricities. | Retirement communities—Fiction. | Zombies—Fiction. | Stepbrothers—Fiction. | Humorous stories. | Mystery and detective stories.
Classification: LCC PZ7.1.W975 Ern 2018 | DDC [Fic]—dc23
LC record available at https://lccn.loc.gov/2017036919

10 9 8 7 6 5 4 3 2 1

LSC-C

To my parents and grandmother,
for reading to me tirelessly as a child
& to my daughter, Abigail,
for letting me do the same.

Foreword

When I first read *Ernestine, Catastrophe Queen,* I was instantly hooked on its strong, smart heroine. Ernestine is laugh-out-loud funny and totally unforgettable. She likes taking charge and being right — and she usually is. Most important of all, she'll do whatever it takes to protect her family and friends. She's a character that every kid can look up to. Ernestine's story also has an important message: sometimes relying on yourself isn't as rewarding as relying on others.

This is a clever, rollicking mystery with a lot of heart, and I hope you love solving it along with your new friend Ernestine.

—James Patterson

ERNESTINE
Catastrophe Queen

HERBERT EDWARD
McGOVERN
1940 – 1977

Chapter One
The Apocalypse Begins, Sort Of

MONDAY, 11:58 PM

The zombie apocalypse was coming.

Tonight, in fact.

At least it would if almost-thirteen-year-old Ernestine Verna Montgomery had anything to say about it. In her opinion, it really should have arrived years ago, but that was life for you. Things never did go the way they should. Sometimes, rather than waiting around for the zombie apocalypse to happen all on its own, you had to go ahead and bring the undead back to life yourself. No sense in waiting around for someone else to do it for you.

Which was why Ernestine was hanging out in the

graveyard with her ten-year-old stepbrother, Charleston Wheeler, of course. Why else would anyone hang out in a graveyard at almost midnight on a bitterly cold February night? Or any night, for that matter?

"So, did you get the chicken blood?" she asked, her pajama-ed posterior slowly going numb through her winter coat. She was sitting on a weathered gravestone, which wasn't the coziest of places to sit at the best of times. On her lap she held a very thick, very battered notebook in which she kept track of all the bits and pieces of arcane zombie lore she'd picked up over the years from comic books, horror movies, and some very strange websites.

"Sorta." Charleston pulled out a plastic-wrapped package of chicken drumsticks. "Turns out you can't just go to the grocery store and buy a can of the stuff. But these are chicken body parts, so they've gotta have blood in them. I mean, body parts are full of blood, right?"

"I'm not sure." Ernestine squinted down at her notebook for confirmation of this new theory while wishing she'd brought a flashlight. The street was only a few yards away, so she'd thought there'd be plenty of city light to see by. However, she hadn't taken into consideration all the trees, whose skeletal branches wove together to form a delightfully creepy barrier. Ernestine approved of the haunted-forest ambiance it lent to the haunted-cemetery vibe but had to admit the crumbling tombstones and mausoleums could definitely use some mood lighting. Again, that was life for you. The universe never set the stage properly. "Couldn't you have gotten a live chicken?"

"I dunno. It's not like you can pick one up off the shelf next to the cereal."

"Did you try that market over on Bancroft near Ottawa Park? The one where Mr. Talmadge says you don't want to ask any questions about where the venison comes from?"

"Look, you want live chickens, *you* do the shopping. This was the best *I* could do." Charleston pushed his silver-rimmed glasses back up his nose as he thought over what she'd just said. "Hey! I'm not murdering a live chicken!"

"Who said anything about murdering it? It's not like we need *all* of its blood. It can keep most of it. We could've just— you know—*poked* it or something. It'd be like donating blood."

Charleston's breath puffed out like a ghost in the frigid night air. He stomped his feet on the ground to warm them. "Yeah, but I'm not sure the chicken would have liked it."

"Charleston." Sighing, Ernestine laid her pencil in her notebook to mark her place before shutting it. "We are not here to protect poultry rights. *We are here to start the zombie apocalypse.*"

"Then why do we even need a chicken? It's human brains zombies eat, not chicken brains!"

"Only if they haven't taken simple, sensible precautions," Ernestine pointed out, hefting her baseball bat onto the tombstone so it would be handy if she needed to bash in some undead heads. Then she opened up her notebook and carefully crossed *chicken* and *bat* off her list of items required for the apocalypse. "The humans, I mean. Not the chickens. I'm not sure chickens know how to take precautions."

"Good point." Charleston fixed his glasses again. They were always slipping down his nose because, like everything they owned, they'd been purchased secondhand. Though a little more than two years younger than Ernestine, Charleston was quite a bit smaller, only coming up to her shoulder even when she wasn't perched on top of a tombstone. He was really skinny, too, just like his dad, Ernestine's new stepfather, Frank. A snub-nosed face peered out from beneath a lot of shaggy blond hair, while his glasses magnified an already enormous pair of blue eyes almost to the point of transforming him into an anime character.

They weren't related, so Ernestine didn't look at all like her stepbrother, of course. A tall girl, she was one-fourth African American, and her biracial heritage showed in the golden-brown hue of her skin and hair. Her eyes were gray, which Ernestine always thought was an indecisive color. Meanwhile, her hair couldn't decide if it wanted to be kinky or straight, so it compromised by sort of doing both and sort of doing neither. Her hair and eyes might be indecisive but the rest of Ernestine most definitely was not.

When Charleston saw her take out her baseball bat, he picked his up, too. No doubt he figured that if Ernestine needed hers, the zombie hordes were scheduled to arrive at any moment. If there was one thing she'd taught him in the six months since Frank married Maya, her mom, it was that you never knew when you might need to beat something's brains out. Best to always be prepared.

The zombie they were planning on raising was from the grave of one Herbert Edward McGovern, born 1940 and died 1977. Ernestine would have preferred a fresher grave because, really, how much damage could a decades-old corpse do? It would probably spend all of its time trying to make sure its head didn't fall off or forgetting where it had left its ears. Or maybe being embarrassed that its clothes had all decayed away a long time ago. Even a zombie probably didn't want to be naked and undead in the city. What would people say?

Unfortunately, that was the newest grave in the long-aban-doned cemetery. It sat plunk in the middle of the city's Old West End, right across the street from the crumbling mansion known as MacGillicuddie House for Elderly and Retired Art-ists, Both Performing and Otherwise. That was the apartment building where their parents supposedly did the maintenance. The minute they had moved in, Ernestine had known it was destiny. She'd been looking for a handy place to start the apocalypse for some time now, and here the universe just went and handed her hundreds of perfectly good dead bodies nobody else was using. It was definitely Meant to Be.

So what if most of the corpses were all about a hundred years old and probably no more than a bunch of mildew-y old bones? If you were going to start an apocalypse, you had to begin *somewhere*. Ernestine could move on to fresher corpses once she got the hang of things.

"Okay, we've got chicken blood, more or less. And salt." After rummaging about in her backpack, Ernestine set the canister of Morton salt up on the stone. "Now, we just need some grave mold."

Charleston wrinkled his nose at all of the weathered stones. "Looks pretty moldy around here to me."

"Yeah, but it's all frozen." Maybe they should have waited until spring to start the apocalypse, but really, what else are you going to do in the middle of a boring February without much snow? Sledding was out and so was building snowmen and having snowball fights. You could either watch TV or raise an undead army. That was pretty much it.

"But that's good," Charleston argued. "If the zombie is

frozen, it'll be fresher. You know, like sticking stuff in the freezer. Like peas or green beans."

Ernestine mulled that one over while Charleston continued to hop up and down to keep his feet warm. He also took a few practice swings with his baseball bat at imaginary zombies.

"Good point. All right, the only other thing we need is human blood." Hopping down, Ernestine pulled an enormous carving knife out of her backpack.

"Hey, whoa! You're not sacrificing me!" Charleston protectively lifted up his baseball bat, more bug-eyed than ever behind his glasses.

"Don't be ridiculous. *Of course* I'm not sacrificing you. I just need a little bit of your blood. It'll be just like a pinprick. Only, you know, bigger." Ernestine took a step toward him, but Charleston ran around to the other side of the gravestone.

"You can't have any of it!" he protested as the two of them danced around and around the stone.

"Stay still, you big baby!"

"You touch me with that, and I'm telling Dad that you tried to murder me!"

"I'm not trying to *murder* you, I'm trying to *assault* you. It's totally different; ask any prosecutor. Now, *stay still!*" Ernestine dodged a swing of the bat and pounced on Charleston, knocking him to the ground. Knife and baseball bat discarded, the two of them grappled for a minute before Charleston managed to wriggle out from underneath her.

"You can't have *any* of my blood!" he shouted loud enough to wake the dead. "I'm using *all* of it! Every last drop."

"*Fine,*" she huffed. "We'll use my blood, and you can handle the gross, disgusting, slimy chicken parts that are probably covered in salmonella if you'd rather die a horrible, lingering death from a bacterial infection instead of getting your finger nicked, you big baby."

"I would, thanks." Charleston tore the plastic wrap off the package of chicken. The drumsticks slid out of the Styrofoam tray and glopped wetly onto the grave. "Blech."

"Just remember to grab them after the zombie claws its way out of the ground. We can use them for supper tomorrow night." As the only responsible, sensible member of the family, the grocery budget usually fell to Ernestine.

"Don't use all the salt. We'll need some of that for supper, too," advised Charleston as she poured a ring of it around herself. He usually cooked the dinner, which was good since Ernestine had no time for that sort of thing when she had much more interesting things to be doing. Like raising the dead, who weren't all that particular about what they were served as long as human brains were included. "What's the salt for, anyhow?"

"The evil undead can't pass over it," Ernestine explained

knowledgably, getting ready to cut her finger with the carving knife. "That way, the zombie can't grab me and suck my brains out once it's risen from the grave."

"Oh." Charleston looked blank for a moment, an expression almost immediately replaced by panic. "Hey, whoa! I'm not staying out here so it can chew on my brain, either!"

He hopped over the circle of salt and clung to Ernestine's back like a monkey, almost knocking her over.

"Don't be such a scaredy baby! Why do you think I told you to bring a baseball bat? You'll be fine."

"Yeah, as long as I stay inside the salt circle with you." Charleston clung all the tighter to the back of her coat, making it rather difficult to wield the carving knife. Ernestine stood up on tiptoes to make enough room for them both. "By the way, it's midnight. I just checked my watch."

"Okay, let go of my elbow, will you?" Ernestine managed to shake him off enough to raise the knife and jam its tip into her finger. "*Ack!* That hurt."

"Told you."

Several drops of blood splashed onto the frozen ground. Ernestine lifted her arms, knife still in hand, and faced the moon. Well, technically it was the streetlight over by the MacGillicuddie House, but close enough.

Clearing her throat, Ernestine chanted, "*Quantum materiae*

materietur marmota monax si marmota monax materiam possit materiari! Quantum materiae materietur marmota monax si marmota monax materiam possit materiari! Quantum materiae materietur marmota monax si marmota monax materiam possit materiari!"

"What's that mean?" Charleston whispered in awe when she stopped to take a breath.

"I dunno. Something Latin I found online." Ernestine shrugged. "It doesn't really matter. See, everybody knows Latin is a dead language, and zombies are dead, too, right? You've got to use a dead language to summon the dead. It's the only way they'll understand what you're saying."

"Oh." Charleston nodded. "That makes sense."

After that, they were both quiet for a while, breathing in the night air and waiting for the zombie to claw its way up out of the earth. Far away, they could hear the sounds of the freeway. From closer by came the tinkling music and laughter of a party in full swing over at MacGillicuddie House for Retired Artists, Both Performing and Otherwise. There should have been a few ghosts stirring about, moaning and making other ghastly noises in the surrounding abandoned mansions, but if any were awake, they were too scared of the hipsters slowly invading the neighborhood to call attention to themselves.

Finally, Charleston asked, "How long do you suppose it's gonna take?"

"I don't know," Ernestine admitted, teeth chattering in the cold. Now she was actually grateful to have her stepbrother burrowed up against her like a frightened bunny since he was at least a *warm* frightened bunny. "I've never dug my way up out of a grave before. But the ground is frozen, and I bet they didn't bury him with a pickaxe or anything. Most people never have any foresight. When I die, I'm leaving specific instructions in my will to bury me with a cell phone and a shovel."

Just then, something made a very loud metallic *CLANG* on the other side of the street over by MacGillicuddie House. Charleston yelped and tried to climb up onto Ernestine's shoulders in fright, knocking her out of the salt circle and onto her knees.

"It's over there!" he shouted, pointing toward the enormous brick and wrought-iron fence that ran all around Mac-Gillicuddie House's vast yard. "It just went in the front gate! I can see it moving!"

"Get off!" Ernestine wiggled him off her back and into a frosty clump of grass. Getting to her feet, she quickly stuffed all her zombie-raising paraphernalia into her backpack. "That can't be our zombie. It couldn't climb out of the ground without us seeing it."

"Well, it's *somebody's* zombie 'cause there's definitely something over there!"

"That's probably just a guest going to Mrs. MacGillicuddie's party."

"It wasn't! I know it wasn't!"

Ernestine looked uncertainly from Herbert's grave to the wide-open gate across the street. She hated to leave a job unfinished. What if whatever was in the garden was just a drunken guest of one of the artists in residence over at MacGillicuddie House? What if her zombie finally sprouted up out of the grave, only to find nothing to eat?

"*Ernestine.*" Charleston scrambled to his feet and tugged at her coat sleeve.

"Oh, all right." Ernestine hefted her backpack onto her shoulders. "Whatever it is, I suppose we might as well bash its brains in just to be on the safe side."

As they ran through the cemetery, Ernestine kept an eye out for open graves in case it turned out Zombie Herbert really had gotten lost on the way out of the grave. If that was her zombie over there, shouldn't there be a big mound of dirt where it had clawed its way up out of the earth? Maybe it had burrowed sideways like a mole and come up across the street in the garden or something. After all, it was a zombie, right? How hard could it really be to confuse it?

Reaching the chained entrance gate, Ernestine pried it open just enough for Charleston to squeeze through. He'd had the presence of mind to grab the raw drumsticks off the grave and now carried them gloppily in his hands. Ernestine slid through after him, but before they could bolt across the street, a car swerved around the corner on two wheels, squealing and sending clouds of smoke up to dissolve into the black night sky.

It wasn't any ordinary car, though. Ernestine immediately recognized it as Mrs. MacGillicuddie's baby-blue 1937 Studebaker limousine, driven by someone who clearly should not be behind the wheel.

Slamming down onto all four wheels, the car sped up and narrowly missed a fire hydrant before bouncing over several flower planters, freeing a mailbox from its bolts so it could learn to fly. If a nearby park bench could have gotten up and run away on its iron legs, it probably would have. Fortunately, the driver seemed to have grown tired of terrorizing inanimate objects, cranking the wheel hard to the left.

Aiming the car toward the graveyard on the left side of the street.

Straight toward Ernestine and Charleston.

Chapter Two
Even Zombies Like to Party

TUESDAY, 12:23 AM

"EEE-III-AAA-YYY!" Charleston shrieked, still clutching his armful of chicken parts. Ernestine grabbed him by *his* most convenient part (which happened to be his arm) and dragged him across the street just in time to avoid being turned into pre-zombies.

The antique limo swiped the graveyard's wrought-iron gates, breaking apart the chain and padlock. Then, as though the driver was playing a game of tag with Charleston and Ernestine, the car turned again, hurtling toward the brick wall surrounding MacGillicuddie House.

Ernestine ducked into the garden to escape, but Charleston

froze like a deer (or zombie) in headlights. Running back out again, she tried to tug him into the garden with her, but he remained rooted to the ground.

"Charleston!" Ernestine cried, but he just pressed the poultry parts tightly against his body and huddled for impact as the driver hit the brakes, causing the tires to shriek and burn into the ground.

Shoving her stepbrother as hard as she could, they both tumbled out of the way of the car's massive silver grille just in time. Instead of their bodies, it bit into the brick wall as the car came to a halt in a cloud of blue smoke.

Coughing and sputtering, they both rolled over and looked at the dented fender a few inches away from their heads.

"*What were you doing?*" Ernestine demanded, scowling at Charleston. Being afraid always made her irritable.

"You said to make sure we saved the drumsticks for supper." From behind his glasses, Charleston blinked at her like this was obvious.

"Not if it means ending up as a zombie!"

"Wouldn't I just be a corpse, not a zombie?"

"Well, sure, not right away." Exasperated, Ernestine helped her stepbrother up. Charleston never did make any long-term goals. Nobody ever *starts* out as a zombie. It's something you have to work toward, obviously.

The driver's side door flew open and out tumbled their landlady, Mrs. MacGillicuddie, owner of MacGillicuddie House, an apartment building that served as a retired artist colony. Which was sort of like an ant colony only filled with loopy old artists rather than mindless insects. Mrs. MacGillicuddie lived on the ground floor in an apartment approximately the size of a small neighborhood. The rest of the three stories she rented out to retired painters, musicians, and actors, while Ernestine's family lived in the attic and took care of the building.

Mrs. MacGillicuddie herself was eighty years old with jet-black hair, lots of makeup, and a face that had had so much cosmetic surgery done to it that a very exclusive clinic in Switzerland threw a party every year in her honor. Tonight she wore a silver dress, a mink coat, and a real diamond tiara on her head because, as Mrs. MacGillicuddie had once explained to them, when you were eighty, you never knew how many more opportunities you might get to wear the family jewels.

What she wasn't wearing were her glasses, which might possibly explain why she had almost turned Ernestine and Charleston into zombies-in-waiting.

"Oh, hello, darlings!" she trilled as she spotted them. "I didn't see you there!"

"Mrs. MacGillicuddie," Ernestine said sternly. "You *know* you're supposed to be wearing your glasses when you drive."

"Don't be ridiculous, darling!" Her landlady waved her gloved hand about dismissively. "I can see perfectly well without those silly things! However, with all of the fog about tonight, I thought I'd better pull over before something else jumped out at me the way that awful mailbox did. What it was doing in the middle of the road, I don't know!"

"Where's Eduardo?" Ernestine demanded, referring to Mrs. MacGillicuddie's butler and limo driver.

Eduardo himself answered the question by tumbling out of the car, dressed as a Roman general for reasons unknown. After the wild car ride, his feathered helmet was askew on his head and he seemed a bit unsteady on his legs. Still, he managed to remain impressively upright, which was just as well given that he also held a swan in his arms.

Ernestine and Charleston stared at them both. This was not, exactly, what Ernestine had in mind for an apocalypse. Their zombie was missing and now they seemed to have gained a swan.

"Oh, the swan's ours!" The Swanson twins, Libby and Mora, tittered as they climbed out of the back of the limo and saw Charleston and Ernestine's looks of confusion. They had just moved into apartment 3A the previous week, and by the standards of MacGillicuddie House, the twins were quite young, being only about sixty years old, and they were identical, right down to every last wrinkle. They had once been famous acrobatic dancers, known for their ability to each simultaneously balance a spinning plate upon a big toe while balancing on a tightrope. How a person discovered they had this ability, Ernestine didn't know, but evidently the Swanson twins had found a way.

Tonight, they wore their signature swan costumes, which involved sparkly white swimsuits with enormous white feather headdresses, more white feathers around their wrists, and extremely high, sparkly heels that Ernestine suspected you had to be a certified acrobat to even buy, let alone walk in. They made the stiletto high heels Mrs. MacGillicuddie always wore seem downright sensible.

As soon as the Swanson twins made it out of the car, they were followed by Mrs. Talmadge, a pink-haired, retired British pastry chef who lived in apartment 2C.

A pink-haired, retired British pastry chef who was carrying the front end of a whole roast pig. Well, Ernestine assumed it was whole. Right now she could only see its snout, an apple shoved into its mouth.

"Oh, hullo, luv!" Dressed as an egg with horns, she gave Ernestine a cheerful little finger wave. "Have you come for the party?"

"No, I'm looking for my zombie. I seem to have lost it."

"Oi, keep on moving there, Pansy." The roast pig poked at Mrs. Talmadge. For one startled moment, Ernestine thought that not only was it a zombie roast pig, but one that had also learned to talk in spite of the apple stuffed in its mouth. Then Mrs. Talmadge tugged the pig free of the car, allowing her husband, Mr. Talmadge, to emerge.

"Vegan garbage," he muttered. Mr. Talmadge carried a rubber knife and had cereal boxes strapped all over his body. "Frou-frou rabbit food, that's what he was trying to serve us. What she was thinking having him cater, I don't know."

"I thought there was a party going on in your suite, Mrs. MacGillicuddie." Charleston peered through the wrought-iron bars of the fence to confirm that, yep, there were indeed the silhouettes of people clearly having a very good time in Mrs. MacGillicuddie's half of the mansion's first floor.

"Oh, there *is,* darling! A costume party for Mardi Gras!"

"But it isn't Mardi Gras yet," Ernestine pointed out.

"Well, I don't want to be throwing a Mardi Gras party when *everyone else* is throwing a Mardi Gras party, now do I? How *gauche* would that be?" Mrs. MacGillicuddie took the swan from Eduardo and set it down on the ground so it could follow along next to her on its leash. "We just had to run out and get some meat for Mr. Talmadge since he doesn't like the vegan canapés dear little Dill was serving, and some swans for the Swansons here! Eduardo had forgotten them, the silly boy!"

Eduardo, who hadn't been a boy in at least fifty years, leaned over to murmur into Mrs. MacGillicuddie's ear. As he did so, the feathers on top of his helmet swiped across Ernestine's face like a mop. She sneezed and swatted them away, as he murmured in his posh Spanish accent, "I thought the sight of Libby's swan might get Mr. Sangfroid more excited than his heart could take."

Mrs. MacGillicuddie giggled and said to Eduardo, "Oh, you *are* terrible!"

Mr. Sangfroid lived in apartment 2D and had once been an art curator. These days, he spent most of his time as a professional cranky old man, always complaining about something. Why a swan might make him grumpier than usual, though, was a mystery to Ernestine. However, before she could ask, Mrs. MacGillicuddie cried, "Come join us, my darlings! I'm sure your parents won't mind!"

"Okay." Never one to mind staying up late and missing school, Charleston stepped agreeably forward, only to jump backward again when the swan hissed and flapped her wings at him.

He followed her beady gaze down to the dismembered poultry parts in his arms. To the swan, he said, "Oh. Don't worry. They weren't relatives. Well, maybe distantly, I guess."

"No, thank you," Ernestine said firmly to Mrs. MacGillicuddie, still wiping feathers off her face as Charleston made friends with the bird. "We have school in the morning, and we have to find our zombie. We seem to have misplaced it."

"Oh, well, if you find it, tell it's welcome to come, too! My son and his awful daughter are in there somewhere, so it'll have plenty to snack on!"

"I'll keep that in mind," Ernestine said dryly as Eduardo helped a second swan out of the Studebaker. She watched as the swans, Swansons, millionairess, chefs, and manservant all went inside. Shaking her head, she said, "C'mon, Charleston, let's go find our zombie before it can eat someone."

They headed into the front garden, which was full of very strange sculptures made by Charleston's father, Frank. At the moment, it also contained a lot of musicians taking a break from the party.

"You cats on your way to the party?" called out a large, elderly African American man. He had a rich, deep voice and wore a very impressive black leather coat. His name was Mr. Ellington and he lived in apartment 3C. He had played saxophone with the Hep Cats since sometime in the middle of the previous century. Tonight, all of the Hep Cats were wearing purple and green peacock masks, probably because of the early Mardi Gras party Mrs. MacGillicuddie was throwing.

"Not tonight. We have school in the morning," Ernestine called back. "Hey, have any of you cats seen a zombie go by?"

"Not tonight."

Leaving Mr. Ellington and the other musicians behind, they continued on their way through the darkened garden, careful not to trip over, run into, or get impaled upon any of Frank's many interesting sculptures made out of things like old washing machines, discarded VCRs, chainsaws, and obsolete cell phones.

Over by the side porch, they ran into an excitable Mr. Sangfroid as he waved his cane disapprovingly at his neighbors from across the hall, Mr. Theda and Mr. Bara.

"Those movies of yours aren't art!" he ranted, almost whacking Charleston in the head with the pronged foot of his cane. "They're garbage! Pretentious hoodlumism attacking our culture!"

Mr. Theda was a retired horror movie villain, currently dressed as a pasty-faced Dracula, while Mr. Bara had once been a movie special effects expert. Their movies were the sort that tended to be released straight to video back in the days when people watched things on videotapes rather than streaming them on their TVs and phones.

"They're social commentary," Mr. Bara said with great dignity. Or at least as much dignity as he could manage given that he was currently dressed as a mutant alien chicken from a movie called *The Perils of Poultry: Sometimes, They Eat Back,* which Ernestine had once watched late at night when she was four. She hadn't been able to sleep with a feather pillow ever since, secretly convinced that it might come to life and eat her. Possibly with a side of coleslaw.

When not dressed as a monster, Mr. Bara had a bald head, very dark skin, and always wore a thick gold hoop in one ear. Ernestine had once asked him what his ancestry was, and he had told her he was ten percent Abatwan, thirty percent Basajaunak, thirty percent Zerzurian, and thirty percent Gandharvian. When she did a search online to figure out what those were, she discovered that Mr. Bara was actually one hundred percent none of her business.

"Bah! They're the end of civilization, that's what they are!" Mr. Sangfroid yelled. Though he technically hadn't dressed for the party, Mr. Sangfroid was so old and leathery, he looked exactly like an unwrapped mummy. He was the only one among the residents who wasn't an artist, having instead been an art curator and critic. These days, no one was willing to pay him for his criticisms, but that didn't stop Mr. Sangfroid from offering them anyway. No one in the house liked him, but he had once done Mrs. MacGillicuddie a great favor. What that favor might be, no one knew, but whatever it was, their landlady was still apparently in his debt.

Dodging another swipe of his cane as he tried unsuccessfully to whack the antenna off Mr. Bara's head, Ernestine cleared her throat and said, "Uh, speaking of the end of civilization, have either of you seen a zombie pass by?"

"Just the one standing in front of us," Mr. Theda sneered, whirling his cape menacingly.

Ducking under Mr. Sangfroid's cane, Ernestine dragged Charleston forward. "We'll take that as a 'no.'"

The garden path narrowed to a dark ribbon of bricks as it squeezed between the house and fence. The shadows seemed to swallow up the sounds of the party taking place on the other side of the house. Between the brick wall rising up on one side and the house on the other, the narrow passageway felt like a tomb. Which was exactly the sort of place no one wanted to hang out in, whether they were a zombie or not.

"Ernestine, are you hyperventilating?" Charleston asked.

"No," Ernestine gritted through her teeth.

"It sounds like you're hyperventilating."

"I'm not hyperventilating! Brave warriors of the apocalypse do *not* hyperventilate! I'm just breathing deeply, okay?" Ernestine hooked her thumbs around the backpack straps circling her shoulders and forced herself to be calm before admitting, "I just don't like tight spaces, okay? That's all."

"I guess zombies don't, either." Charleston shrugged as he studied the darkened windows staring down at them. "Hey, you don't think the zombie could have gotten inside, do you? Maybe it's in one of those rooms, eating someone."

"Nah, it's too quiet in there. If it was eating someone, we would hear it." Ernestine didn't want to take the time to pry one of the windows open and peer inside. She wanted to get off the garden path. *Now.* Not discuss zombie table manners.

"Some people are quiet eaters. Why not some zombies, too?"

"Charleston, would you just move!" Shoving him forward, they finally burst out into the backyard from behind an elephant made out of old carburetors and a thick mess of network cables. Charleston let out a yelp. "Over there!"

Following his outstretched finger, Ernestine spotted a shadowy figure lurking beneath the laundry room window. As they watched, it turned and shuffled along the path ahead of them, unaware of their presence.

"Excellent." Ernestine stood up on her toes in delight. "Be quiet, Charleston. We don't want to startle —"

Before she could finish her sentence, Charleston — who clearly had not been listening to her — screamed, "ZOMMMBIEEE!"

Leaping over a row of dead hosta bushes, Charleston ran toward the zombie with his baseball bat raised while Ernestine clapped a hand to her head in frustration and yelled,

"Don't hit it too hard or it'll fall apart, and we'll have to put it back together again!"

Great. Just great. She finally managed to raise a zombie and Charleston was about to break it. How did you even put a zombie back together again, anyhow? Duct tape? Superglue?

Apparently, the zombie didn't want to find out, either. Rather than shambling forward to slurp out their brains, the figure cringed in terror behind the gazebo in the middle of the garden, further obscuring its face. But before Charleston could get close enough to bash its head off, he stumbled over a low stone bench and into the koi pond, landing with a splash as the thin layer of ice covering the pond crackled apart.

Ernestine grabbed his coat collar and hauled him out of the slush. Sputtering, he yanked a dead lily pad off his head as Ernestine fished around in the bottom of the pond for his baseball bat.

"Charleston, in the zombie apocalypse, there are two things that are very important. One, don't drown." Ernestine shoved the baseball bat back into his hands. "Two, don't let your weapon drown, either."

"Are th-th-there any r-r-r-rules about l-l-losing your z-z-z-zombie?" Charleston asked through chattering teeth as he tried to wipe off his wet glasses with the hem of his equally wet coat.

"What?!" Ernestine looked around the garden frantically, but Charleston was right. Their zombie had disappeared.

They ran over to the gazebo. Well, Ernestine ran. Charleston mostly squished along and tried not to freeze into an icicle.

"Charleston, are you *sure* that was a zombie you saw?" Ernestine squinted at the dormant shrubs and dead flowers.

"D-d-d-definitely." Charleston shrugged, still shivering. "I m-m-m-mean, what else could it be?"

"It's just that it ran *away* from us and our nice, delicious, juicy brains. Doesn't that seem kind of weird to you? What sort of zombie doesn't try to crack open our skulls or something?"

"Yeah, that does seem kind of w-w-w-weird," Charleston admitted, his lips beginning to turn blue. "But it was definitely a zombie. Maybe our b-b-b-brains aren't ripe since we're kids. You know, kinda like green f-f-f-fruit."

"There's nothing wrong with *my* brain! I bet it's perfectly delicious," Ernestine huffed, taking off her coat and handing it to him as she swept her flashlight beam around the garden for footprints. Terrific. Just terrific. She'd finally managed to raise a zombie only to immediately lose it—*twice!* How embarrassing.

"How d-d-d-did we raise the wrong zombie, anyhow?" Clutching her coat about him and still dripping, Charleston followed Ernestine as she spotted something on the ground beneath the laundry room window.

"What do you mean, 'wrong zombie'?" Ernestine asked defensively.

"Well, n-n-n-nothing dug its way out of Herbert's grave, right? So the zombie m-m-m-must have come from one of the other graves."

Rather than answering, Ernestine picked up the object lying on the thick mat of autumn leaves. It felt cold and heavy to the touch.

"What's that?" Charleston asked.

"It's a crowbar."

"D-d-d-did the zombie drop it?"

"I don't know. Maybe? I guess?"

Ernestine blinked at the curved strip of metal. What kind of zombie carried a crowbar around? Of course, zombies *did* try to break in windows, but they did so by just pounding on the glass with their hideously decayed hands until it broke. They didn't use tools, did they? Where would a zombie even get a crowbar, anyhow? Unless someone had the foresight to bury them with one, of course. You know, just in case they had to pry the lid off their coffin. But even if they had, why go after the window instead of the much-easier-to-get-into door a few feet away?

"I c-c-c-can't believe we started the end of the world

only to lose our zombie," Charleston moaned, smacking his hand to his face. "Oh, m-m-man. We're going to be in so much trouble if it eats s-s-s-someone."

"I don't know. It seemed like a scaredy zombie to me, what with all that shuffling and hiding and everything. I can't see it eating anyone unless they're, like, really slow or stupid, and that's hardly our fault if they are," Ernestine said vaguely as she unlocked the back door and went inside, taking the crowbar with them.

"Oh, it f-f-f-feels good to be in where it's warm!" Charleston stuttered, dripping pond water onto the floor like some sort of monster from the blue lagoon.

"Here, let's put our coats in the dryer so they're ready for us to wear to school tomorrow." Going into the laundry room, Ernestine stuffed them into one of the dryers. As she did so, she noticed that the window above it had been wedged open a fraction of an inch. The lock had been broken for a while now, but the scratches on the sill looked new.

They also matched up perfectly with the crowbar when Ernestine laid it against them.

Pulling out her notebook, Ernestine made two notes in it. They read:

Fix the laundry room window
Zombies maybe use tools???

Tapping her pen against her chin, Ernestine said, "Charleston, how could the zombie know *that* window was broken...and that it would be the easiest to open? And since when have zombies been stealthy?"

"What do you mean? In the movies, they're always sneaking up on people." Charleston had found a pile of their clothes in a laundry basket that his dad, Frank, had forgotten to take upstairs. Squatting down behind a washing machine, he changed into a dry pair of pajamas. "Ernestine, we can't let our zombie actually eat anyone. It just wouldn't be right. We've got to find it before it hurts anyone."

"I guess," Ernestine agreed reluctantly, still not entirely convinced they had raised a zombie. Sure, it would be nice to think she had released the ravenous undead on the city, but she didn't want to take credit for something she hadn't actually accomplished.

On the bright side, *someone* had tried to break into the house. Maybe it wasn't a zombie, but it *might* be a bloodthirsty killer, which was at least a step in the right direction.

Though why that someone had bothered to actually break in, Ernestine didn't know. Sure, in theory the doors were kept locked, but in practice, Mrs. MacGillicuddie was usually throwing a party that anyone was invited to. Zombies and bloodthirsty killers included.

This quickly became evident when a bloodcurdling scream ripped through the house.

Ernestine shot out into the main hallway that ran like an artery through the entire house. More screams followed, along with the excited rumble of voices that always accompanied interesting things when they happened around a large group of people.

"Oh, this is more like it!" Ernestine beamed approvingly at Charleston as he staggered out of the laundry room, glasses askew and still trying to button his shirt. "Let's go see who Herbert's trying to eat!"

"I hope it's not the Swanson twins. They said they were going to teach me how to walk a tightrope."

"You want to learn how to walk a tightrope?"

"Seems like a good way to get around if the streets are filled with the zombie hordes."

This was an excellent point, and Ernestine was chagrined that she hadn't already thought to include it in the zombie survival guide she was planning on publishing. However, before she could pull out her notebook, they had reached the swinging door that led into the front foyer.

Rather than swinging forward, though, it thumped against something solid.

"Oof!" Ernestine said as she bumped against it.

"Oof!" Charleston gasped as he bumped against her.

Mr. Ellington, the saxophone player from 3C, cracked the door open and let them through. He had been the something solid the door had hit a moment before. Even though he was a very strong man, he had difficulty opening the door enough to let them wriggle into the foyer.

The reason for this became immediately clear once Ernestine and Charleston were inside. A very large crowd of elderly partygoers had jammed the hallway as the Swanson twins, each clutching a swan, climbed out onto either end of a tightrope hooked to the balcony three stories above. Swans and Swansons alike appeared riveted by whatever was going on in the middle of the foyer beneath the chandelier's blazing light.

"Fifty on the skinny grocer!" One of the twins yelled merrily down into the crowd.

"The chef has a meat cleaver, Libby!" shouted the other twin, who must have been Mora. "I say seventy on him!"

"What the—" Ernestine began, only to be cut off by Mr. Ellington.

"Mr. Talmadge is going to fight Dill, the vegan grocer from around the corner." Mr. Ellington crossed his arms and shook his head as though that explained it all. And maybe it did. Just not to Ernestine or Charleston.

"Why?" Charleston asked, spotting a platter of vegetable

canapés and scooping up a handful of miniature baked potatoes and a couple of mushroom tarts. Ernestine grabbed a canapé herself and squeezed her way forward to get a better look.

"Because they both want to open up a restaurant in the empty building next to Dill's vegetable co-op," explained Mr. Ellington.

That didn't make a bit of sense to Ernestine, though Charleston nodded thoughtfully around a mouthful of potato and hummus as though it did to him. Personally, Ernestine didn't really care what the reason was. While she thought that learning to wield a meat cleaver against an opponent was excellent training for fighting zombies in the coming apocalypse, she also knew she'd be the one stuck cleaning the blood off the floor if Mr. Talmadge actually managed to whack anything vital off of Dill.

Plus, she quite liked Mr. Talmadge and would prefer not to see him sealed inside a jail cell like Jell-O in a plastic cup, just waiting to be cracked open by the first zombie someone was thoughtless enough to leave the prison gate open for.

"Last call for bets!" Mrs. MacGillicuddie called out cheerfully from the middle of the room as Eduardo counted the wads of cash people kept shoving at him. Her nephew Lyndon seemed to be trying to set up his own betting ring over in the corner but everyone kept ignoring him. "Twenty-to-one odds on Mr. Talmadge, fifty-to-one odds on the skinny grocer! Sorry, Dill, darling."

"Pin him up against the door, Parsley, or whatever your name is!" Libby Swanson leaned forward to call out, accidentally dropping her swan in the process. "Oopsy!"

The outraged swan flapped its wings as it landed, causing the crowd to skitter out of its way. Ernestine almost fell down but was able to grab Mr. Theda's cape just in time to keep herself upright.

Spotting her, Mr. Bara pulled her to the front of the crowd so she could see better. Now that she had a clear view, Ernestine watched Mr. Talmadge and Dill circling each other. Burly Mr. Talmadge had once been personal chef to rocker Alice Cooper. From the stories he liked to tell, this wasn't the first time he'd brought a meat cleaver to a fight. Meanwhile, Dill looked around dazedly like he wasn't entirely sure how all of this had happened. Especially given that his weapon against the meat cleaver appeared to be a dinky paring knife.

"You know, it really just isn't one of Mrs. MacGillicuddie's parties until someone tries to murder someone else," Mr. Theda drawled to his partner.

"I'm taking *one-hundred*-to-one odds that it's Talmadge." Lyndon wiggled hopefully through the crowd to stand next to them. He had a desperate look on his skinny, hang-dog face, possibly because he'd yet to get a single person to place a bet with him in spite of all the knives flashing about.

"You're taking bets on whether someone actually dies?" Mr. Bara slowly cocked an eyebrow in such a way that Lyndon blushed.

"Well, it's not like I'm actually trying to kill someone!" he protested, hunching his shoulders. "I'm just—er—trying to make money off of it. Nothing wrong with that, right?"

"Are you taking bets on whether one of them will come back as a zombie afterward?" Ernestine asked, feeling that Lyndon—as usual with Mrs. MacGillicuddie's nephew—was missing the real opportunity here.

Lyndon blinked. "Is that likely?"

"*I* don't know. Aren't *you* the one taking bets?"

"Mother! I insist you put an end to this farce this instant!" Mrs. MacGillicuddie's son, Rodney, pushed his way through the crowd. He wore the costume of an Egyptian pharaoh and had swelled up his chest pompously, his moustache quivering with rage. Nearby, his daughter Aurora Borealis was dressed as a black cat. Or at the very least, a black cat who wore a miniskirt and stiletto heels. She was old enough to be in college but had decided to try and be an Instagram star instead. Somehow, Aurora Borealis had already managed to amass a hundred thousand followers—and she certainly hadn't done it by hanging out with a bunch of elderly artists. Right now, she sat on the steps next to the ornate Cupid statue holding up the bottom of the banister, only looking up from her jewel-encrusted phone to throw a bored, pouty look at all of the chaos.

"Daaaaaaddyyyyyy," she whined, "is it time to goooooo yet? This party is sooooo *lame*. Nothing interesting *ever* happens at *any* of Grammy's parties. I've, like, already lost a million followers."

"Rupert, you put that meat cleaver down right now!" Mrs. Talmadge bellowed through the crowd. "He's only got a paring knife! I'll go get the bread knife for him, luv! Make it a fair fight and all!"

That immediately brought about a new round of betting as the promise of a new weapon seemed to substantially improve Dill's odds, though Dill himself looked far less convinced.

"Mrs. MacGillicuddie, I *really* don't think this is a good idea." As Ernestine tugged at her landlady's fur coat, she swept the room with her eyes. There was so much chaos, her zombie could stumble in here and graze like it was at a five-star buffet without anyone ever noticing. Even her parents, Frank and Maya, had wandered out of their artist studio down to the third-floor balcony to see what all of the commotion was about.

Just as she spotted them, Ernestine noticed that the immense crystal chandelier dangling from the ceiling nearby had begun to sway far more violently than it had any reason to, as though all of the excitement below had gotten it worked up, too. Easily ten feet tall, its curly silver arms, glittery pendants, and bright lights hung close to the third-floor balcony where the Swanson twins were still balancing precariously on their tightrope.

The light fixture had to weigh a couple of hundred pounds, Ernestine realized in horror as she watched it sway. Heavy enough to turn them all into humanburger patties, if it fell. She frantically tried to get her mother and Frank's attention, but they were already heading down the stairs toward her.

The Swanson twins had realized something was wrong, too. Perhaps they had seen Ernestine's panicked pointing. Or maybe they had finally noticed the way their tightrope was quivering from the breeze from the shaking chandelier. Either way, they looked upward in alarm just as half of the bolts holding the chandelier popped out of the ceiling, showering the crowd below with dust and plaster.

"Is it snowing?" Mr. Talmadge asked in confusion, cleaver in hand.

"Twenty-to-one odds that it is!" Lyndon shouted, waving his arms frantically in effort to be noticed through the crowd.

"No! Look!" Ernestine cried, pointing upward.

"What is it, darling? *Oh, my!*" Mrs. MacGillicuddie gasped.

"Oh, *help!*" the twins screamed.

Before anyone could say or do anything else, several more bolts gave way. The base of the chandelier, still attached to part of the ceiling, cracked and lurched downward, exposing the electrical wires above. For one breathless moment, it seemed like they would hold.

Then, in a shower of sparks, the wires snapped apart. Slicing through the tightrope, the chandelier plummeted to the floor.

Directly toward Ernestine and Mrs. MacGillicuddie.

Chapter Three
The Apocalypse Is Put Temporarily on Hold

TUESDAY, 12:51 AM

With a massive thrust, Ernestine flung both herself and Mrs. MacGillicuddie out of the way. The chandelier crashed to the ground, smashing apart the marble floor. Broken stone and shattered crystal exploded across the crowd as they all fell down, covering their heads with their hands.

"Ernestine!" The silver platter Charleston had been holding clattered down and skidded right over to Ernestine's nose as her stepbrother raced over to help her up. All around them, partygoers sat among the wreckage of the chandelier—along with water-stained books, broken musical instruments, and several dozen moldering photo albums. All of which had, until recently, been stored in the attic above.

"Goodness, darling!" Rolling over, Mrs. MacGillicuddie blinked in amazement at the mess now filling her lovely foyer.

Standing up, Eduardo flicked a single crystal shard off his red Roman general's cape, tucked the purple silk handkerchief behind his breastplate, and gave her a hand getting to her feet.

"Is anyone injured?" he asked, in his Spanish accent.

"My meat cleaver has seen better days." Mr. Talmadge sadly held up the wooden handle in one hand and the enormous blade in the other.

Mr. Theda was trying to tug his silk-lined cape free of one of the chandelier's silver arms, but he wasn't having much luck until Mr. Bara came to his aid. Mr. Ellington dumped broken crystal out of the mouth of his saxophone, while Mr. Sangfroid ranted, "This is what comes of letting hippies into the place! No-good beatniks!"

"Could someone help us?!" wailed one of the Swanson twins. They were both dangling from the third-floor balcony railings. They'd lost their glittery white shoes in the crash, their elderly bare toes digging into the wall for support.

"Ten to one odds that they fall before someone can!" Lyndon waved about some money but everyone ignored him.

"Are our swans all right?" Libby asked anxiously. A flutter of feathers and some irritable honking confirmed that the swans were, in fact, just fine and quite ready to go home. In fact, one of them had snatched Aurora Borealis's phone away from her, possibly in an attempt to call a ride.

"Ooo! Animals always get extra likes!" Grabbing her phone back from the swan, Aurora Borealis took a selfie with it, though neither of them quite looked their best, as the swan had lost quite a few of its feathers, which now stuck out of Aurora Borealis's hair instead.

The other partygoers got unsteadily to their feet as well. Surprisingly, no one had broken a hip.

"Thank goodness for titanium!" Mrs. MacGillicuddie beamed, knocking her fist against her hip and then holding up her arms. "The elbows, too!"

"Mother! This really is the last straw!" Rodney staggered to his feet from beneath a pile of old people. His pharaoh's head-dress was askew on his head, while his toupee had slunk down into the safety of his collar. "I am having my personal doctor evaluate your mental fitness! Your lifestyle at your age and your insistence on throwing all of these wild parties—in the middle of the week, no less—is alarming to say the least! I don't think you should manage the family's money any longer!"

"Oh, put a sock in it, Junior." Mrs. MacGillicuddie shoved

his overcoat at him. Behind them, Aurora Borealis had finished posting to Instagram but still hadn't gotten up, apparently too busy eyeing a pair of the Swanson twins' shoes glittering amidst the debris. "And it isn't 'the family's money.' It's *my* money. What happened to all of the millions your father left you? And you think *I'm* not fit to handle money? Now take that vapid creature you spawned and go home before I have the swans attack you."

"But my car isn't here! I told my driver not to return until two. What am I supposed to do? Take a *taxi?*" Rodney looked ill at the thought. Eduardo moved discreetly behind him in case he was called upon to catch his employer's son. As a result, Ernestine was the only one to notice Aurora Borealis snatching up the twin's shoes and trying them on her feet. She seemed pleased with the results, though one of the swans nipped at her disapprovingly. Lyndon should have noticed, too, as he was standing right next to her, but he seemed to be in a state of shock that he hadn't been able to make any money off the evening. He still clutched a couple of limp bills in his hands.

"You can take my limo. It's, er, parked out front." Waving her hand airily, Mrs. MacGillicuddie turned her attention to removing the Swanson twins from where they were decorating her balcony. Meanwhile, Mr. Sangfroid jabbed at one of the photo albums that had fallen down from the attic above as though trying to prod it into getting up and going back upstairs.

"Ernestine!" Ernestine's mother, Maya, swept her into a paint-spattered hug. Her skin was a richer brown than her daughter's, with deeper golden undertones. Freckles speckled her cheeks, and she had lovely hazel eyes. Unlike Ernestine's indecisive hair, Maya's hair was wonderfully thick and springy, cut short and worn naturally around her face.

Ernestine hadn't felt afraid until she felt her mother's arms around her. It wasn't until she snuggled against her warm skin and smelled the faint turpentine scent of her mother's fingers in her hair that she realized she could have died before she'd ever had the chance to witness the apocalypse.

"My baby! I'm so proud of you! You saved Mrs. MacGillicuddie's life!" Maya exclaimed.

Ernestine immediately stiffened at the mention of her mother's pride. Her mother shouldn't be proud. She should be *terrified*. Absolutely sick with worry.

"I almost *died*, Mom." Ernestine wriggled out of her mother's grasp and crossed her arms. "You're proud that I almost died?"

"I'm proud of the way you can take care of yourself in any situation, Nestea." Her mother smiled and laid her hand on Ernestine's shoulder. "It makes me glad to know that you can take care of yourself even when I can't be there. Just like you did before."

"Before when?" Charleston asked as his father, Frank, released him from a hug.

The smile slid from Maya's face. It was like a cloud had passed across the sun that normally lit up her personality. She glanced at Ernestine and began, "Back when Ernestine was five —"

"*Nothing happened.*" Ernestine snatched her backpack up from the ground, her gaze daring anyone to contradict her. No one did.

Together, they all trouped up the stairs to the attic loft where they lived. Though MacGillicuddie House was a retired artist colony, it needed some less-retired people to take care of it. Technically, those people were Ernestine's mom and stepdad, though they spent most of their time painting and making weird sculptures instead of repairing things. Still, as they were — again, technically — the building's maintenance people, they got to live in the half of the attic that wasn't full of junk. Fortunately, it was also the half of the attic that hadn't been attached to the now-fallen chandelier.

As they reached the balcony, Ernestine looked at the gaping hole in the ceiling above. Wires dangled uselessly in the air. Through the cracked plaster, she could see into the rafters above. The wheel of an ancient baby carriage jutted out through this new opening, threatening to take a wild ride down into the foyer below.

"You need to check all of the light fixtures tomorrow," Ernestine warned her mother and stepfather severely as they pushed open the door to their home. "I know you have a gallery opening this Saturday, but *there are more important things than a gallery opening*. People could have died, you know."

"Not with you here to save them." Maya's voice wavered a bit as she said it, but she gave Ernestine another squeeze. "And besides, we could hardly have known that chandelier was loose. It looked fine."

"I hope the vibrations from my metal cutter didn't jiggle those bolts loose." Frank looked worriedly towards the work space where he created his sculptures. It was separated from the living room and kitchen by curtains made out of old bedspreads and quilts. "I had it running for most of the day. Mr. Talmadge asked me to make a sculpture out of old refrigerators and ovens for the new restaurant he's opening after he overheard Mora say that Dill was planning something similar for *his* new place."

Ernestine knew from many weekends spent trying to find a quiet place to study just how noisy that metal cutter could be. You could hear it all the way down on the second floor.

Everyone else just took out their hearing aids, but Ernestine didn't have the luxury of just yanking her ears off. Well, at least not yet. That might be one upside to the apocalypse that hadn't occurred to her before.

Still, she didn't think it was powerful enough to shake the chandelier loose. Unless it had flung itself off the ceiling in protest, sick of listening to all of that noise.

"You guys *have* to do your job. You can't always rely on me to take care of things," Ernestine pointed out. "When the zombie apocalypse comes, you're going to have to fight to keep me from getting eaten."

"The zombie apocalypse is going to be righteous, man." Frank raised his clenched fist in a salute and beamed at her.

With a sigh, Ernestine gave up and went to bed. Charleston tagged along behind her. They shared a bedroom inside the cavernous attic at the very top of MacGillicuddie House. The rest of their home was mostly taken up by their parents' art studio, with a small space left over for boring things like a kitchen, a bathroom, and a couch, coffee table, and TV that served as a living room. Colorful quilts and blankets marked off the various spaces, including Frank and Maya's bedroom on the other side of the attic, leaving Ernestine and Charleston with the one room separated off by actual walls (well, the bathroom also had walls).

Charleston peeled off his boots, plunked his glasses onto the nightstand, and was snoring in the bottom bunk before Ernestine had even finished climbing the ladder up to the top bunk. Typical. He'd probably sleep right through the apocalypse when it finally happened and wake up in the morning to wonder where all of the bones had come from.

The night hadn't exactly gone the way Ernestine had planned. She tried not to feel too down about it as she plumped her pillow and pulled the blankets up to her chin. If she *had* raised a zombie, she'd raised the wrong one and then lost it. Humiliating. On the other hand, if she *hadn't* raised a zombie, she was still incompetent and plus she'd have to figure out who had been trying to break in. Humiliating *and* tiresome.

Either way, she'd have to beef up security around here, and push back ending the world.

Oh, well. Tomorrow was another day, Ernestine supposed, her optimism returning as she drifted off to sleep. There'd always be time to start the apocalypse after school.

In the morning, she went through her usual before-school routine. After brushing her teeth, shoving her hair up into a messy bun, and putting on her uniform in the bathroom, Ernestine went back to the room she shared with Charleston and yanked him out of bed. It seemed mean, but he slept like the dead so there was just no nice way to wake him up. Charleston's face flopped onto the floor, his cheek smeared against the wooden boards, his legs still propped up on the mattress. He snorted, drooled a bit, and went on sleeping.

"Get up." Ernestine nudged his cheek with her toe. More drool slid out of his mouth and onto her shoe. Ernestine sighed. "If you don't get up, I'm putting rats down your pajamas."

"You don't have any rats," Charleston muttered, squishing his face into the floor.

"Oh, I'll find some," Ernestine said darkly and then went off to make them both scrambled eggs and toast for breakfast. Eventually, Charleston stumbled into the kitchen, more or less dressed. Well, mostly less. His pants were inside out, his shirt untucked, and he kept trying to tie his sock around his neck. Meanwhile he'd used the tie for a belt. It was anyone's guess where the belt had ended up. Charleston slumped into a chair, drooped his chin onto the table, and opened his mouth to push his eggs directly into it from the plate. Ernestine sat down next to him and flipped open her notebook to go through her Morning Checklist.

"Do you have everything you need for school?" she asked Charleston, who mumbled some sort of indistinct response. Ernestine narrowed her eyes at him and decided to be more specific. "Homework?"

"Yup."

"Textbooks?"

"Uh-huh."

"Student ID?"

"Yeah."

"Zombie survival guide?"

"Of course."

Ernestine had put Charleston's zombie survival guide together herself. It was a duplicate of one she always kept on hand for the day she'd need it. On the front cover, in thick black permanent marker, she'd written, "PANIC!!!" Usually, those sorts of guides told you not to panic, but Ernestine figured that in the case of the zombie apocalypse, if you weren't panicking then you probably hadn't grasped the full scope of the situation.

Inside, she'd written all sorts of helpful hints, starting with "Barricade all doors and windows," followed by, "But first make sure there aren't any zombies inside." Maybe that second one should have gone first, but honestly, if you couldn't figure that out on your own, it was probably your destiny to be snack food.

Maya wandered into the kitchen, a paintbrush tucked behind either ear, and paint drying in her curls.

"Morning, guys." She kissed Ernestine on the head and ruffled Charleston's hair. "Oooh, did you make me coffee, Nestea? Thank you."

"Don't call me Nestea. I hate nicknames. Future presidents don't have nicknames. Well, except for maybe 'Future President.'" Ernestine paused, thinking that one over. She'd be quite pleased if everyone got into the habit of calling her "Future President." Or better still, just "President." "I've also made you a list of things that need to be done today. Including checking *all* the light fixtures in the house."

As Maya yawned and poured herself a cup of coffee, Ernestine pushed a neatly written list across the table. She'd even drawn little boxes next to the items so her mom could *X* them out as she completed each one, something Ernestine personally found very satisfying. "In addition to cleaning up the mess in the foyer, there's a leak in one of the pipes in the basement, which is interfering with Mr. Sangfroid's water pressure. Mr. and Mrs. Talmadge need their kitchen sink unclogged, there's litter in the front lawn, graffiti spray-painted on the garden wall, and Mrs. MacGillicuddie has a loose floorboard that sent her cat flying yesterday. Oh, and the lock on the window in the laundry room is broken, which I'd swear it wasn't two days ago when I cleaned out the dryer filters."

"Mm-hmm," her mom agreed vaguely, clearly not ready to start the day just yet. Ernestine always sprang right to work as soon as she got up in the morning, and therefore didn't understand why so many people seemed to need to ease their way into the day.

Heaving a sigh, Ernestine laid the list on top of her mom's coffee cup so she couldn't possibly miss it. Maya was an amazing artist and all, but she wasn't very practical. She spent all her time thinking about things like contours and contrast and pigments and the meaninglessness of modern existence. Which was fine, but it didn't pay the bills very well. If modern existence had any meaning at all, it was probably that you *had* to pay the bills until the zombies came and ate you. Mrs. MacGillicuddie was a big fan of Maya's paintings and Frank's sculptures, so she'd hired them to be the maintenance people for her apartment building/elderly artist colony. But if they didn't do the work, she'd fire them eventually. Possibly. Maybe.

Honestly, probably not, but Ernestine still didn't want to risk it.

She liked it here. The people were nice and weird and it was a great place to spend their last days on earth before zombies ate almost everyone, leaving behind only a plucky band of humans to fight them off. With Ernestine as their leader, of course.

"*Mom,* you've got *responsibilities,*" Ernestine pressed.

"And *you* sound just like my mother." Maya took an irritable sip of her coffee. Ernestine's grandmother was a civil rights activist and college professor. She never, ever forgot to fix anything in her house and spent most of their time on FaceTime chastising Maya for being lackadaisical and disorganized. "Stop worrying about things around here, Nestea! We'll take care of everything while you're at school. Though I wish they didn't make you wear those dreary uniforms. It's fascist."

"Right on, man," Frank agreed as the smell of coffee drew him to the kitchen from the other side of the attic. He was incredibly tall, incredibly skinny, and like Charleston, had rumpled blond hair and glasses. Unlike Charleston, he also had a rather scraggly beard. "Like, who are they to tell you how to dress? How you look should be an expression of your inner spirit, you know?"

"Uh-huh," Charleston agreed, and then started snoring into his eggs.

"It's a *very* good school, and we're lucky to go there." Ernestine gritted her teeth as her mom started to doodle a sketch of Ernestine's profile on her neat list of chores. When the zombie apocalypse came, she was totally going to have to lock her mom and Frank in a closet to keep them from getting eaten.

Personally, she quite liked her uniform because it looked an awful lot like a suit. Which made it very unlike Maya's flowy dresses and very much like the suits her grandmother always wore, even on Saturdays and Sundays. That was exactly how Ernestine would dress once she was President of the United Post-Apocalyptic States.

If Ernestine liked her uniform, she liked the school even more. A friend of Mrs. MacGillicuddie ran a top-notch private school and had agreed to let Ernestine and Charleston go there as charity cases so long as they passed the entrance exam. Ernestine had received perfect marks, of course, but Charleston had flunked miserably. Fortunately, Mrs. MacGillicuddie *really* liked Maya and Frank's artwork and had more money than she knew what to do with. So she gave an amazingly generous donation to the school to build a new auditorium. After that, the friend didn't mind what a terrible student Charleston was and let him go there, anyhow.

Oh, well. Fighting an army of the undead would instill some discipline in him. Nothing like almost getting torn apart by a mob of ravenous zombies to teach you to pay attention to things.

That was why Ernestine always paid very close attention to everything in school. You never knew when you might pick up something that could come in handy in the apocalypse. For example, in science class she'd learned about the importance of purified water, which could be crucial when fighting zombies. You didn't want to get your intestines torn out because you drank bacteria-filled river water and got so distracted with running to the bathroom that you didn't notice the zombie horde hiding in the next stall. And all because you hadn't paid attention in science class. You'd never forgive yourself.

Grabbing her backpack and a still-snoring Charleston, Ernestine dragged them both downstairs to catch the city bus. They had to edge their way around all the broken crystal in the foyer to get to the exit.

While they did so, Mr. Theda stood at Mrs. MacGillicuddie's door, trying to get in. Their landlady wore an elegant silk nightgown, furry stiletto heels, a diamond necklace big enough to qualify as a medieval knight's breastplate, and sunglasses. She kept one hand pressed against her forehead and winced each time Mr. Theda raised his voice, but she still kept her other arm stretched out to block him from getting in.

"By rights, they should be mine!" Mr. Theda insisted, pulling his Dracula cape around his shoulders with a flourish. Why he was still wearing it, Ernestine didn't know, but combined with the way he had styled his hair into two horn-like peaks, he looked like he had arrived in a puff of brimstone. "You know they should be!"

"They're mine, they've been mine for years, and they'll stay mine!" Mrs. MacGillicuddie responded tartly.

Lowering his voice, he cocked one eyebrow into the

signature *V* all his villains used right before they unleashed evil mayhem on the world. "You'll regret this."

"Not as much as you will if you keep this up, *Frankie Nelson*."

Mr. Theda gasped, and if he didn't quite vanish in a cloud of smoke, he did at least manage to make his cloak swirl about him as he fled back upstairs.

"What do you think *that* was all about?" Charleston muttered as they stepped outside. Ernestine was surprised to discover that he'd been awake enough to hear any of it.

"That Mr. Theda doesn't like to be called Frankie Nelson, I guess."

"I thought Mr. Theda's first name was Theodore, not Frankie."

Ernestine shrugged. Whatever his first name was, it didn't seem to concern either zombies or world domination, so she wasn't very interested.

In spite of their near-deadly fall the night before, the Swanson twins were out in the front garden, practicing their routine.

Their act would have been pretty impressive even if the twins weren't sixty years old. They stood facing each other, each movement a mirror image of the other's. As one lifted her left foot up with toes pointing to the sky, the other did the same with her right foot. Then they both spread their arms out like the wings of a swan and turned carefully around on one foot. Each gesture occurred so exactly in time with the other that Ernestine would swear they had computer chips implanted in their brains to control them.

"Wow!" Charleston clapped furiously, now fully awake. "That was amazing!"

"Thank you." Bringing their feet back down, they took identical, graceful bows.

"Hey, when you were up on that tightrope last night, did you see any zombies?" Ernestine asked curiously.

"Zombies!" One twin clutched a hand to her throat. Ernestine thought it was the one named Libby, but it was hard to tell for sure. "Are there zombies about? Mora, do we have any organic pest spray that might keep zombies away?"

Ernestine said, "No, there's just the one, and if you find any pest spray that works, please let me know. I'm putting together a zombie survival guide so we don't all get our guts torn out during the apocalypse. I'd like to keep the cleanup to a minimum."

"Goodness!" Libby opened her eyes wide.

"If you see it, try not to let it eat anyone, and I'll take care of it after school." With a wave good-bye, Ernestine and Charleston headed on their way.

They got there early, which was just as well since Ernestine needed to go to the library to print off a list of suggestions she'd made for Principal Langenderfer on how to keep the school safe and free of zombies. Ernestine summarized them for her during a meeting she'd requested in the principal's office. She hadn't planned on giving it to her until next week, but with a possible zombie on the loose, Ernestine figured she'd better step things up a bit.

"First, why do we have to practice fire drills?" Ernestine asked, handing over her proposal in its plastic sheeting. She made sure to sit upright, speak clearly, and maintain eye contact, all important skills for getting someone to listen to you. She'd also worn her blazer and skirt rather than a jumper and a cardigan so she'd be sure to look more businesslike. "I mean, seriously? If there's a fire and you don't know to run *out* of the building rather than staying in it, I don't think practice is going to improve your odds of survival. Our time would be much better spent practicing what to do in case of a zombie attack. There are *nuances* there that could make the difference between life and death. Will you be safer staying inside the building and barricading the entrances or fleeing to wide open spaces where you can at least see the zombies coming? Making the right choices could make all the difference on where you end up on the food chain."

"Wow. This is quite a…thorough analysis of the, uh,

situation." Principal Langenderfer appeared to be struggling to find the right words as she flipped through the first twenty pages or so of the report.

Ernestine glowed with pride.

"You even made charts. Goodness…"

"Yes, as you can see, I outlined a few scenarios. For example, I don't think it's a good idea for everyone to eat together in the same location. It gives the zombies one target. All they have to do is break into the cafeteria, and it's lunchtime for *everyone*, living *and* dead. On the other hand, if you separate the lunch groups out into individual classrooms, you're guaranteed a much higher likelihood that at least some of the students will survive. Rather than losing a whole school of kids, you'll just lose one small group of them. I mean, that's *got* to impact your insurance rates, right?"

Principal Langenderfer sent her to see the school psychologist. Again.

Which Ernestine didn't mind at all. Mr. Price always made her a cup of hot chocolate and never forced her to talk about bad stuff that had happened in the past. That scored a lot of points with Ernestine. The past was over and done. Why get all obsessed with it when there were plenty of future disasters that needed worrying about right this second?

No, Mr. Price always listened to her when she explained

how to survive zombie attacks and asked good questions. He also took lots and lots of notes about what she said. So Ernestine was pretty sure she'd managed to teach him a thing or two, which he'd definitely appreciate when the apocalypse finally got underway.

Of course, she didn't mention to him that she might have raised a zombie last night. First, she didn't want to admit that she'd misplaced it. And second, she still wasn't *entirely* sure it had been a zombie sneaking around the back of the building. She'd hate to tell everyone to be on the lookout for a ravenous zombie when what they should be looking for was a bloodthirsty, psychotic murderer instead. You just didn't want to get the two confused. It could lead to all sorts of misunderstandings.

"Maybe we should put up missing posters around the neighborhood for the zombie," Charleston suggested after school as they stood by Herbert's gravestone. "You know, like they do for missing dogs and cats."

A light snow fell from the leaden sky, decorating the grass around his stone marker with lovely white flakes. What the grave *wasn't* decorated with was a hole. The hole of the ravenous undead clambering out of the ground to wreak havoc on the city.

There weren't even any teeny tiny holes, like maybe he'd

been poking his fingers up out of his casket. Ernestine had hoped she'd awoken Herbert just a little bit. Enough to make him at least climb halfway out the grave to see who was trying to raise him.

"I don't know, Charleston. I think it would have crawled out by us if we'd actually raised one," Ernestine sighed as they lugged their backpacks across the street to the mansion.

"Oh, yeah? Then who tried to break in last night?"

"Well, it *might* have been a zombie," Ernestine admitted reluctantly, "but it might also have been just your normal, average, run-of-the-mill homicidal maniac."

"Huh." Charleston thought that one over. "That could be interesting, too."

"I think so, yes. So let's keep a look out for one of those, too."

A chunk of missing bricks marked the spot in the wall where Mrs. MacGillicuddie had almost turned Ernestine and Charleston into windshield smears. Coincidentally, as they reached the sidewalk, one of the bricks flew out of the gate and whizzed right past Charleston's nose.

Just as Ernestine had reached the most logical conclusion that a poltergeist must have invaded the garden, Dill the vegan grocer shot out of the gate with a yelp, clutching his delivery basket and running with a high-kicking step that made his legs look like spokes on a wheel.

"AND STAY OUT!" Mr. Talmadge roared, bursting out of the gate after him with a brick raised in one hand. He screeched to a halt when he saw a disapproving Ernestine and shocked Charleston. He lowered the brick and looked sheepish. "Oh. Er. Hullo, you two."

"Mr. Talmadge," Ernestine said sternly, "while it's always a good idea to practice your skull-bashing skills for when the apocalypse begins, you almost whacked Charleston in the face with a brick!"

"Oh," Mr. Talmadge said again, looking even more chastened. Aged around seventy, he had flames tattooed all around his neck and wrists. Ernestine assumed this was some sort of chef's joke. "Sorry 'bout that. But ruddy Mrs. MacGillicuddie won't do anything about the…the…*travesty* that culinary quack has planned over on Delaware Street! It's a sign of the end of times, it is!"

Ernestine perked up at this. She didn't really know Dill very well, but if he was planning on ending the world, too, perhaps she should get to know the competition.

"Do you mean the vegan restaurant Dill would like to open?" Charleston asked, carefully prying the brick out of Mr. Talmadge's fingers and stacking it with the rest of the pile just inside the gate. "But how could she stop that?"

Mr. Talmadge blushed so deeply that it looked as though

his tattoos had set his face on fire. He muttered something about never minding and that it didn't matter, anyhow, but just because he was old that didn't mean he couldn't still cook as well as he could when he was younger and if anybody should understand that, it was Mrs. MacGillicuddie, so he just couldn't believe…

The rest of his grumblings trailed off as he marched back into the house. Ernestine and Charleston exchanged bewildered looks.

"Wow. It seems like everyone's angry at Mrs. MacGillicuddie all of a sudden," Charleston said as they trudged through the garden. "Her son. Mr. Theda. Mr. Talmadge."

"That's hardly everyone, Charleston," Ernestine pointed out.

Still, he had a point. Ernestine had always thought that everyone loved Mrs. MacGillicuddie. Well, everyone except for her son. Clearly, that wasn't the case.

How many other people held mysterious grudges against her? Just Mr. Theda and Mr. Talmadge? Or were there more?

How many of them would have been just as happy if the chandelier last night hadn't missed?

And what if last night's accident hadn't been an accident at all?

Chapter Four
Tidying Up Before
the Apocalypse

To Ernestine's surprise, Frank and Maya had actually managed to clean up both the fallen chandelier and all the debris
it had created. True, a crater had carved out a large chunk of
the foyer, but given that the floor was actually an elaborate
marble mosaic of Apollo and Artemis, Ernestine supposed
that it might take a while to fix it. A draft swirled down from
the attic above through the hole in the ceiling, and the lack
of a light plunged the hall into a murky twilight.

Upstairs, the broken chandelier jutted out of Frank's

workspace, a clear indication that he planned on incorporating it into one of his sculptures. A swan sat in a large galvanized tub of water, floating happily as Maya painted its portrait.

Ernestine found her list of maintenance tasks still lying on the kitchen table. Several coffee rings marred it, but no one had bothered to X off a single task.

"Mother, you and Frank need to fix these things!" Snatching it up off the table, she marched over to her mother's studio and shook the piece of paper in exasperation.

"We will, Nestea! We will!" Maya got up and tried to give her a paint-smeared hug, which Ernestine dodged because she didn't want to mess up her uniform. Her mother compromised by kissing her on top of her head. "Cleaning up that chandelier took the better part of the day, and someone had to do something with the swans."

"So you solved that problem by painting their portraits," Ernestine observed dryly as Maya's attention slid back to her artwork.

"Mmm, what was that?" she asked vaguely as she considered the way the light of the setting sun was making the swan's wings glow red as though tinged with blood.

"Nothing." Ernestine rolled her eyes at Charleston. On the other side of the attic, behind an enormous curtain, they could both hear the sounds of power tools that meant Frank was hard at work on his latest masterpiece. With their gallery show coming up this weekend, neither one of them was likely to get anything else done for the rest of the week. Not that Mrs. MacGillicuddie would care if the mansion fell down around them, so long as everyone had a marvelous time while it happened. "C'mon, Charleston. It looks like we've got work to do."

"Oh, man. I really wanted to watch TV." Charleston flopped onto the couch and burrowed his head into the pillows as though he could hide there.

"And *I* wanted to start the apocalypse. We can't always get what we want, you know." Ernestine heaved a sigh. "You make some sandwiches, and I'll get the toolbox."

Changing out of her uniform, Ernestine put on overalls and covered her hair with a red handkerchief. She grabbed her toolbox and an ancient, dog-eared book left behind by the previous maintenance man called *The Handyman's Handy Helper!* Ernestine liked a book with an exclamation mark in the title. If you weren't going to be enthusiastic about the book you were writing, then why write it at all?

Charleston was waiting for her out in the kitchen. He'd changed into old jeans and a plaid shirt. He handed her a mayonnaise-pickle-and-bologna sandwich while he munched on one of his own. Ernestine handed him his half of the list, and they went to work.

Her first stop was 2C, where Mrs. Talmadge peered anxiously over Ernestine's shoulder as she poured a big bottle of gloopy stuff down the drain of the kitchen sink and asked her, "Aren't you a little young to be handling dangerous chemicals?"

"Not at all!" Ernestine replied confidently since she firmly believed that one was never too young to handle dangerous anythings.

Mrs. Talmadge was on the plump side and had once been a chef to various punk rock bands back in the nineteen-seventies and eighties before eventually becoming Marilyn Manson's pastry chef. She kept her white hair dyed bubble-gum pink and wore about a dozen earrings in her left ear. They all looked like nuts, bolts, and possibly a corkscrew.

"Mr. Talmadge seemed a little, um, irritated with Dill," Ernestine said delicately as she put down the bottle and took off the heavy rubber gloves and goggles she had been wearing. "*And* with Mrs. MacGillicuddie."

"Oh, *that*." Mrs. Talmadge tutted. "He's just worried about what his old mates the Dead Kennedys would say."

"I'm sorry, what was that?" Mr. Talmadge knew some dead people named Kennedy? Where on earth had he found some dead friends to hang out with? Perhaps he could give her some pointers.

"That was back when I was still cooking for Sid," Mrs. Talmadge continued mistily, not exactly answering Ernestine's question. "That's Sid Vicious, of course, dearie."

"Did Sid viciously kill them, which is why the Kennedys were dead?" Ernestine asked. If so, maybe she could get his number so she could ask a few questions about how he'd brought them back afterward.

"No. Personally, I blame MTV." Mrs. Talmadge peered into the bag Ernestine had brought downstairs along with the drain cleaner. With her thumb and forefinger, she pulled out one of the drumsticks they'd dumped on Herbert's grave last night. "Speaking of dead things, what are these, dearie?"

"Oh. Those. Those are tonight's supper. Hey, you haven't seen any zombies wandering around today, have you?"

"Do you count Mr. Sangfroid when he's overdone it on his medication?" Mrs. Talmadge pulled some dead grass off one of the chicken legs.

"Did he try to bite you?"

"Not this time, no."

"Then I don't, unfortunately." Ernestine ran water down the drain until she was sure it had cleared up. "It should be good to go now, but if any body parts come up, let me know."

"Uh, is that likely, dearie?" Mrs. Talmadge peered down the drain anxiously, apparently unaware that there might be a minor zombie apocalypse going on in the neighborhood.

"Depends on whether the zombie apocalypse has started," Ernestine explained helpfully. "If it has, then you're likely to find body parts *anywhere*."

Next, Ernestine went to fix Mr. Sangfroid's leaky pipe. When he answered his door, he was holding the enormous, dusty old photo album that had fallen from the attic when the chandelier crashed down.

"Isn't that Mrs. MacGillicuddie's photo album?" Ernestine asked pointedly.

"That's none of your business! You're just the hired help!" Mr. Sangfroid snapped the album shut as though *she* was the one doing the peeking. "And why didn't you come sooner? Why aren't your parents here? Maybe I should be contacting Children's Services, eh?"

"Maybe you should," Ernestine retorted, spine very straight. "I think they should know about an adult harassing a child."

The Adam's apple in Mr. Sangfroid's throat bobbed up and down as he glared back at her in outrage for daring to stand up for herself. However, rather than slamming the door on her as she had expected, Mr. Sangfroid followed her down into the warrenlike basement so he could rant at her some more, this time about the end of the world. Unfortunately, his apocalypse was a lot less interesting than the average kind.

"Rubbish! That's what those Talmadges are! Cooks! Kitchen help! Not true artists!" He pounded the dank floor with his cane as Ernestine unlocked and then relocked various small rooms, looking for the correct pipes. Each resident got a storage room along with their apartments above. "And what of Mr. Theda and Mr. Bara, eh?"

"What about them?" Ernestine located the pipe in a room full of debris from MacGillicuddie House's glory days, including several very ugly paintings, a broken mirror or two, and an absolutely ginormous frame that had freed whatever it once held many years before.

Ernestine tried to reach the pipe but couldn't. Mr. Sangfroid watched disapprovingly as she hopped up and down, trying to get to it, but didn't offer to help.

"Cheap, low-brow entertainers, that's what they are!" Mr. Sangfroid harrumphed.

Ignoring him, Ernestine tested the empty frame to confirm it was sturdy enough to hold her weight from where it was propped up against the wall. It was, and she climbed up on it. Mr. Sangfroid's eyes widened at the sight, but he *still* didn't offer to help. "Those horror movies of theirs appeal only to the low-brow, you know. Just like those Swanson twins. Common dancers! Not even ballet dancers! Little better than chorus girls. Why, it's no wonder their parents—"

Mr. Sangfroid suddenly clammed up. Ernestine stopped winching the pipe to stare at him. "No wonder their parents what?"

"None of your business," he snapped. "I disapprove of gossip!"

Straightening his back and jutting his chin out at her, he marched off with one final parting shot. "It's just a pity that chandelier didn't take care of Mrs. MacGillicuddie *before* she could invite in any more trash like your parents and you nosy kids!"

"Well!" Ernestine slid down off the picture frame as it began to crack under her weight, hands on her hips. "If you think things are bad now, wait until the zombies move in!"

He made her so mad that it wasn't until she was out in the garden looking for Charleston that she realized she'd forgotten to lock that last door down in the basement. Meanwhile, she couldn't find Charleston anywhere, even though litter patrol in the garden was the second item on his list, so he should have been on it by now. Hopefully, that didn't mean he'd been hideously eaten or bloodily murdered on the way. She'd never had a stepbrother before, and she quite liked him, even if they did have to share a room. She'd prefer it if he didn't get either hideously eaten *or* bloodily murdered. He was fine just the way he was.

If Charleston was missing, Mrs. MacGillicuddie's 1937 baby-blue Studebaker limousine had returned. That meant Rodney and his daughter must be skulking around someplace like the ghouls in one of Mr. Theda's movies.

Speaking of which, Ernestine found several crumpled flyers that the wind had torn off telephone poles and then deposited in the shrubbery along the wall. A fanged and clawed Mr. Theda sneered out at her from the page, advertising a showing of his movies over at the old Palace Movie Theater by the university, featuring a special performance by the Swanson twins. Though retired, Mr. Theda was actually more popular than ever, thanks to Mr. Bara's social media savvy. The two had quite the online following and made an extremely comfortable living showing up at horror movie, sci-fi, and comic book conventions.

The flyer reminded Ernestine of Charleston's suggestion to put up missing zombie posters. If nothing else, it would raise awareness on a very important matter of public health.

Tucking the flyers into her pocket, Ernestine went in search of her stepbrother, finding him at the site of the very first chore on his list. Only rather than fixing a squeaky floorboard in Mrs. MacGillicuddie's apartment, he was standing on an ottoman while wearing an enormous flow-ered hat, high glittery heels, and a long lavender gown while a seamstress did something to the hem that seemed likely to end in Charleston stitched to the furniture.

"I don't even know what to say," Ernestine said when she stepped into the palatial room full of lemon trees and gold furniture. Charleston just shrugged and went back to eating brownies from the plate he was holding.

"*So* sorry, darling," Mrs. MacGillicuddie drawled from where she lounged on a leopard-print fainting couch. She wore a hot pink silk robe with a feather boa and stiletto heels. Heirloom jewels encrusted her from the top of her head to the tips of her fingertips right on down to her feet where she wore emerald-and-diamond anklets worth more money than most people made in a lifetime.

As Mrs. MacGillicuddie had said before, at her age you never knew when it might be your last chance to wear your jewels. Especially your no-good-lying-cheating-dirty-rotten-underhanded-crook-of-an-ex-husband's family jewels, may he rot in his grave until he rises as a zombie to shamble about so Mrs. MacGillicuddie could whack off his head with her cane. (A delighted Mrs. MacGillicuddie had added that last part after Ernestine told her about the coming apoca-lypse.)

When Ernestine was eighty, she wanted to be *exactly* like Mrs. MacGillicuddie.

Several other people filled the room aside from Charleston and the seamstress. Rodney sat on a purple chair beneath two potted lemon trees, looking like he'd been sucking on the fruit dangling above his head. Fluffy-Wuffy-Kins, Mrs. MacGillicuddie's cat, gleefully shed long, white hair all over his suit as Aurora Borealis preened in front of her phone, taking a selfie so all her followers would know that she was still as gorgeous as she was ten minutes ago.

A man Ernestine didn't recognize sat on a gilt chair covered in zebra print while scribbling down a bunch of notes. Kind of like Mr. Price, the school psychologist. Meanwhile, Mrs. MacGillicuddie's nephew Lyndon tried to blend in with another lemon tree. Ernestine suspected that when the end of the world came, he'd be one of the first ones to get eaten because he'd be too busy trying to figure out how to make money off the zombies to pay attention to avoiding them. He'd probably just walk right up to the first zombie he saw and ask it if it wanted to get rich quick. He always had some sort of scheme that he was trying to get people to invest in, having already wasted his inheritance on bad investments.

"As I was saying, Mother, last night was the final straw! You're deranged." Rodney peered over at the guy taking the impressive amount of notes and said, "Did you get that? Are you making a note of the fact that she's deranged?"

"Rodney, that chandelier *might* have *re*arranged my body parts had it hit me, but that hardly makes me *de*ranged!" Eduardo hurried forward to fill Mrs. MacGillicuddie's cup with tea as she waved it about irritably. He then discreetly removed a Fabergé egg from Aurora Borealis's purse and returned it to its rightful place next to a Chihuly sculpture on a seventeenth-century desk Aurora Borealis had stuck her gum under. Ernestine noticed she was wearing the white sparkly shoes she'd stolen from the Swanson twins the night before.

Turning back to Ernestine, Mrs. MacGillicuddie begged her, "*Don't* be upset with Charleston, darling. I'm *dreadfully* afraid I forced him to remain with us so Peggy here could hem my negligee. He's *exactly* my size, you know."

Ernestine approved of the way Mrs. MacGillicuddie tended to speak in italics. No sense in saying anything if you didn't feel emphatic about it.

"He's half your size!" Ernestine protested.

"Not on the ottoman and in my stilettos," Mrs. MacGillicuddie trilled, while Peggy the seamstress looked up with a mouthful of pins and nodded in agreement. "I *tried* to get Rodney there to do it, but he's *much* too busy consulting with that shrink he brought along to try and prove I'm crazy."

"You *are* crazy!" Rodney puffed up his chest and then whispered to the psychiatrist, "You got that, too, didn't you? Put down that she shows clear signs of dementia."

"Plus, she said she'd give me twenty dollars," Charleston interjected from around a mouthful of brownie.

"Oh, Charleston," Ernestine groaned, setting her toolbox down next to the loose floorboard Eduardo helpfully pointed out for her. "You can't put a price on your dignity."

"I can on mine, and it's twenty dollars."

"That reminds me." Getting up from her fainting couch, Mrs. MacGillicuddie tottered on her stilettos over to one of the lemon trees. Reaching a hand into the pot, she rummaged about until she came up with a stack of neatly wrapped bills. This she promptly handed to Ernestine. "For you, darling, for saving me last night from that *awful* chandelier while my *devoted* son stood by and watched, hoping I'd die so he'd get to inherit even more of the MacGillicuddie fortune."

"Mother!"

"Wait, you're giving *her* money, Grammy?" Aurora Borealis froze in the act of sliding an antique ashtray into her purse. "But *she* isn't even very *pretty!* And she doesn't have any followers on Instagram. You don't, do you?"

That last comment was aimed at Ernestine, who was too busy thumbing through the stack of cash to bother answering. They were all fifties and there seemed to be about two hundred of them. That made...

Gosh. That made ten thousand dollars.

"Mrs. MacGillicuddie, this is too much." Ernestine held the money out to her landlady. "I can't possibly accept ten thousand dollars."

"Ten thousand?" Lyndon gasped. Then, in a low whisper to Ernestine, he added, "I've got this fantastic business I'm putting together to set up hot chocolate cafés all along the equator in Africa, if you're interested."

Ernestine blinked. "Er, I don't think so, no."

"Ten *thousand!*" Aurora Borealis whined. "But you only gave me *five* thousand for my last *birth*day!"

"She only gave me a card!" For once, Rodney turned his open-mouthed outrage on someone other than his mother. He spent so much of his time with his chest puffed out, Ernestine half-expected him to float away like a balloon.

"At your party, *you* served me avocado, which you know I'm deathly allergic to," Mrs. MacGillicuddie said pointedly, swiping a brownie from the tray Charleston was still holding, and collapsing back onto her fainting couch.

"That was an accident! I forgot to tell the chef!"

"Ha! Who's got dementia now, Rodney?"

Rodney turned to the psychiatrist, only to discover the

doctor studying him beadily as he tapped his lip with his pencil. Meanwhile, Lyndon peered into the barrel of the closest lemon tree as though hopeful of finding it mulched in fifty dollar bills.

"*Keep* the money, darling. Use it to start your adorable little zombie apocalypse. It sounds like grand fun."

"Well, all right." Ernestine didn't feel entirely good about it, but she supposed keeping it herself was better than letting Mrs. MacGillicuddie's awful family get their hands on it. She was going to need a lot of cash to run her campaign for president when the apocalypse was over.

"Wait, what's this about zombies?" Aurora Borealis glanced around like she thought there might be one lurking in the lemon trees along with all of that cash. "Are there dead things around? Ew, gross!"

"There might be," Ernestine warned. "As I was telling Mrs. Talmadge earlier, you never know for sure these days."

As Charleston explained that the ravenous undead might be wandering the neighborhood, Ernestine pulled out a hammer and some nails to fix the loose floorboard. However, when she looked at it, there didn't seem to be anything wrong with it. It didn't stick up at all or look uneven compared to the rest of the floorboards. Yet that was the one Eduardo said had launched Fluffy-Wuffy-Kins into the lemon tree yesterday. Ernestine pressed down on one end with her hand.

WHUMP! The other end sprang up and almost smacked her in the face.

"Oh, *I know,* darling," Mrs. MacGillicuddie peered over the fainting couch at her. "I would have broken my neck stepping on it, if Fluffy-Wuffy-Kins hadn't stepped on it first, the brave, adorable, widdle darling."

"Is that why his face looks so squashed?" Charleston asked, earning him a one-eyed glare from Fluffy-Wuffy-Kins, whose face really did look like it had been flattened by a floorboard.

Huh. Ernestine inspected the floor, her spider-sense tingling. Well, maybe it was her zombie-sense. Either way, *something* was tingling because something else wasn't right. Two accidental almost-deaths in one day was one accidental almost-death too many.

Then Ernestine spotted it. She bent closer to get a better look and noticed sawdust in the cracks.

The board wasn't loose. It had been neatly and deliberately sawed in two.

Mrs. MacGillicuddie hadn't accidentally almost-died. She'd been purposefully almost-*murdered*.

Chapter Five
A Little Late-Night Murder

"MURDER!" Ernestine screeched, pointing dramatically at the floorboard.

Everyone stopped what they were doing and looked at her. Lyndon pulled his arm out of the lemon tree. Aurora Borealis pulled her nose out of her phone. Rodney pulled himself up to his full height. Even the psychiatrist ceased scribbling in his notebook for the first time since Ernestine arrived. Only Charleston kept on calmly eating his brownies.

Extremely pleased to have all attention focused on her, Ernestine smoothed down her overalls and cleared her throat. "Ahem. Mrs. MacGillicuddie, I believe someone is trying to murder you. Unfortunately, zombies don't seem to be involved, but in my opinion, it is still an urgent matter that needs to be addressed. Because I don't think the chandelier fell last night by accident."

"Oh, darling! How *thrilling!*" Rather than the horror Ernestine was expecting, Mrs. MacGillicuddie positively beamed. "It's been *ages* since anyone last tried to murder me. No one has bothered at all since Rodney tried to kill me with that avocado."

"Mother!" Rodney cried. "That was an honest mistake! I thought it was asparagus you were allergic to!"

"Yes, I'm sure that's *exactly* what you would have said in my eulogy!"

"It could be Eduardo they were trying to murder," Charleston pointed out from a mouthful of brownie as the seamstress hastily gathered her stuff up to go, clearly unnerved by all of this talk of zombies and murder.

"Oh, *that* wouldn't be at *all* fair!" Mrs. MacGillicuddie pouted. "Someone tried to murder him just last year, didn't they, Eduardo? You naughty boy!"

Eduardo bowed modestly.

"Did they do it with a zombie, a chandelier, or a trick floorboard?" Ernestine inquired. Perhaps Eduardo's would-be murderer was back.

"No, tried to strangle him with a leash at last year's Purebred Pampered Puss Pet Pageant."

"It's very competitive," Eduardo murmured as though that explained everything.

"Mother!" Rodney barked, clearly feeling it was time he took control of the situation. "This is too much! I'm having you committed to a home for the elderly and insane!"

He turned optimistically to the psychiatrist, who made a face and shook his head. Deflating like a pricked balloon, Rodney turned to his mother and tried wheedling. *"Please,* Mother? It's in your best interests. That's all I want."

"I already live in a home for the elderly and insane, and I quite like it here. NOW. GET. OUT." She jammed the tip of her cane into his derriere, causing her son to yelp and scurry out of the room, followed by Aurora Borealis, the seamstress, and the psychiatrist.

As the doctor passed by Ernestine, he handed her his business card. "If you want to use some of that cash and come see me sometime, I can tell we have fertile ground to discuss."

"Well, you don't really need to fertilize the ground before you raise the zombies, but I'd be more than happy to give you some pointers," Ernestine told him, immensely flattered. "I have a whole zombie survival guide put together. It will definitely be a bestseller when the zombie hordes finally arise to devour us all, you know."

"Er—" The psychiatrist seemed to be thinking twice about giving her a card that had his address listed on it, but in the end, he let go of it, anyhow.

"Lyndon, darling, you'll find a stack of fifties in a secret panel behind that cuckoo clock on the wall over there," Mrs. MacGillicuddie said wearily, having just noticed that Lyndon was trying to pry a lemon open with his bare hands.

"Oh!" Hastily, he dropped the lemon into the pot. "I, uh, wasn't—"

"Oh, get it and get out!" She jabbed her cane in his direction, causing him to leap up, swing the cuckoo clock open, and grab his cash.

"Thank you, Great-Auntie Edna!" he babbled. "Incredibly generous of you! Can't thank you enough! Don't know what I would do without you!"

"Inherit a third of my fortune and promptly lose it all, I suspect," she sighed to Ernestine and Charleston as he departed. "You know the last business venture he tried to get me to invest in involved trying to sell frozen yogurt to Eskimos in the Antarctic."

"But there aren't any Eskimos in the Antarctic," Charleston pointed out. "They live in the Arctic."

"Yes, I know, darling. Why do you think I wouldn't invest?"

"Lyndon is one of your heirs?" Ernestine asked curiously as she helped Charleston out of his heels and fancy dress.

"Yes, darling. There aren't any heirs on my side of the family, and Rodney, Lyndon, and Aurora Borealis are the only surviving heirs on my husband's side. Of course, they won't get all my money. A few million here and there will go to others outside of the family, but the bulk of it will be split between the three of them. Awful people, but they *are* family, I suppose." As Mrs. MacGillicuddie talked, Eduardo brought her the sort of fancy, curvy, gilded phone Ernestine had only ever seen in one of Mr. Theda's old movies. "Now do get out, you two! You're lovely, but I need to call my personal beautician to come over and fix me up. I want to look my best if I'm going to be almost-murdered again. Fancy being almost-murdered with curlers in your hair or a mud mask on your face!"

Mrs. MacGillicuddie shuddered as though the thought of it was the most appalling thing she'd heard all evening.

"Gosh, it sounds like a lot of people have reasons to want Mrs. MacGillicuddie dead," Charleston remarked as they left the room. He looked a bit like a talking chipmunk as his cheeks stored enough brownies to last him the remainder of the winter. "Her family inherits if she dies. Mr. Theda was threatening her. Mr. Talmadge is mad at her, *and* armed with kitchen knives."

"And Mr. Sangfroid was telling me that *he* wished she was dead," Ernestine said, recalling their earlier conversation as she and Charleston headed back up to the attic. "He said it was a pity the chandelier didn't kill her last night. He doesn't like that she's letting people like us and the Swanson twins live here."

"What's wrong with us and the Swanson twins?" Charleston asked in astonishment.

"Apparently we're garbage and just haven't noticed it," Ernestine said grimly.

Charleston sniffed his shirt and muttered, "I think I'd notice if I was garbage."

Back up in the attic, Ernestine went into Frank's studio to take a look at the remains of the chandelier. Most of it was just twisted metal and shards of crystal, but the base was still attached to a chunk of the ceiling with a few bolts.

Inspecting the bolts, Ernestine sucked in her breath. "Charleston, look at this."

"Can't. I don't feel so good." Clutching his stomach, Charleston slumped down onto the couch. "I may have eaten too many brownies."

"The screws were deliberately unscrewed!" Grabbing him

up off the couch, she propelled him over to the broken light fixture. "Look, you can see the scratch marks."

Looking at them now, each bolt was longer than her longest finger and almost as thick as her wrist. Whoever had loosened them must have had a difficult time of it, as the wrench had cut deep grooves into the reddish-brown metal.

"How do you know they're new? Maybe they had a hard time putting it in a hundred thousand years ago or whenever." Charleston belched and grabbed his tummy again. "Uuuuggghhh."

"Because those scratches are shiny. If they'd been made when the chandelier was put in, they'd be rusty by now, too."

"Yeah, but they'd had to have snuck through our apartment to do it. Unless—oh, jeez, Ernestine—you don't think your mom and my dad did it, do you?" He looked green at the thought. Well, mostly he just looked green. It might not have been the thought causing it.

"Don't be stupid, Charleston. Our parents could never get themselves organized enough to murder anyone." Ernestine pondered his point for a moment. How could anyone have made it through without Frank and Maya noticing? Easily, as far as she was concerned. Her mom got so wrapped up in her artwork that she didn't notice all sorts of important things, and as far as Ernestine could tell, Frank was every bit as bad. Then she remembered what Frank had said the night before. "He had the metal cutters running for most of the day! With the curtains pulled across their studios and those metal cutters going, you could march a high school band through here, and Frank and Maya would never even know anyone had been inside! And—oh, Charleston!—*look at this!*"

"*Urp.*" Rather than looking, Charleston slapped a hand over his mouth and ran for the bathroom.

Ernestine waited patiently until he'd finished puking up the brownies, rinsed his mouth out, and collapsed once again on the couch. Then she held up the slender thread of fishing wire she'd found. "Someone loosened the bolts, then attached a wire to the chandelier. While all the fighting was going on, that someone tugged on the wire to make the chandelier fall onto the crowd below."

"But who?" Charleston asked weakly. "I didn't see anyone pulling on it."

"Neither did I," Ernestine admitted. "But the fishing line is so thin, I don't think anyone could see it unless they knew it was there. And with all of the cheering and the fist-pumping going on during the fight, anyone could have yanked it down without anyone else noticing a thing."

"Who do you think was supposed to get murdered?" Charleston asked, sliding down off the couch. "Do you think it was Mrs. MacGillicuddie? Or Eduardo? Or maybe even the Swanson twins? They were the ones most likely to die in the accident since the chandelier smashed right through their tightrope when it fell. It was just chance that Mrs. MacGillicuddie was even under it. Hey, I'm hungry again. Let's go help the Talmadges make supper."

That was an excellent point about the Swanson twins. Although, what about that floorboard? Ernestine wondered as she followed Charleston down the stairs. If someone wanted to kill the twins, that didn't add up.

Maya and Frank were actually already down in the Talmadges' kitchen, helping them chop vegetables. Normally, Mrs. Talmadge would be fixing Mrs. MacGillicuddie's supper, but after all of the excitement last night, Mrs. MacGillicuddie had decided to go on a juice cleanse to make sure she looked fantastic in case she was murdered. As she said, "No one wants to be an unattractive corpse on the society page, darling. Imagine the embarrassment!" So the Talmadges had invited Ernestine and her family to their apartment for dinner instead.

After last night, Ernestine was a bit afraid that Mr. Talmadge might go bonkers at the sight of the carrots and start throwing knives around, insisting that they have their chicken with ham on the side and a nice salmon mousse for dessert.

But he just placidly chopped some rosemary instead.

"Mr. and Mrs. Talmadge, can you think of anyone who might want to kill the Swanson twins?" Ernestine asked, pausing from her work. "Well, you know. Aside from zombies, who I think it's safe to assume want to kill everyone."

"Who? Libitina and Morana?" Mrs. Talmadge asked, surprised.

"Um, I think?" Ernestine had never actually heard their full names before. Which, if Maya had named *her* Libitina or Morana, she'd make sure that no one ever heard it, either.

"Lots of disappointed boyfriends, I suspect," Mr. Talmadge snickered, dicing a pile of carrots with several rapid whacks of his meat cleaver.

"Now Rupert, luv, that isn't nice. You make them sound like maneaters."

"From what I hear, they broke a lot of hearts."

"Oh, and who did you hear that from?" Mrs. Talmadge stopped stirring whatever was in a saucepan on the stove and put one hand on her hip.

"Mr. Sangfroid. Apparently he used to date Libitina many, *many* years ago." If Mr. Talmadge was snickering before, he positively guffawed now. Until the disapproving glare of his wife caused him to sober up. Chastened, he concentrated on chopping the rest of the carrots.

"But Mr. Sangfroid hates the twins." Ernestine recalled how angry he had been when speaking of them. Angry enough to murder someone, it seemed like. "He said they were garbage."

"You don't hate someone like that without having loved them first," Mr. Talmadge said wisely. His wife nodded, too, even though that didn't make a bit of sense to Ernestine.

"Love, man," Frank agreed sagely. "It's a many-splendored creation."

Ernestine had absolutely no idea what that meant, either, but as she loathed admitting that she didn't know something, she decided to just google it later. Of course, it was entirely possible it only made sense to Frank and no amount of googling would make it sensible to anyone else.

"How about Mrs. MacGillicuddie? Can you think of anyone who might want to kill her?" asked Ernestine as Mrs. Talmadge showed Charleston how to pour the sauce over the leftover chicken legs from last night's cemetery expedition.

"Her family," everyone responded in unison and then looked at each other.

Maya's face scrunched up as she set the table with silverware and plates. "Oh, that's rather sad, isn't it?"

"Yes, families should be very protective of each other," Ernestine told her mother meaningfully.

"*And* supportive," Maya agreed, hugging her as though they were on the same page. "And encourage them to be individuals who seek out their own destinies."

Ernestine pulled away and crossed her arms. "In the zombie apocalypse, no one will have a destiny to seek out if we don't keep *a very close eye on* each other."

Maya winced and let her go. In a slightly wobbly voice, she said, "The apocalypse sounds awful. Like when I was a girl and my mother would never let me out of her sight, not even for a moment. I ran off when I was eighteen and never looked back."

"Grandma probably wanted to make sure nothing terrible happened to you," Ernestine pointed out, satisfied by the stricken look her words brought to Maya's face.

Mr. Talmadge broke the awkward silence that followed by saying to Maya, "You sound like me. I ran away from home when I was fourteen. I was living in London back then. Got me first job cleaning up at the Black Swan Pub. You had to be tough, you did. Not like these days, eating all these froufrou garden weeds and worrying about whether your food had legs to try and run away with…"

He had started to ramble on, but a whack on the shoulder with Mrs. Talmadge's wooden spoon brought him back to the present. Mr. Talmadge looked around sheepishly. "Sorry. I know I do go on about the old days sometimes."

When dinner had finished cooking, they sat down together to eat it. Ernestine pointed out to Mr. Talmadge that zombies, like him, felt meat should be a staple of any proper diet, while Mrs. Talmadge asked Frank and Maya about their gallery opening on Saturday.

"Yes, Saturday *is* a big day," Ernestine agreed grumpily. "We should *all* definitely pay attention to what a *big* day Saturday is."

Charleston was the only one who noticed her tone. "What do you mean? It's the fourteenth, isn't it? That's Valentine's Day, right?"

It was, but that wasn't what made it a big day for Ernestine. "Oh, never mind."

After supper, Maya and Frank went off to work on their very big, important artwork for their very big, important day, while Charleston tried to sneak off to watch a competitive cooking show with Mr. Talmadge. Ernestine caught him and marched him upstairs to do his homework.

"You have a math test tomorrow!" She pointed at the note in his agenda book. Their teachers made them fill it out at the end of each school day so they wouldn't forget anything. "And you're barely passing as it is. We have to maintain good grades or they'll kick us out! And then you'll have to go to the public school, and you'll never get into college."

"So what?" Charleston sulked, opening his math book without enthusiasm as a bored-looking swan wandered past.

"So what?!" Ernestine repeated, shocked. *"So what?!"*

She sat down next to him and folded her hands on the table. "Have I taught you *nothing*? When the apocalypse comes, it will be the stupid people who get eaten first. If you don't exercise your brain properly, it gets all mushy like a rotten apple. That makes it easier to suck out when they crack open your skull! So, if you don't want to be a zombie Slurpee, *you will pass your math class with at least a B!*"

"Fine." Charleston thunked his head against his open book. He did, however, study with Ernestine for the next two hours. At the end of that time, she was reasonably sure he'd get at least a C on the test and not rot away into zombie baby food. Not tomorrow, anyway.

In bed, with Charleston snoring down below, Ernestine took out a flashlight and read some of her comic books underneath the covers. You never knew when you might have missed something critical, so it was always a good idea to go back and reread things as many times as possible. She was looking for anything that might suggest that sometimes zombies didn't look or act like zombies while actually *being* zombies. Just in case it really had been a zombie trying to break in last night and not a homicidal maniac.

Eventually, she gave up and turned her flashlight off, safe in the knowledge that she probably wouldn't get eaten tonight. Probably.

In the deep dark of the night, something woke her up out of a sound sleep. Ernestine shot upright, immediately on the alert. She'd heard a noise downstairs in the foyer, she was sure of it. The Hep Cats didn't have any gigs tonight, there wasn't a party going on in Mrs. MacGillicuddie's suite, and no one else had any plans to be out late as far as Ernestine knew. So whatever was going bump in the night had an excellent chance of being either a murderer or a zombie. Whichever it was, Ernestine was quite sure she didn't want it sneaking up on her while she slept.

Crawling down out of her bunk, she pulled on the zombie mask she'd worn last Halloween and then shook Charleston's bed violently. When he rolled over and squinted blearily at her, she shoved her face down by his and moaned, "Brains…braaaaaaaiiiiins…"

"*AAAUUUGGGHHH!!!*" Charleston screamed and skittered backward, slamming against the wall.

"What sort of zombie attack response was *that?*" Ernestine yanked off her mask. "If I'd been a real zombie, what good would going, 'AAAUUUGGGHHH' do? A zombie isn't going to run away because you yelled at it!"

Charleston flopped against his mattress. "I gotta get my own room. One with a lock on the door."

"Yeah, good luck with that."

As Charleston mushed his glasses onto his face, Ernestine handed him his baseball bat, while keeping a second one for herself. "I think something's trying to break in downstairs. Let's go kill it."

"Couldn't we just tell my dad and your mom about it?" Charleston pleaded.

"No, they'd just paint it or wrap it up in aluminum foil and tie it to a sculpture. C'mon."

Weapons held aloft, the two of them tiptoed past the sleeping swans, out of the attic and down the back stairs to the third floor, where they switched over to the better-lit front stairs. The stairs zigzagged around the foyer so that you could see down all three stories. Peering over the railing, Ernestine couldn't see anything but shadows below. Which didn't mean anything because everyone knew that both zombies *and* murderers loved to lurk in shadows.

"You know, getting a good night's sleep is highly recommended before taking a test," Charleston hissed on the way, apparently holding a grudge.

"So is surviving until morning," Ernestine pointed out.

No one appeared to be up at the moment, not even Mr.

Ellington and the Hep Cats, who frequently stayed up until the wee hours of the morning even when there wasn't a party going on, scatting and reminiscing about the time Jack Kerouac threw up in Mr. Ellington's saxophone. Even the mice seemed to have called it a night.

Reaching the bottom of the steps, they both stood still, listening. Far, far away, Ernestine could hear the sounds of cars on the expressway. Much, much closer, she could also hear the slow shuffling of feet.

"Erk." Charleston strangled a gasp in his throat, his eyes bugging out in fear. Ernestine elbowed him and put her finger to her lips.

The back door. Something was definitely lurching about somewhere near the back door. Right next to the laundry room with the broken window latch. Ernestine and Charleston peered slowly around the edge of the elaborately carved banister. When nothing tried to murder and eat them, they slowly tiptoed forward.

A long, long, loooooong wood-paneled hallway led to the back of the house, with doors off of it leading to various rooms. Through the mudroom, a pale square of light marked the window in the back door. Moving silently, they stepped closer and closer with Charleston huddled against Ernestine's back. Closer…closer…

Something rose up out of the shadows, so nearby that it loomed up and over them, its hideously decayed face just barely visible from the security light in the backyard.

"ZOMMMBIEEEEEEEE!" Charleston screamed and swung at it with his baseball bat. He missed and knocked Ernestine into the wall in the process. Then he threw his bat at it, and retreated behind Ernestine in a state of panic.

The zombie screamed, too, but at least it had the sense to snatch up the bat and take a swing at Ernestine.

"Oh great, Charleston. Arm the zombie, why don't you?" Ernestine snapped in exasperation as it tried to play t-ball with her head. She ducked and struck back at it with her own bat, smacking it right in its zombie gut. It grunted in pain as a bit of it fell off, which distracted the creature long enough for Ernestine to aim for its head.

Rats. Displaying amazing reflexes for something half-decayed, it swerved backward just in time, and her bat whistled right past its nose.

"You're not eating our brains!" Ernestine screamed and swung again.

Apparently that was too much for the zombie. It threw Charleston's bat at Ernestine, knocking her down and gaining enough time to run out the back door. By the time she reached the backyard, there wasn't a zombie in sight.

Seriously, had her zombie been an Olympic runner in life or something? Zombies were supposed to shuffle slowly along since necessary body parts were probably hanging on by just a tendon or two. They weren't supposed to sprint zestfully along as though they'd been working on their glutes with an undead personal trainer.

Charleston joined her at the doorway, glasses askew on his face.

"That was sorta embarrassing," he admitted.

"You think?" Ernestine wanted to bang her head in frustration. Zombies were not supposed to be this hard to catch.

Behind them, the hallway lights flipped on. Ernestine and Charleston both screamed and clutched at each other in terror, rather proving Charleston's point about the whole embarrassing aspect of the night's fiasco.

It was not, however, the zombie back for a better look and possibly a nibble. Instead, it was Mrs. MacGillicuddie, dressed in a leopard-print robe and purple turban, green creamy stuff spread all over her face. Eduardo popped up behind her, green goo spread all over his face, too, and a shotgun crooked in his arm.

Ernestine and Charleston shrieked again.

"Goodness, darlings. What is all this racket about?" Mrs. MacGillicuddie demanded.

Half an hour later, Ernestine and Charleston were sitting around Mrs. MacGillicuddie's kitchen table, china cups of hot chocolate in their hands, compliments of Eduardo. Mrs. MacGillicuddie was there, too, her face still slathered in beauty cream. A Ziploc bag lay in the middle of the table, and they all peered at it with interest. It contained the bit of zombie that had fallen off during the fight, proof they had a zombie problem on their hands. Ernestine couldn't have been any more delighted.

"How shocking!" Mrs. MacGillicuddie said as she sipped at her cup. "I've never had a zombie problem before. Rats and cockroaches, yes, but never zombies! It's positively thrilling!"

"I know!" Ernestine enthused, glad someone appreciated what a positive turn of events this was. At this rate, she might be able to achieve a full-scale, city-destroying, rotting-corpse infestation by the end of the week!

"And here you thought it hadn't worked," Mrs. MacGillicuddie said as though reading Ernestine's thoughts.

"Wait. How did you know about that?" Ernestine asked, positive she hadn't said anything to Mrs. MacGillicuddie about Monday night's failure. She turned and glared at Charleston, who suddenly found the marshmallows bobbing in his cup to be awfully interesting.

"What?" he asked guiltily.

"Charleston, you do not run around telling people that you tried to start the apocalypse and failed. You only brag about it when you're sure it succeeded! Otherwise, you're not an evil genius, you're just some idiot with an undead problem!"

"Ha! That's my son, Rodney." Mrs. MacGillicuddie leaned back as Eduardo sat a china plate of chocolate chip cookies on the table. *"He's* an idiot with an undead problem. Only *I'm* the undead he has a problem with! Eduardo, be a darling and make me some warm milk, please. I'll never be able to sleep knowing I was almost eaten by zombies if I don't have some warm milk first."

Eduardo did as she asked, pouring it into a pink teapot. As Ernestine watched, he pulled a bottle out of his pocket and discreetly tipped a bit of whatever it contained into the pot.

"MURDERER!" Ernestine shrieked, springing out of her chair so quickly, she knocked it over. She yanked the bottle out of Eduardo's hands and gave it a sniff. It smelled dreadful.

Eduardo muttered something in Spanish, rolling his eyes to the ceiling. Mrs. MacGillicuddie snatched the bottle from her. "Don't be so dramatic, darling. It's just bourbon."

"Mrs. MacGillicuddie!" Ernestine exclaimed, shocked.

"Well, you don't think the milk is going to put me to sleep all by itself, do you, darling? It's just milk from a cow. It's not like their udders have any magical properties."

"It could still be poisoned bourbon," Charleston pointed out, munching on a hopefully unpoisoned cookie.

"Oh, darlings. Don't be so silly. Here, put some in a bowl for Mr. Fluffy-Wuffy-Kins to try. That'll prove to you that it's fine." Mrs. MacGillicuddie tipped some of the bourbon–milk mixture from the teapot into a saucer and sat it down on the floor for the cat.

"You can't give a cat bourbon!" Ernestine said, shocked all over again.

"Whyever not? I do it all the time. Keeps Fluffy from clawing the curtains in the night."

Fluffy-Wuffy-Kins settled down daintily at his dish and lapped at the milk. The four of them leaned toward him, waiting to see if he keeled over.

"See, he's fine." Mrs. MacGillicuddie poured milk into cups for all four of them as Eduardo took a delicate sip from his. "Now we all need a cup to sooth our nerves."

"You can't give kids bourbon!" This time it was Charleston who was shocked. Ernestine had sort of given up on it.

"Whyever not? I gave it to Rodney all the time when he was little, and he always slept right through the night." Just as Ernestine and Charleston were trying to wrap their minds around Mrs. MacGillicuddie's questionable parenting skills, Fluffy-Wuffy-Kins screeched a horrible screech. Mrs. MacGillicuddie froze in the act of lifting her china cup to her lips.

Back arched, tail stiff as a board, Fluffy-Wuffy-Kins hacked like he was about to spit up a hairball. Eduardo jumped backward to protect his purple slippers.

Only Fluffy-Wuffy-Kins didn't spit out a wad of half-digested fur.

He keeled over on his side, dead as a doornail.

HERBERT EDWARD McGOVERN 1940 – 1977

Chapter Six

Sometimes It Takes More Than One Try to End the World

WEDNESDAY, 2:23 AM

Eduardo immediately clapped one hand over his mouth and the other over his stomach, and ran to the bathroom to throw up the milk he had just drunk. Mrs. MacGillicuddie scurried after him, pulling out an impressively high-tech phone for someone so elderly as she shrieked, "Don't die on me, Eduardo, darling! I shan't be able to carry on if I lose both you and Fluffy in one night!"

Ernestine and Charleston stared down at the sad furry body lying on the floor.

"Well," Charleston said, trying to find a bright side. "At least we know it was probably Mrs. MacGillicuddie the zombie was trying to kill. We must have caught it right after it poisoned her bottle of bourbon."

"I don't think zombies normally poison a person before they eat them," Ernestine pointed out. "Zombies just sort of grab the first person they see and gobble them down, Charleston."

"People like salt and spices on their food. Why shouldn't zombies be the same way?" Her stepbrother argued. "You don't know. Maybe zombies season us before they eat us."

Ernestine opened her mouth to explain that zombies weren't exactly picky eaters when someone pounded on the kitchen door that led out into the house's main hallway.

"Is everything all right in there? We heard screaming!" a voice cried anxiously.

Ernestine unlocked the door, allowing Mr. Theda, Mr. Bara, and a typically irate Mr. Sangfroid to tumble into the room. The Swanson twins followed after but had some difficulty getting through the doorway as each was dressed in an elaborate, spangly peacock outfit complete with iridescent stiletto heels, and headdresses as wide as their outstretched arms.

"We're used to hearing *some* screaming around here, but never this much." Mr. Bara said, the thick gold hoop he wore in one ear glinting as he looked around as though expecting to find a zombie massacre.

"What sort of wild hootenanny is she throwing now?" Mr. Sangfroid demanded, practically trembling with rage before turning on the Swanson twins. "This is all your fault, you know!"

"Our fault?" They each pressed a hand to their chests in identical gestures of shock. "What have we done?"

Mr. Theda spotted poor Fluffy-Wuffy-Kins's body on the kitchen floor and fell to his knees next to him, crying out, "Alas, poor Fluffy-Wuffy-Kins! We knew him well, Sharav! A fellow of infinite jest, of most excellent fancy!"

"That's from Shakespeare's *Hamlet*," Mr. Bara explained gravely.

"Fluffy-Wuffy-Kins knew Shakespeare?" Charleston asked.

"Your first name is Sharav?" Ernestine inquired.

"Get out of my way, darlings!" Mrs. MacGillicuddie screamed as she dragged a semiconscious Eduardo back out into the kitchen. "I'll drive him to the hospital myself if that blasted ambulance isn't out front."

After that, the night got even more exciting. The ambulance was, in fact, waiting outside to rush Eduardo to the hospital to get his stomach pumped before Ernestine needed to try out her zombie-raising skills on him. A whole squadron of police officers also arrived, drenching the mansion, the neighborhood, and rather a large portion of the cemetery in red and blue light, almost as though Fluffy-Wuffy-Kins's passing warranted a whole fireworks show.

Detective Kim, a young officer dressed in an impressively crisp suit and tie in spite of the late hour, sat Ernestine and Charleston down along with Frank and Maya to ask them what they saw.

Taking charge of the interview, Ernestine explained that the not-dead Mrs. MacGillicuddie was a significantly smaller problem than the definitely-dead zombie who had been on a murderous rampage earlier in the evening.

Detective Kim blinked rapidly at her. "Er—you think it was a, um…zombie that tried to poison Mrs. MacGillicuddie?"

"Possibly but not necessarily," Ernestine replied primly, sitting very straight on the edge of an enormous settee. Charleston had slipped so far back into the cushions that he looked like he might get swallowed by them. Even Maya and Frank were having a hard time not falling backward. "The zombie was definitely trying to eat her, but I haven't been able to ascertain yet whether he was also trying to season her first."

"Season her?"

"With the botulin. You did say you thought it was botulin

that was in the bourbon bottle, right? If it was avocado, I might suspect her son, Rodney, but I'm not so sure if it's botulin."

Detective Kim remained silent for a very long time before turning to Charleston. "Do you have anything to add to this statement?"

"Nope," a muffled voice somewhere deep inside the pile of velvet replied. "Sounds about right to me."

To Ernestine's outrage, Detective Kim dismissed them to their parents' custody rather than inviting her to help him investigate the case further. She'd been about to show him the chunk of zombie she had stored in a Ziploc bag in her pocket, but after that, she wasn't about to trust him with important evidence. He didn't seem at all interested in the fact that there was a zombie wandering around, possibly gobbling up taxpayers.

What was the point of finally unleashing an undead army on the city if no one was going to notice it? Ernestine wondered in disgust. The whole *point* of the apocalypse was for people to realize it *was* the apocalypse. Not go about their business as usual while their friends and neighbors tumbled several notches down the food chain.

"Oopsy, I forgot my slippers back in Mrs. MacGillicuddie's kitchen!" Ernestine smacked her head with her hand as they reached their attic apartment.

"You were wearing slippers?" Charleston asked, earning him a whack in the ribs from her elbow. "Right! Your slippers. How could I forget about the slippers you were, uh, wearing?"

"Ernestine, I'm not so sure about you wandering around..." Maya began, but Ernestine was already shooting down the stairs.

"It'll take just a second!"

Not only had the police not secured the kitchen door against zombies, they didn't even notice the almost-thirteen-year-old girl slipping through it, either. Ernestine shook her head at their shoddiness. Clearly, you wouldn't be able to count on police protection when the apocalypse came. She couldn't even get them to care about the zombie *already* wandering about.

All sorts of enormous old antiques, heavy draperies, and exotic plants filled Mrs. MacGillicuddie's apartment to a distracting degree. Combined with all of the sparkling crystals, animal prints, and gold leaf, the effect seemed to have dazzled the police into a state of utter confusion as they wandered about, prodding things in a futile search for evidence.

Well-accustomed to all of the gaudiness, Ernestine easily slid from behind the marble bust of Mr. MacGillicuddie's great-grandfather to beneath a grand piano near where Detective Kim was continuing to conduct his interviews. However, in the cramped space beneath it, Ernestine immediately began to feel panicky. Stuffing her fists in her mouth to keep from hyperventilating, she quickly scampered over to a jungle's worth of ferns. The closeness of the space still bothered her, but not enough to trigger a full-on anxiety attack, allowing her to eavesdrop on the detective in relative peace.

As she peered out from between the fronds, he rubbed his temples and said to the Swanson twins, "So, let me get this straight. You're saying you actually *saw* a zombie, too?"

"Yes, on our way back from practicing our routine over at the Palace Theater," one of the twins agreed chattily. Like Ernestine and Mrs. MacGillicuddie, they always seemed quite pleased to be the center of attention. "We had just put our peacocks back in their kennels inside the carriage house, and we were walking through the garden—"

"When it ran right past us! I almost died of fright, didn't I, Libby?"

"Horrible creature, wasn't he, Mora?" Libby shuddered, the blue and green feathers on her headdress shivering along with her.

"Just dreadful!" Mora reached out and took her sister's hand for comfort. "Although…"

"Although what?" Both Detective Kim and Ernestine perked up.

"Well, if he *was* a real zombie, that is." Mora looked at her sister uncertainly.

"Whatever can you mean, Mora?" Libby cocked her head, almost sweeping a passing police officer off his feet with all her feathers.

"It's just…it's rather far-fetched that it could be a real zombie, isn't it? And Mr. Bara was a top-notch special effects expert back in the days when you had to be a *real* expert to turn an actor into a monster. Not the way they do it these days with those awful computers."

"You think the zombie had the look of one of Mr. Bara's creations?" Detective Kim scribbled furiously in his notebook.

"Well, it looked quite real, so if it wasn't an actual zombie, then yes. I did think it looked like something he would put together for Mr. Theda so they could both have a little fun scaring us."

"But, Mora!" Aghast, Libby snatched her hand back from her sister. "They said the zombie was seen inside this very apartment, trying to murder Mrs. MacGillicuddie!"

Mora covered her mouth in shock, her eyes wide. Her voice wavered, "Oh, then it couldn't have been them! They'd never do such a terrible thing! Libby, you realize what that means, don't you?"

"We could have been eaten by a zombie!" Libby swooned

backward onto the couch, landing in her twin's arms. "We must find that strange little Montgomery girl and see what she suggests we do. She seems to know quite a bit about those awful creatures."

Ernestine preened with pride even if Detective Kim looked skeptical. He didn't seem as certain as the twins that neither Mr. Theda nor Mr. Bara could commit murder. Ernestine had to admit she was with Detective Kim on that one. *Everyone* was capable of murder. Anyone who has spent any time at all out on a school playground could tell you that.

Detective Kim escorted the Swanson twins out and brought Mr. Theda in. Settling on the couch that had almost eaten Charleston, Mr. Theda crossed his legs so that one foot rested on his knee and held one hand aloft. He looked like a king sitting on his throne.

"*Dreadful* business." Maybe it was all his years playing cultured-but-homicidal villains in B horror movies, but Mr. Theda managed to make the word "dreadful" sound quite ominous. As though he knew for a fact about other impending events that people should be dreading.

"Yes." Detective Kim shifted around uneasily, looking at Mr. Theda as though he worried that the retired movie star might be keeping a dungeon in the basement that the police should know about. As it happened, Ernestine knew that Mr. Theda *did* have a dungeon but he kept it in his apartment. It had been a set for his movie, *Sometimes They Come Back No Matter How Many Times You Slam the Door.* Now he and Mr. Bara used it as their dining room. "Can you explain to me how you and Mr. Bara came to be standing outside Mrs. MacGillicuddie's door earlier tonight?"

"Well, I had some, ah, *business matters* that I needed to discuss with her." Suddenly, Mr. Theda no longer looked like a king. He looked as nervous as a zombie's appetizer.

"At one o'clock in the morning?"

"It's of a very sensitive nature," Mr. Theda huffed. "I didn't want anyone eavesdropping on our private conversation."

"Mm-hm." Detective Kim looked skeptical. "And why was Mr. Bara there?"

"Moral support?" Mr. Theda looked around shiftily. His gaze fell on an enormous antique cupboard over by the equally enormous (if much newer) television. His eyes widened in horror, as he straightened upright, both gestures missed by Detective Kim as he consulted his notes.

"I see here…" he began, only to be cut off by Mr. Theda, who suddenly gave a very good imitation of a frail, elderly gentleman having a heart attack.

"My heart! Oh, my heart!" Clutching his chest, Mr. Theda

fell backward onto the cushions with his head rolling and his face contorted in pain.

Leaping to his feet, Detective Kim pulled out his phone. "I'll call an ambulance!"

"No, no, dear boy!" Mr. Theda gasped. "Mr. Bara has my pills. Quick, go get them from him!"

Detective Kim rushed out of the room. As the other officers had been assigned the task of taking the Swanson twins upstairs, no one other than Ernestine was there to witness Mr. Theda leap up and rush over to the cupboard, slamming the doors shut. Mission accomplished, he threw himself back onto the couch and resumed his fake swoon just as Detective Kim hurried back in with a glass of water and Mr. Bara.

"Here are your heart pills." Mr. Bara gravely handed Mr. Theda two "pills" that Ernestine bet were really breath mints. To Detective Kim, he said, "Perhaps we could resume this interview another time? Sterling needs some rest while I call his doctor."

Detective Kim could hardly say no. Instead, he gave Mr. Bara a hand lifting Mr. Theda up and escorting him to their apartment upstairs.

As soon as they were out of the room, Ernestine bolted out of her hiding place and over to the cupboard containing whatever Mr. Theda had been so determined to hide.

Upon opening it, Ernestine expected to find poison or some other nefarious object.

Instead, she found videotapes.

Lots and lots of VHS tapes. The sort Frank frequently used in his sculptures since no one else had much use for them anymore. Picking one up, she read its label:

Torrid Dilemmas, Season 1, Episode 12, Frankie Nelson

Ernestine had absolutely no idea what a torrid dilemma might be or why Frankie Nelson might be having one. She did, however, know that Mrs. MacGillicuddie had called Mr. Theda "Frankie Nelson" just yesterday. Grabbing a tape, she shoved it into her robe and scampered out of the apartment. Only to smack right into Detective Kim, followed by her mother.

"What are you doing here again?" the detective demanded, snagging her by the robe before she could squirm past him.

"Let go of me!" Ernestine wrenched herself free and pulled herself up haughtily. Glaring over his shoulder at Maya, she said very precisely, "I don't like people grabbing me."

Detective Kim gaped at her. Ernestine balled her fists, bracing herself for an argument. Ernestine didn't mind arguments at all. She quite liked them because she was very good at winning them.

Instead of scolding her, Detective Kim said, "I apologize, Ernestine. But you understand you can't wander around a crime scene, don't you? You could destroy evidence."

"She came back downstairs to get her slippers." Maya joined her daughter, putting an arm protectively around her. "Did you find them, Ernestine?"

Ernestine admitted that she had not. Then, because Detective Kim had actually apologized to her, she said, "But I think you should know that someone tried to break in through the laundry room window the other night."

As Ernestine led them down the lengthy hallway to the back of the building, Maya whispered into her ear, "By the way, your slippers are upstairs in the bathroom."

"Oh!" Ernestine cocked her head and widened her eyes, looking as innocent as possible. "That's where I left them!"

"Right." Maya clearly didn't buy the act but she didn't say so in front of Detective Kim.

Ernestine showed them both the broken window and the crowbar, which she had hidden behind the washing machine.

"Oh my," Maya gasped, reaching out to take the crowbar from Ernestine.

Both Ernestine and Detective Kim thought that a strange response.

"It's just…" Maya stammered. "That's my husband's crowbar."

Chapter Seven
Zombie Shopping

WEDNESDAY, 4:30 AM

"That's *Frank's* crowbar?" Ernestine demanded, aghast. How on earth was she supposed to tell Charleston that his dad was a murderer? Maybe she could get the zombie apocalypse started before her stepbrother could notice that his father had been dragged off to prison. "How do you know it's *his* crowbar? A crowbar is a crowbar. They all look the same!"

"Because, look, there are grooves on this end from the time he tried to use it as a femur in a sculpture of Lennon. John, not Vladimir, I mean." The curls on Maya's head shook as she babbled, more embarrassed, it seemed, than appalled to find out her husband was a murderer. Even Ernestine was rather shocked by that, and she knew from personal experience that her mother had *terrible* taste in men.

"Are you saying that your husband broke into this building?" Detective Kim scribbled furiously in his notebook. Ernestine noticed for the first time that his suit and tie looked a lot less crisp than they had when he entered the building an hour or so before. MacGillicuddie House seemed to have that effect on people. "Would he have cause to want to see Mrs. MacGillicuddie dead?"

"What? No!" Now Maya did look appalled. "Goodness, no! He's the maintenance man, so he has a set of keys. He wouldn't need to break in. And he wasn't even the one who lost the crowbar. It was me."

"*You're* the zombie?" Her mother could definitely be spacey when Ernestine needed her to be focused, but she certainly had never seemed in need of brains before.

"Goodness," Maya repeated, blinking rapidly. "Wow. There are certainly all sorts of wild speculations flying around tonight, aren't there?"

"I don't know about 'wild.'" Ernestine crossed her arms grumpily. When did people start referring to the coming zombie apocalypse as "wild speculation"? Even the Center for Disease Control was preparing for it.

"I lost it the other day after I helped Mr. Talmadge get

one of the Swanson twins' peacocks back into the carriage house after it got loose. The door jammed, so I had to use the crowbar to pry it open. Then the peacock startled at the sight of Mora in her swan costume, and Mr. Bara had to help me chase it down. In all of the chaos, I must have left it out by the carriage house door."

"Where pretty much anyone could have picked it up." Detective Kim ran his fingers through his short black hair, making it stand up as though he had just poked his finger into a light socket. MacGillicuddie House also tended to have that sort of effect on people.

"I'm afraid so." With an apologetic grimace, Maya handed the crowbar back to him. "On the bright side, I suppose that rules out any of the residents of MacGillicuddie House, doesn't it? I mean, no one who lives inside the house would have reason to break into it, right?"

The detective made some sort of noncommittal answer, thanked them both, and sent them on their way. Ernestine could think of two problems with Maya's statement. The window had been jimmied open the other night, not tonight. Plus, someone inside the house could easily have done it to throw suspicion on someone outside of the house.

As they climbed back up the stairs, Maya said seriously, "Ernestine, with some sort of crazed murderer wandering around, I don't want *you* wandering around at night as well."

"Mom, there are always crazed murderers around," Ernestine pointed out. "They're usually just masquerading as normal people."

"Still, until this crazed murderer is caught, I think you and Charleston need to spend more time around the apartment. After Rocco…"

"After Rocco, I would think you'd want to keep an eye on me *all* the time!" Ernestine shouted, balling her hands into fists.

Aghast, Maya stopped on the steps. "Ernestine, I didn't understand what you meant at that time! And I'm so sorry for it. All I've ever done is to try and encourage you! My parents never gave me any freedom, *never* trusted me out of their sight—"

"Maybe that's because they *shouldn't* have trusted you." Cutting her mother off a second time, Ernestine had said the most hurtful thing she could think to say before continuing, "I mean, all you care about is your big, important day on Saturday, *not anything else that might be going on.*"

Her mother remained frozen on the steps as Ernestine marched off, the victor of the battlefield.

Not that victory felt that good. In fact, for some reason, it felt an awful lot like defeat.

Stomping into her room, Ernestine shut the door so she wouldn't have to see her mother's sad face when she followed her daughter into the apartment a few minutes later. Charleston was already in bed. Well, mostly in bed. He had actually only half made it onto the mattress before passing out from exhaustion. His head, chest, and arms had made it in, but the rest of him dangled onto the floor.

With a sigh, Ernestine heaved him the rest of the way in, shoved a pillow under his head, and covered him up with a blanket.

She waited long enough to be fairly certain that both Maya and Frank were asleep, and then, grabbing a flashlight, crept back out into the living room. It had been an eventful night and she had school in the morning, but there was no way Ernestine was going to bed without first watching the tape that had frightened Mr. Theda so much. After all, he had spent years starring in hundreds of low-budget horror movies. What, exactly, could horrify the horror star?

Snoozing sounds from behind the curtain separating Maya and Frank's bedroom from the rest of the attic confirmed that they were both asleep. Tiptoeing past it, she lifted the curtain to Frank's cavernous workspace and started sorting through his junk. She knew what she was looking for was around here someplace. She swept the flashlight beam over all sorts of strange discarded junk: an answering machine, floppy disks, CRT monitors, broken microwaves...

A-ha! There it was!

From the bottom of the junk pile, Ernestine tugged free an antiquated VCR. Lugging it out into the living room, she hooked it up to the TV, popped in the videotape, and sat back to watch what was on it.

A sunset and palm trees filled the screen. As passionate music played, letters swirled over the pink and gold colors to give the title of the show: *Torrid Dilemmas*. Well, Ernestine already knew that. Even if she still wasn't sure what might make a dilemma "torrid."

Then a very handsome young man with a very full head of hair and a shirt he seemed to have forgotten to finish buttoning burst through a door, snatched up a young woman with an equally full head of hair, and declared, "Darling, I can't live without you! Forget my inheritance! I want nothing to do with it if it means I can't be with you!"

Ernestine slid right off the couch in shock.

The handsome young man was Mr. Theda.

"Whatcha watching?" Charleston yawned, padding out into the living room with a blanket wrapped around him.

"The end of Mr. Theda's career, if it ever got out." Getting up from the floor, Ernestine made them a bowl of popcorn to share. Then they both settled down to finish watching the episode.

Mr. Theda's plotline was only one of many on what turned out to be a soap opera from the early 1970s. An online search revealed that it had only been on a season and a half before being canceled by the network. It must not have been very popular, because no one had bothered to upload a single episode to YouTube, and Google turned up only a single image related to it.

When Ernestine clicked on the page linked to it, none of the actors were named, but in the background, a young Mr. Theda could clearly be seen smoldering over the shoulder of his on-screen girlfriend.

Oh, my.

It was just as well that it would be almost impossible for his fans to stumble across this picture without first knowing what to look for. Because Ernestine couldn't imagine many things more embarrassing for the King of Horror Movie Villains (as Mr. Theda had been crowned by his fans) than to be seen spending most of the episode weeping and begging his girlfriend to run off with him.

"Is it supposed to be a comedy?" Charleston asked, snorting back a laugh. "This is supposed to be funny, right?"

"I don't think so." Ernestine popped the tape out and pushed it back into its sleeve.

"Wow. If any of Mr. Theda's fans found out…"

"He'd be laughed out of the next convention he showed his face at," Ernestine concluded. She looked down at the tape in her hands. "There can't be that many of these left in the world. I mean, not many people had VCRs when this show was on."

"Really?" Charleston looked at it curiously. "What did they do when they wanted to watch something?"

"Just watched it when it was on, I guess."

"Weird." Charleston shivered, obviously pleased not to have lived through the Dark Ages. "No wonder Mr. Theda is so annoyed with Mrs. MacGillicuddie. She could ruin his career, if she wanted to."

Ernestine nodded slowly. "The question is, is he annoyed enough to murder her?"

"If anyone wants to murder Mrs. MacGillicuddie, my bet is on her family," Charleston said. "Not only are they annoyed with her all the time, they'll inherit about a billion dollars when she dies. Plus, Rodney already tried to poison her with avocado."

"Accidentally, he says. And it's about half a billion they'll all inherit, actually." Ernestine absently unhooked the VCR and took it back to Frank's workspace. "Five hundred thirty five million, if the gossip around here is to be believed."

"That's a lot of reasons to murder someone."

"It is." Glancing at the time, Ernestine groaned. "Come on, Charleston. It's time to get ready for school."

"Oh, *man*." Charleston flopped down face-first on the couch. "Nooo…"

"Charleston, school is like the apocalypse. Complaining about it isn't going to make it go away."

By the time they finished getting dressed, Maya had gotten up and started to make them eggs and toast. More or less awake for once in the morning, Charleston gave her a hand, adding goat cheese and chives to the mixture, before swapping out the ordinary white bread she was going to use for ciabatta.

"Aren't you the chef!" She smiled at him, and Charleston blushed, flattered.

"Yeah, yeah. You'll be the one feeding us dandelion salads and pigeon pies after the apocalypse." Grabbing a spatula, Ernestine shoved some eggs onto the bottom slice of toast, squished on the top slice, and handed one to Charleston. "Let's go. We've got an almost-murder to solve today. Which, by the way, Mom, is the eleventh. That makes Saturday the fourteenth, you know. Can you think of anything important that happens on February fourteenth?"

"The gallery opening?" Maya asked, perplexed.

"Valentine's Day?" Charleston suggested.

"Oh, never mind!" Dragging her stepbrother by the hand, Ernestine stomped out of the attic.

From around a mouthful of sandwich, Charleston demanded, "What's with you?"

"Nothing." Taking a bite of her own sandwich, she had to admit that it tasted amazing.

"You know, for someone who always seems to have something to say about everything, you can be very good at saying nothing when somebody wants to know anything!"

"Thank you!" That perked Ernestine right up, causing a pleased smile to spread across her face. "I've been practicing for when I'm president. It's very important for a politician to talk a lot while saying nothing, you know."

As they reached the second floor landing, Ernestine's ears perked up. She gestured for Charleston to stop and held her finger up to her lips for silence. Carefully peering over the balcony, she could see Mr. Sangfroid's cane waving in the air by Mrs. MacGillicuddie's tiara.

"You'd better get them out of here!" Mr. Sangfroid jabbed his cane in Mrs. MacGillicuddie's direction, nearly knocking the tiara from her bouffant black hair. Charleston joined Ernestine to sneak a look over the balcony railing.

"And *you* had better stop threatening me!" Lacking its usual lazy drawl, Mrs. MacGillicuddie's voice slashed right back at him. With one clawlike hand, she grabbed his cane and wrested it away from her head. "I've had a *very* trying night."

"There are things I could tell about the MacGillicuddie family that would turn your hair white if you only knew." Thrusting out his chin, Mr. Sangfroid hobbled forward to glare right into her face. "Things that could keep you from ever showing your face in polite society again!"

"Darling, they aren't *my* family. They're my husband's, and I haven't had to suffer through 'polite society' since he was kind enough to kick the bucket before I had to murder him myself!" She shoved the cane back into his arms. "And *nothing* will *ever* turn my hair white. Now get out of here, you horrible old troll!"

"You'll be sorry!" Mr. Sangfroid pounded his cane against her door as she slammed it in his face. "Last night should have proved that to you!"

Unfortunately, right about then, a bit of egg fell out of Charleston's gaping mouth to splatter onto Mr. Sangfroid's bald head below.

"Oops." Charleston quickly swallowed the rest of his mouthful.

"You vile little eavesdroppers!" Mr. Sangfroid roared, shaking his cane up at them. "You'll be sorry, too!"

"Let's take the front stairs." Grabbing Charleston by a backpack strap, Ernestine pulled him away from the back stairs as Mr. Sangfroid limped onto the first step.

"Who do you think Mr. Sangfroid wants gone from the house?" Charleston wondered as they trotted down the hallway toward the other set of stairs.

"Us or the Swanson twins," Ernestine said, making a face.

"He practically cackled when he pointed out that Mrs. MacGillicuddie almost died last night. Hey, you don't think Mr. Sangfroid could be involved somehow, do you?" he asked as they went down the grand staircase.

Looking up at the hole in the ceiling, Ernestine replied, "When it comes to murder, I don't think you can rule *anyone* out."

Outside, they waved at the Swanson twins, practicing their acrobatic routine on the frosty grass. Icicles hung from Frank's various sculptures, transforming the garden into an icy wonderland.

"Have you heard anything about how poor Eduardo is doing?" one of the twins called as she vaulted up to stand on her sister's shoulders.

"Not really," Ernestine admitted, her attention on Mr. Talmadge as he looked around furtively and slipped out the front gate. "But I suspect it takes more than a bit of poison to keep Eduardo from fulfilling his duties."

She steered Charleston out the gate, but when he would have turned right to go catch the bus, she pulled him to the left. "Let's take the long way to the bus stop, okay?"

"What?" Charleston looked appalled at the thought of all that extra walking so early in the morning. *"Why?"*

"Zombie hunter's intuition."

With Charleston tagging along reluctantly behind her, Ernestine trailed Mr. Talmadge down the block and around the corner. She made sure to keep at least a block behind him so he wouldn't notice them, peering around corners to make sure she knew the next direction he was heading.

He walked about three blocks and stopped in front of a dilapidated storefront next to Mitzy's Coffee Shop and Bakery. The picture of misery, he shoved his hands into the pockets of his leather jacket and hunched his shoulders. With his heavy black boots, he kicked at an empty soda can rolling around in the gutter.

"Ernestine." Charleston tugged at his stepsister's coat.

"Shh!" Hidden behind the corner of Dill's organic grocery store, Ernestine watched as two other thickset gentlemen joined him. From the looks of all the scars on their hands, she'd be willing to bet that they were chefs, too. They both looked to be a few years younger than Mr. Talmadge.

"Well, then, mate. You got the money?" the one on the left asked in a British accent. Like Mr. Talmadge, he looked like an aging punk.

"Naw," Mr. Talmadge replied gruffly. "She won't give me

my inheritance early. I'm sorry, boys, but I'm telling you, you front me the money for this place and we'll make a go of it." He looked up at the vacant storefront wistfully.

The one on the right laughed, and Ernestine instantly disliked him. That was the laugh of someone who usually laughed *at* other people and rarely *with* them. In other words, the sort of person she really hoped the zombies ate first when the apocalypse came.

"Ernestine." Charleston pulled harder on her coat, no doubt worried that they'd miss the bus and have to hoof it all the way to school.

"Shh!" Ernestine hissed again. "I think this is important!"

"Rupert, you haven't made a go of it since the early aughts," the guy on the right snickered. "Do you think we don't know your last place folded? That you had to retire because no one would hire you after that?"

"That you got put out of business by a sushi place?" Now the left-hand guy was laughing, too. "You're lucky your wife made enough money for you both to retire on."

Ernestine wanted to march over there and give them a good piece of her mind. When she finally found her missing zombie, these two were definitely going to be on the dinner menu.

Meanwhile, Ernestine had to slap away Charleston's hands as he pulled at her coat with increasing urgency.

"You're over, mate. A has-been." The guy on the right waved his hand dismissively.

"Shown how it's done by some vegan nutter." Shaking his head, the guy on the left jerked his thumb toward Dill's place. Ernestine ducked quickly behind the brick wall and glanced upward. The sign no longer said *Dill's Organic Produce*. It now read *Dill's Delicious Vegan Delicacies*.

Peeping out again, she heard Mr. Talmadge plead one last time. "I'm good for the money, boys. I stand to inherit a lot one of these days."

"Unless it's today, you can forget about it. We're selling the place to the nutty vegan." The two future causes of zombie indigestion turned around and walked off, leaving Mr. Talmadge standing forlornly in front of the empty storefront.

"Ernestine!" Fed up with being ignored, Charleston grabbed her and shook her so hard her teeth rattled. Ernestine opened her mouth to tell him off for grabbing her, but stopped when she saw the way his eyes were bugged so far out they might have been detachable.

"What?" she demanded, yanking his hands off her shoulders.

"ZOMBIE!" Charleston twirled her around the corner and pointed toward the army surplus store across the street.

His cry startled the figure rummaging through the Goodwill donation bins in the alleyway next to the store.

He wore what appeared to be several tie-dye shirts layered together, baggy pants, garden gloves, and a sunhat pulled low over his head. Before Ernestine could do more than confirm that he definitely had some sort of unfortunate skin condition that made him look all rotten and bloated, he skittered down the alleyway and disappeared.

"Come on!" Ernestine cried, rushing after him.

Just as they reached the alleyway, however, strong hands grabbed them both by the scruff of the neck.

"Oi! What're you two doing here?" Mr. Talmadge swung them around to face him.

Ernestine wasn't sure what to say, a rare occurrence in her life. She usually had something to say about everything, and if she didn't, she was more than happy to make something up just to have an opinion. However, she couldn't help but wonder if rather than looking into the face of her friend, she was staring into the eyes of a murderer.

Mr. Talmadge had been begging Mrs. MacGillicuddie to lend him money just yesterday morning. From the sound of the conversation, he wanted to buy the space from those two jerks to start a restaurant. With money he didn't have. He'd said that he was going to eventually inherit a lot of money. Could it be Mrs. MacGillicuddie who was going to leave him all of that money when she died?

Could he have been the one to loosen the screws on the chandelier, hoping to kill Mrs. MacGillicuddie, plus the Swanson twins and who knows how many more people, if Ernestine hadn't been there? Could he have staged the fight, drawn the crowd to the right spot, and then used the fishing wire to yank the chandelier down? Could he have disguised himself as a zombie, broken into Mrs. MacGillicuddie's suite, and slipped the poison into her bourbon?

Would he kill the two of them if he suspected them of suspecting him? Would there be another unfortunate "accident" at MacGillicuddie House, this one successful?

Before Mr. Talmadge could wonder at her unusual silence, Charleston solved her dilemma for her. Hopping from one foot to the other, he pointed down the alleyway and stuttered, "Z-Z-Z-Z-ZOMBIEEEE!"

"We followed it from MacGillicuddie House." Ernestine crossed her arms, stuck her nose up in the air, and glared at him disapprovingly as though he had just interrupted some Very Important Work. Which he actually had. "We would have been able to apprehend it, too, if you hadn't stopped us just now."

Squinting off down the alleyway in the direction the zombie had disappeared, Mr. Talmadge said, "Wasn't it just a chap looking for clothes? When have you ever met a zombie who cared about the way he was dressed?"

"When has anyone ever met a zombie doing anything?" Ernestine countered. Then she marched off down the alleyway, dragging Charleston along behind her.

"But I don't want to get eaten!" he protested.

"And *I* don't want to get murdered."

"Aw, Mr. Talmadge wouldn't murder us!"

"Someone we're friends with is trying to murder someone else we're friends with," Ernestine pointed out as they reached the end of the alleyway, where it spilled out onto the next street over. There wasn't a zombie in sight. Unless you counted several dozen people who looked like they were probably shuffling their way over to Mitzy's for a mocha or frappucino.

"Unless it's someone in Mrs. MacGillicuddie's family who is trying to murder her. Mr. Sangfroid did say he knew things about them that would turn her hair white. Given all the dye she pours on it, whatever their secrets are, they've got to be pretty impressive."

"Hm, maybe." Right now, Ernestine didn't know what to think, also an unusual experience for her, and one she didn't at all like.

A search of the street didn't turn up any zombies. They tried asking a few passersby if they had seen anything, but all they got for answers were weird looks. Giving up, they headed off to school on foot, arriving late. This was one more first in a day of many for Ernestine.

When she reached science class, Ernestine discovered Mrs. Hawthorne temporarily outside of the classroom due to Riccardo Chapa having thrown up as soon as the day's lab assignment called for them to prick their fingers to do a simple blood test. Boy, if he thought that was bad, wait until he saw arms and jaws and ears falling off the undead hordes.

Deciding she'd better take advantage of the situation to apprise her classmates of the fact they were about to be eaten, Ernestine hopped up on Mrs. Hawthorne's desk.

"All right, listen up, people," she shouted. "The end is at hand. And I *don't* mean the end of the semester. I mean the end of the world. The zombie apocalypse is upon us and only the smart, the strong, and those with a plan will survive. Fortunately for you, *I* have a plan."

Ernestine handed out the photocopies she always kept on hand for the day she'd need them. One side had a neatly typed survival strategy, while the other displayed a close-up still from a movie depicting someone getting rather graphically eaten by several half-decayed corpses. Nothing like a little shock value to get people to grasp the gravity of the situation. If you wanted people to panic, then by golly, sometimes you had to give them something to panic about.

The entire class was in the process of securing the perimeter by barricading the windows with their chairs when Mrs. Hawthorne came back in. Possibly, she might have been open to hearing what Ernestine had to say had Rainbow LeBoux not swung a chair at her head while screaming, "ZOMMMBIEEEE!"

Possibly, but even Ernestine had to admit the odds had never been good.

Ten minutes later, she found herself back in Mr. Price's office, another cup of hot chocolate in her hands.

"So, Ernestine…" For a moment, Mr. Price seemed to be at a loss for words. He fixed himself a cup of hot chocolate and began again. "I hear you had an interesting night last night."

"I know, right?" Ernestine sat up straighter, pleased *someone* finally understood the gravity of the situation. "I mean, who knows how many people our zombie has infected by now? It's probably a full-scale epidemic, and I can't get *anyone* at the CDC to take my call!"

"Zombie…CDC…" Mr. Price repeated, looking completely flummoxed. Then he shook his head and said, "I meant Eduardo and Mrs. MacGillicuddie. Your mother called the school this morning. She thought we should know in case you were having trouble coping."

"Oh." Ernestine slumped back in her chair. *"That."*

"It seems like that might stir up some bad memories," Mr. Price said gingerly, "of Rocco."

Right. Rocco. Also known as He-Who-Must-Not-Be-Named. Or at the very least, He-Who-Must-Not-Be-Named-If-You-Didn't-Want-Ernestine-to-Add-You-to-Her-Zombie-Hit-List. Which was actually quite extensive. And which Mr. Price totally knew.

"I'd prefer it if you didn't say that name, thank you kindly," Ernestine replied coldly. "I thought we'd agreed on that."

"I know, Ernestine. But given the events of last night... and this morning..."

Ernestine sat up very straight, really quite angry. So angry, in fact, that she had to hold her hot chocolate very carefully to keep from slopping it because her hands were shaking so badly. "For the record, *I* saved Mrs. MacGillicuddie's life. *Three times.* Once from the chandelier, once from the zombie, and once from whoever was trying to poison her. I would think that would garner me some sort of respect. But, oh no, everyone thinks that makes me deranged. And all because I *also* had to save myself from Rocco, who you seem so keen to talk about. If you find him so fascinating, why don't *you* go talk to him? I'm sure he's got plenty of free time up in the state penitentiary! For my own part, I've got a zombie apocalypse to stop, and I can't get anyone to take me seriously, including you! I bet you don't even believe in zombies, do you, Mr. Price?"

Ha! Take that! Ernestine set down the hot chocolate and crossed her arms defiantly.

In response, Mr. Price loosened his tie and unbuttoned his shirt to show her the t-shirt he wore underneath. It read: *Brains: It's What's for Dinner* with a funny cartoon zombie drooling over a brain-burger beneath the words.

Well! Ernestine certainly hadn't expected that.

"I don't know what to say," she admitted.

"Welcome to my world," Mr. Price replied dryly. "Ernestine, I'll admit that I don't think the zombie apocalypse is upon us, but I also think it makes the world a lot more interesting to believe in zombies. However, I also know from your file that Rocco is a big fan of zombies. He even used to dress up as them and go to conventions."

Mr. Price seemed determined not to drop the subject of Rocco. Stupid Rocco. A charming snake-in-the-grass Maya had dated for a few months when Ernestine was in kindergarten. It hadn't been long, but that had still been enough time for Ernestine to decide that Rocco deserved to be eaten by one of the zombies he loved so much. "*I* don't know what Rocco does with his time these days, and *I* really don't care. But when I finally *do* start the zombie apocalypse, he's going to be in for a really, *really* big surprise from his favorite creatures."

"So that's why you're so focused on the apocalypse." Mr. Price nodded like it all made sense. "You want Rocco to feel betrayed in the same way you felt betrayed."

Not liking the implication that he finally had her pegged, Ernestine said, "Just think about how much *better* everything is going to be when zombies attack! Having a common goal brings people together. You want world peace? Then what you need is a zombie apocalypse. Having the undead swarm all over really forces you to put your priorities in the right place. No one will have time for wars or polluting the environment or dating really horrible creeps who do mean things to their kids. Or—or—or putting their stupid *art careers* ahead of their kids! They won't forget that it's *your birthday* on Saturday, and all because some dumb gallery opening is the same night! It'll make families come together and be real families because *nothing* is going to make you have an epiphany like a zombie munching on your brain."

Finished, Ernestine sat back smugly and sipped her hot chocolate. Let Mr. Price try and peg her now. She knew enough about psychology to know that there were multiple layers of dysfunction there. Ha! No one was ever going to accuse *her* of being easy to understand.

Nonplussed, Mr. Price stuttered various nonsensical things, trying to wrap things up unsuccessfully. Eventually, he decided she probably wasn't a threat to society, added some more notes to her file, and sent her back to class.

"You know, Ernestine, none of our other top students have ever had a file half as thick as yours," Mr. Price sighed, making Ernestine glow with pride. She liked being the best at things.

Rather than heading directly to her next class, Ernestine marched back to Mrs. Hawthorne's classroom. Her science teacher had done a bang-up job of getting the room back in order. You'd never know it had been ready to withstand a zombie invasion. Mrs. Hawthorne definitely needed to be on Ernestine's post-apocalypse clean-up crew.

"I'm really sorry about Rainbow almost hitting you with a chair. I told him to wait until he could see the whites of their eyes, but I guess he got a little carried away." Ernestine set a Styrofoam cup of hot chocolate down in front of her science teacher. "I wanted to bring you a cup of coffee since I know that's what you normally drink, but Mr. Price thought you might already be feeling a little jittery."

"I can't imagine why," Mrs. Hawthorne said dryly, accepting the cup and taking a sip.

"Well, yes. Everyone should feel a bit skittish with zombies around." Ernestine pulled out the Ziploc bag containing last night's zombie body part and plunked it onto the lab table. "Speaking of the undead, would you mind taking a look at this and telling me if zombie molecular structure is any different from that of a not-dead person, please. I'm sort of curious."

"Good lord. Where on earth did you get that?" Mrs. Hawthorne picked the bag up with a pair of tweezers and looked at it like it might try to tear her head off. Which it might.

"Got it off of a dead guy." Ernestine hopped up onto a stool and folded her hands on the table, patiently waiting for her answer.

Mrs. Hawthorne unzipped the bag and used her tweezers to pull out the disgusting hunk of decaying flesh. She poked at it a couple of times and it wiggled gelatinously. Then she popped it under a microscope and studied it for a while, making very intelligent *hmmmm*-ing sounds as she did so.

"Well?" Ernestine asked eagerly. "Is it different?"

"It's latex," Mrs. Hawthorne said flatly, dumping the zombie part back in its bag and handing it to Ernestine.

"What?" Ernestine was taken aback.

"I have no idea what on earth it is, but it's made up of latex rubber."

"Since when do zombies turn into latex?" Ernestine asked incredulously.

"Never, as far as I know." Mrs. Hawthorne picked up her cup of hot chocolate and turned back to her stack of grading.

"Huh." Scowling, Ernestine skulked off to her next class.

So last night's zombie was a fake. But what about that homeless-looking guy this morning? There had definitely been something funky about his skin. But was he rotting or just in need of a good dermatologist? And had he been the one to break into the house the other night? Or was Mrs. MacGillicuddie's would-be murderer disguising himself or herself as a zombie?

It looked like Ernestine had a zombie that definitely wasn't and a zombie that maybe was.

Plus a houseful of geriatric suspects and a suspiciously greedy family, though thankfully that last one was not her own.

Finally, she needed to remind her mother of the real reason why February fourteenth was important, while also getting everyone to stop talking about Rocco forever.

The apocalypse was turning out to be far harder to start than Ernestine had thought.

Chapter Eight
Lost: One Zombie

"How'd the math test go?" Ernestine asked Charleston on the bus ride home.

"Piece of cake," Charleston said. "Speaking of which, I don't suppose we have any, do we?"

"No, and we don't have time for that, anyhow." Ernestine handed him a thick stack of papers. She'd placed a picture of a half-decayed zombie at the top of the sheet. Beneath it, in seventy-two-point capitalized font, she'd typed, **MISSING ZOMBIE!** Then, in smaller letters, she'd added: *Zombie lost from St. Millicent Cemetery on Tuesday, February 10th. If found, please return promptly to grave marked Herbert Edward McGovern,* *plot 982. Shovels available upon request at MacGillicuddie House for Elderly and Retired Artists, Both Performing and Otherwise.* "What do you think?"

"I think I hope that no one shows up at our door with it on a leash," Charleston sighed.

"We'll cross that bridge when we come to it." Ernestine waved a hand unconcernedly. Charleston did tend to get hung up on inconsequential details.

They plastered the neighborhood with the signs, including the boarded-up mansions that no one lived in anymore. If you were a zombie taking a break from your murderous rampage, where else would you hang out?

"Far out," said the young shaggy guy working the cash register at the army surplus store near where the zombie had been clothes hunting that morning. "Like, yeah! Zombie revolution, man!"

"No, no. Not revolution. *Apocalypse*," Ernestine corrected. Quite frankly, she didn't think much of this guy's odds should either one occur. Judging by his outfit, he had yet to figure out how to wield an iron against his shirt and pants, let alone a weapon against a zombie's cranium.

"Zombies? *Zombies?*" demanded the old guy in fatigues who owned the store. He had long hair that would never pass any kind of military inspection and eyes that popped so far out of their sockets Ernestine privately wondered if they were attached by retractable strings. "The undead have arisen?"

"Not all of them." Charleston handed him a flyer. "Just one."

The pop-eyed guy took one look at it, and went, "AAAAUUUUUGGGGGHHHHH!!!"

Then he ran screaming from the store, waving the flyer wildly in the air. Ernestine, Charleston, and the shaggy guy stared after him.

"Finally, a sensible reaction," Ernestine said with satisfaction.

"He's kinda paranoid," the shaggy guy explained.

"Just because you're paranoid, that doesn't mean there aren't zombies coming to eat your brain," Ernestine warned ominously. The shaggy guy gulped and nodded, looking nervously around in case they had already arrived.

Finished putting up their signs, Ernestine and Charleston returned home, stopping by Mrs. MacGillicuddie's apartment to see how Eduardo was doing. Walking in, they found all Mrs. MacGillicuddie's family plus the psychiatrist cringing together on the settee while Mrs. MacGillicuddie attempted to load a shotgun. The doctor scribbled furiously in his notebook, but everyone else pretty much seemed frozen in terror. Ripe for zombie-picking, Ernestine thought, shaking her head.

For once, Eduardo was the one lying on the fainting couch in a quilted silk robe and slippers. One hand lay limply against his forehead, and he looked quite ill. That could have been because he'd been poisoned only the night before. Or it could be because Mrs. MacGillicuddie was brandishing a shotgun.

"Come to finish him off, have you?" Mrs. MacGillicuddie demanded of her nephew, son, and granddaughter. She wore a red sequined gown, her tiara smashed onto her bouffant black hair. In her agitation, she'd gotten her false eyelashes askew but had otherwise done an admirable job of shoveling on her makeup without Eduardo's help. Diamonds and rubies cascaded about her ears, throat, and fingers. "Well, you'll have to get through me first! Tried to crush me, and that didn't work! Tried to break my neck, and that didn't work! Tried to poison me, and *that* didn't work! How many different ways do you plan on killing me?"

"Well, that depends on how many times they're planning on bringing you back from the dead," Ernestine pointed out as she ducked behind a curio cabinet when the shotgun barrel swung in her direction. Charleston took coverage in the forest of potted ferns she had hidden in the other night.

"Bah!" Mrs. MacGillicuddie snapped the gun shut with so much force that it went off and decapitated the bust of her former husband's great-great-grandfather-in-law. Everyone dove for cover.

"Mother!" Rodney gasped from underneath Eduardo's fainting couch, while Eduardo simply closed his eyes.

"Never did like him!" Mrs. MacGillicuddie said cheerfully, surveying her handiwork.

Since Mrs. MacGillicuddie really didn't like *them* either, Aurora Borealis joined Rodney in scurrying under the couch, while Lyndon and the psychiatrist shot out of the room, the former trying to interest the doctor in his latest business scheme for drive-through psychiatric services in old fast-food buildings.

"I'm confused," a potted fern said to Mrs. MacGillicuddie in Charleston's voice. "Does this mean you're doing good or bad after last night?"

"Bad," her son and granddaughter said in unison just as Mrs. MacGillicuddie said, "Good."

"Uh, Mrs. MacGillicuddie?" Coming out from behind the curio cabinet, Ernestine went over and gingerly moved the box of ammunition out of the reach of Mrs. MacGillicuddie's lacquered red nails. "How about if Charleston fixes you some hot chocolate?"

"Oh, fine," Mrs. MacGillicuddie huffed, handing her the gun. Ernestine hadn't any idea what to do with it, so she dumped it into a nearby umbrella stand. "But *do* hurry up, darling. I'm quite sure someone will be coming to murder me again shortly, and I must be ready to murder them first."

"But we're here now, Mother. No one can harm you," Rodney pointed out rather condescendingly for someone currently cowering underneath both a couch and a sick butler.

"Harm *me!*" Mrs. MacGillicuddie made a noise of utter disgust. "When I set out to murder someone, *I* don't mess it up!"

"Hear, hear!" Ernestine applauded, approving of Mrs. MacGillicuddie's determination. "Only, why not let the zombies do it? *They'll* eat out your murderer's brains. That would be way more horrible than just getting shot."

"That," Mrs. MacGillicuddie said grimly, "all depends on where you shoot them. Besides, who knows how long this zombie apocalypse of yours is going to take, darling. No offense, but you've gone and lost the one zombie you had."

"That is just a temporary setback," Ernestine replied icily, red spots burning on her cheeks.

"Ew. Zombies." Even under the couch and in fear for her life, Aurora Borealis held out her camera and leaned into Eduardo to take a selfie with him. "Yuck. That is *so* gross."

"You don't really think there are zombies about, do you?" quavered Rodney as Aurora Borealis decided it was safe enough to crawl out now that Ernestine had disarmed her grandmother.

"*I* believe in the unholy undead. After all, I'm looking at three of them right now." Mrs. MacGillicuddie accepted a cup of hot chocolate from Charleston as he returned to the room. "What a good boy you are. You'd make a wonderful cabana boy, you know."

"Mother! That was quite unkind and I refuse to stay here and listen to this sort of talk any longer," Rodney huffed. "We only came by because we care deeply about your health, and you've seen fit to insult us. You're clearly quite out of your mind. I think that's evident to everyone here."

He looked hopefully over at the psychiatrist for support, only to realize the doctor had long since vanished in a puff of panic and self-preservation, leaving the rest of them to fend for themselves.

"Ha! My lawyers will eat you alive in court. If the zombies don't do it first."

They all stormed out. Well, Rodney stormed out. Aurora Borealis was so busy updating her status on her diamond-encrusted phone that she didn't notice he'd left until her father was already outside, whereupon she skittered after him on her stiletto heels. However, she did pause long enough to sneakily scoop up a diamond earring that had fallen from

Mrs. MacGillicuddie's ear and drop it into her purse, unseen by anyone except Ernestine.

The door barely had a chance to shut behind them before Lyndon crept back into the apartment, having apparently failed to interest Rodney's doctor in his latest crazy business venture.

"I'm sorry about all of that, Great-Auntie Edna," he said meekly, wringing his hands. "For what it's worth, I'm very glad you're all right, too, Eduardo."

Eduardo waved his hand dismissively as though to indicate that a minor poisoning or two was an everyday occurrence around here and nothing to get too upset about.

"Lyndon, my husband left you five million in his will." Mrs. MacGillicuddie sipped wearily at her hot chocolate. "*How* have you managed to go through it all, darling?"

"Well," Lyndon's eyes darted about nervously as though he were being interrogated, "in all fairness, that *was* twenty years ago."

"Too true, I suppose." Getting up, Mrs. MacGillicuddie hobbled over to the grand piano. Ernestine wondered if she'd be able to walk without a cane if she'd wear sensible heels instead of insisting on stiletto heels like her granddaughter. Opening up the piano cover, she fished out four stacks of fifties and handed them to him. "*Do* try not to spend it on any more of your frightful business ideas, darling. Spend it on something sensible like caviar or a spur-of-the-moment trip to Tripoli with a gorgeous blonde. Or an alpaca. Those *always* come in handy."

Not needing to be told twice, Lyndon grabbed the money and scampered off. Possibly to Tripoli, with or without a blonde or an alpaca.

Ernestine fetched brooms for both herself and Charleston, along with a dustpan. As they cleaned up the remains of the shattered bust, she asked, "Mrs. MacGillicuddie, I know this is a very personal question, but you mentioned that a few people other than Rodney, Lyndon, and Aurora Borealis are mentioned in your will. Who else inherits when you die?"

"Oh, darling, *that's* not a personal question." Going over to a heavy gilt mirror, Mrs. MacGillicuddie tucked her eyelashes back into place. "Asking a woman her age when she's *clearly* only forty-five the way that impertinent Detective Kim did last night, *that's* a personal question. Anyhow, darling Mr. and Mrs. Talmadge will receive enough to ensure that they can retire comfortably since they've cooked for me all of these years. Eduardo here receives my little vacation cottage down in Florida and enough money to support his family down in Ecuador. Mr. Sangfroid will receive several paintings that my husband's will gave me life estate on—"

"What does that mean?" Charleston asked. Ernestine had

wondered that herself but was planning on googling it later rather than letting anyone know that she didn't know.

"It means that my husband left them to Mr. Sangfroid but the terms of his will let me keep them for as long as I'm alive. When I die, he gets them, and won't he be happy when he does! They're worth quite a lot these days, you know, which should please Mr. Sangfroid immensely. I know he's an awful man, but he did me a great favor once, you know."

"What was that?" Ernestine interjected quickly, eager to know what made Mrs. MacGillicuddie put up with the least popular member of the retirement house.

"Never you mind!" Mrs. MacGillicuddie fluffed her hair and clothing. "*Anyhow,* MacGillicuddie House itself becomes a self-sustaining cooperative because I want it to always be filled with interesting people, not miserable beasts like my son and granddaughter. Oh, and Mr. Theda will receive a special bequest that is absolutely confidential. Only he and I know what it is."

Actually, Ernestine and Charleston knew as well. Or at least, Ernestine suspected she did. If Mr. Theda's bequest wasn't those *Torrid Dilemmas* tapes, Ernestine would let a zombie eat her brain.

"Oh, enough of this *dreary* talk!" Mrs. MacGillicuddie waved her hand dismissively. "What do you say the two of you try and raise another zombie? Get this apocalypse of yours properly under way. I can't wait to see Rodney running around with zombies chomping at his heels. *How* he turned out so awful, I have no idea. It certainly wasn't *my* fault. *I* let the nannies raise him."

So at midnight, Ernestine and Charleston found themselves back in the graveyard again. Only this time, rather than having to make do with dead chicken parts from the grocery store, they had several live chickens with them, compliments of Mrs. MacGillicuddie. Where she had gotten them from at ten o'clock on a weekday night, Ernestine didn't know and wasn't about to ask. Some chickens sat perched atop the tombstones, while several more wandered among the graves.

"You're sure you're not going to murder them, right?" Charleston asked anxiously.

"Don't worry. I brought Band-Aids." Tonight they'd be raising Mrs. Ella James (b. August 5, 1902 — d. September 30, 1972) from her grave.

"All right. Remember, this time we don't want to let the zombie get away," Ernestine warned and then began to cast her zombie-raising spell.

"I didn't think we wanted to let the last one get away," Charleston muttered as he held out a wildly flapping chicken for Ernestine to scratch.

Several irate chickens later, they discovered that it was a lot harder to put a Band-Aid on one than you might think. They had also yet to raise a zombie, but Ernestine was getting there.

Plucking several feathers out of her hair, she jabbed her finger with a much smaller paring knife and chanted, "*Quantum materiae materietur marmota monax si marmota monax materiam possit materiari! Quantum materiae materietur marmota monax si marmota monax materiam possit materiari! Quantum materiae materietur marmota monax si marmota monax materiam possit materiari!*"

Then they sat down on a grave and waited. They drank some hot chocolate from a thermos and then waited some more. The chickens avoided them both. It began to snow, and apparently zombies didn't like to be out in bad weather because not a single one had yet to appear.

"Charleston," Ernestine said suddenly, her breath making a puff of white in the cold air. "Do you think it's possible that Eduardo could have poisoned himself intentionally to make himself look innocent?"

Charleston thought that one over before admitting, "I dunno. He always seems on top of everything so, yeah, I guess if he was going to murder Mrs. MacGillicuddie, I think he'd make sure to have a pretty good alibi."

"Exactly. He's like me. If *I* wanted to murder someone, I'd be sure to cover my tracks, too, even if it meant sipping a bit of poison myself."

Charleston gaped at her for a moment, hot chocolate dribbling out of the corner of his mouth. Finally, he wiped it with his mitten and swallowed, "Uh, should I be worried about going to sleep at night?"

"Everyone should always be worried about being eaten by the undead in the night," Ernestine said, waving her hand dismissively. "The point is, I haven't had him on my list of suspects. Which means that he's smart enough to stay off my list of suspects, so he should definitely be *on* my list of suspects."

Charleston mulled that over, and then suddenly spit out the mouthful of hot chocolate he'd just swallowed.

"Ernestine," he gasped as he jumped down off of the tombstone. "Did you ever fix the laundry room window?"

"No, that was on your list."

"Well, I sort of got distracted when Mrs. MacGillicuddie wanted me to wear her dress!" Charleston grabbed two chickens, stuffing one under either arm. "What if the zombie arose, and we didn't see it again, and now it's inside the apartment building eating everyone's brains!"

"I'd think we'd have heard it, if it was," Ernestine pointed out sensibly, but Charleston just shoved one of the chickens into her startled arms. The bird turned its head and blinked up at her with one eye as though it didn't understand what the fuss was all about, either. "And why are you gathering up all of the chickens?"

"We can't leave them behind to be zombie snacks!" Charleston snatched up two more chickens. Arms filled with squawking, wriggling fowl, Charleston sprinted toward the house.

Ernestine rolled her eyes. If he didn't want the chickens to be snacks, then why on earth was he carrying them *toward* the supposed zombie infestation rather than *away* from it? Grabbing the remaining blood donors, she ran after him. When she finally caught up with him all the way around the house in the backyard, Charleston stood stock-still at the foot of the steps, one bird at his feet and another wriggling free from his arms.

"Look!" he gasped, pointing. Uneven footsteps led a jagged trail through the newly fallen snow to the window, which gaped as wide open as a hungry zombie mouth.

Still clutching her chickens, Ernestine shoved past Charleston and burst through the back door. Where the heck were the zombies coming up out of the ground? They'd have seen them if they'd risen from their graves in the cemetery.

"You check the second floor!" Ernestine gasped as they

sprinted down the hallway. "I'll make sure Mrs. MacGil-licuddie is safe!"

"But you don't have your baseball bat!" Charleston cried.

That was, of course, a problem. However, Ernestine had already spotted Mrs. MacGillicuddie's back door hanging wide open. Which meant that Mrs. MacGillicuddie was about to end up as a midnight snack. Baseball bat or no baseball bat, she was *not* about to let her friend get eaten.

Putting on a burst of speed, the chickens shrieking their encouragement, Ernestine sprinted through the open door, zigzagged her way through Mrs. MacGillicuddie's maze-like suite, and burst into her bedroom.

Where a zombie in a long dress stood over Mrs. MacGil-licuddie's sleeping body, a candelabra raised in its undead hand.

Chapter Nine
When Confronted With a Zombie, Panic

THURSDAY, 12:17 AM

Step four of Ernestine's zombie survival guide stated quite specifically that as soon as you were finished panicking, you should arm yourself with something deadly before confronting the undead. Without something to kill them when you ran at them, you were pretty much offering yourself up as fast food.

Now, confronted not only with a zombie, but a zombie carrying a weapon, Ernestine found herself armed with nothing more deadly than chickens. *Chickens.* It was too humiliating for words.

Oh, well. If all she had for a weapon was chickens, then she'd just have to use chickens as a weapon. As the zombie slashed the candelabra toward Mrs. MacGillicuddie's head, Ernestine screamed, "You wanna eat something? *EAT CHICKEN!*" and flung the birds right at the creature's head.

As these things went, "Eat chicken" wasn't terribly clever. But it was a zombie. Its brain was liquefying in its skull. It wasn't like it would appreciate witty banter, anyhow.

Ernestine's shriek woke up Mrs. MacGillicuddie, who saw the danger and rolled out of the way just in time. Rather than breaking open her skull to reveal a delicious, juicy brain inside, the candelabra tore her pillow apart. A cloud of feathers puffed up into the air, joining those already flying from the furious birds as they landed on the zombie. They took out an entire evening's worth of aggression by pecking mercilessly at its decaying flesh. Ernestine had just wanted the zombie to eat the chickens rather than Mrs. MacGillicuddie, but she was fine if they wanted to eat the zombie instead. Birds. Who would've thought they'd be excellent allies in the coming war against the undead? Ernestine would have to make a note of it in her zombie survival guide.

Worried that her allies might not be able to finish the zombie off all on their own, Ernestine launched herself forward and pummeled it right in the stomach with her outstretched hands.

It turned its hideous, deformed face to gaze at her with a slack jaw and purple, mottled skin. Ernestine swallowed hard, wishing she'd kept one of the chickens to defend herself with. Whatever she had seen in the alleyway this afternoon, the creature before her *definitely* had a skin problem. As in, its skin was rotting away and hanging in flaps off its cheeks, which Ernestine assumed would be a problem for most creatures, even ones who hadn't gotten out of their coffins much the last couple of decades.

While Ernestine was wishing she'd thought to bring along a rain poncho in case it decayed all over her nice coat, the zombie fell to the ground and tried to crawl away. Mrs. MacGillicuddie clutched her satin sheets to her chest and shrieked, "What is it? What is it?"

"Mrs. MacGillicuddie, meet Ella James, deceased! We just raised her," Ernestine yelled as the zombie sprang to its feet. It swung the candelabra at her and would have gotten her on the nose if Ernestine hadn't jerked back in time. Then it kicked her with a stiletto heel, which smarted like anything.

"Ow!" Ernestine grunted, rubbing at her shin as Charleston burst into the room and flipped on the lights.

Just like Mrs. MacGillicuddie, he shouted, "What is it? What is it?"

"What on earth do you think it is?" Ernestine snapped

back in exasperation. The late Ella James tried to kick her again, but Ernestine wrenched its shoe off instead.

Its zombie brain must work pretty well given that it had been dead for the better part of the last century. Because Ella James clearly seemed to realize she was outnumbered and tossed off the last bird to dash past Charleston. He tried to decapitate it with his baseball bat, which was a lot better than flinging it at the zombie and screaming hysterically the way he had last time, but Ella also moved pretty fast for someone who not only was missing a shoe, but who'd lately spent more time decaying in the ground than exercising. Its legs just couldn't be attached all that well anymore, yet it darted right past him, leaving the bat to whiz through the air.

Ernestine wasn't about to lose a second zombie in less than a week. Shoving the stiletto heel into Charleston's hands, she bolted down the hallway and managed to grab the zombie by the hair as it made it to the kitchen. Her victory was short-lived, though. While Ella James's legs were remarkably well-attached, its hair was not. As Ernestine tugged at its curls, they slipped right off the zombie's head. Ernestine blinked stupidly down at the hunk of hair, allowing the creature time to kick her right into an enormous garbage can full of debris from the party the other night.

Quite literally into it. Hitting the rim, she tumbled over the edge and ended up with her face smushed into the remains of a custard tart. Her legs kicked ignominiously in the air while she tried unsuccessfully to get out.

"Ernestine! Are you okay?" Charleston and Mrs. MacGillicuddie each grabbed an ankle and pulled her out.

"I scalped it," Ernestine said bitterly, custard sliding down the side of her face to dribble onto the floor as she held up the zombie's hair. Other than that, the zombie was nowhere to be seen.

"Good heavens, darling! You just saved me from being murdered again!" Mrs. MacGillicuddie cried.

Well, there was *that*, Ernestine supposed, but she'd still lost her zombie. It wasn't like you could order them online when you ran out of them.

"Come on, Charleston! Let's see where it went!" Snatching his baseball bat from him, she barreled out the kitchen door without waiting to see if he was following.

"How — are — the — muscles — of — the — undead — in — better — shape — than — mine?" Charleston panted, catching up with her as she paused on the back porch, her eyes searching the immense, silvery garden for signs of the missing zombie. A clatter by the carriage house caught her attention. Through the light snowfall, she saw the gate to the alleyway swing shut.

Grabbing Charleston by the hand, she ran along the icy path, slipping and sliding as they went.

"Whoa!" Charleston hit a patch of black ice and spun right out of her grip to land in a heap of dead hostas. The force of it propelled Ernestine in the other direction so that she banged into the same marble bench Charleston had the other night. Unlike him, she managed to avoid a dive into the koi pond.

Someone—or some*thing*—else, it turned out, hadn't been so lucky.

As Ernestine landed in the frosty mulch, she saw two feet right by her face. One was bare. The other wore a sparkly iridescent stiletto heel just like the one she'd wrenched off the zombie a few minutes ago.

Sitting upright, Ernestine raised her baseball bat to slug the zombie before it could turn her into a late-night snack.

The zombie, however, didn't move. Perhaps because, other than the feet and legs, the rest of it seemed to be drowning in the pond.

Realizing this, Ernestine leaped up and hefted it out of the pond, only to discover that it wasn't so much of an "it" as it was a cranky old coot.

"Mr. Sangfroid!" Charleston gasped, getting up only to walk over to Ernestine and collapse again. "Is he dead?"

A sputter of water followed by a frozen goldfish confirmed

that Mr. Sangfroid was not, in fact, dead. Though he certainly would have a lot of explaining to do when he woke up.

"Goodness!" Having traded her usual heels for a pair of sensible tennis shoes, Mrs. MacGillicuddie made her way through the garden with remarkable ease. She bent over with hands on thighs to peer down at the unconscious body lying by her koi pond. "Darling little Mr. Sangfroid! Who would have guessed *he* was the zombie? But whatever has he done with the dress he was wearing?"

Ernestine wasn't so sure he was the zombie, which would explain why he wasn't wearing the dress. Something had gone out of the back gate a minute ago, hadn't it?

"Ernestine! Look!" When Charleston fell the second time, he had landed in a giant old rhododendron bush. From beneath its branches, he pulled out a cloth shopping bag from Dill's store. Inside it were the remains of the zombie costume, the mask, and the long dress.

"Well, that settles it." Mrs. MacGillicuddie straightened up. "I suppose I'd better go get my gun so I can shoot him."

"No!" Ernestine and Charleston simultaneously cried out in horror.

"Whyever not?" Mrs. MacGillicuddie blinked in astonishment at them. "What else am I supposed to do with someone who tries to murder me?"

"*Call the police.*" Ernestine pointed at the house. "*And* an ambulance for Mr. Sangfroid."

"Oh, fine," Mrs. MacGillicuddie huffed. "But your way is a lot less fun than mine."

Ernestine thought that probably depended on your point of view. She gazed suspiciously at the back gate. She supposed it *could* have been the wind or a stray cat that closed it—or perhaps the zombie had just stumbled across Mr. Sangfroid and seized the opportunity to make him look like the guilty party.

Glancing back at her elderly neighbor, Ernestine noticed something clutched in his hand. As her landlady hurried back to the house, Ernestine pried it loose to discover it was a damp piece of paper.

No, not paper. Shaking some of the water off of it, Ernestine unfurled it to discover it was a very old black-and-white photograph.

In it, a toddler stood in front of an enormous fancy mirror and looked in delight at her reflection smiling back at her. She wore a short dress, hair pulled into a bow on one side of her head, and chubby legs shoved into frilly socks and patent leather shoes. The mirror was big enough that she could see herself from head to toe while pressing one hand against it.

It was a very cute picture, but there was also something

unsettling about it. Something Ernestine couldn't quite put her finger on. Perhaps it was the mirror, so big and gothic, it could have been a prop in one of Mr. Theda and Mr. Bara's horror movies. Except in that case, the adorable little girl would have been smiling because she'd just eaten the family dog and was thinking about the cat for dessert.

Or perhaps it was because she'd seen the picture before.

"That's it! It's a picture from a photo album he stole from Mrs. MacGillicuddie," Ernestine told Charleston.

"What's that?" Charleston asked as he slipped the frozen koi back into the hole in the ice covering the pond. "When did he steal a picture album from Mrs. MacGillicuddie? And why?"

Ernestine realized that, in all of the excitement of the last couple of days, she had never mentioned the stolen album to Charleston. Honestly, between a missing zombie and an unknown murderer, petty theft had seemed like the least of the problems around MacGillicuddie House. Now, she told her stepbrother about how Sangfroid had picked it up off the floor after the chandelier crashed—and how he had been looking through it when she showed up to fix his leaky pipe.

"Are you sure that was one of the pictures?" Charleston asked skeptically. Flipping it over, Ernestine showed him the writing on the back: *MacGillicuddie House, 1952.*

That was it. No name. No reason to explain why Mr. Sangfroid might have had it in his grasp.

"Don't mention it to anyone else right now," Ernestine warned him, still studying the picture.

The mirror. It still bugged her. And not just because she'd been traumatized by watching Mr. Theda and Mr. Bara's horror movies at too young an age.

It was the mirror's frame, Ernestine realized. It was the same one she had stood on down in the basement the other night when she'd argued with Mr. Sangfroid while fixing his leaky pipe. His eyes had widened in surprise as he looked at her. At the time, she had assumed it was because he was afraid she'd hurt herself, but she should have realized that couldn't possibly have been the case. Mr. Sangfroid was the sort of person who would cheer on the zombies in the apocalypse, not the plucky group of human survivors coming together to overcome them.

No, it was because Mr. Sangfroid had recognized the frame from the picture.

There are things I could tell about the MacGillicuddie family that would turn your hair white if you only knew, he'd told Mrs. MacGillicuddie. Was the story of this little girl one of those things? If so, what had happened to her?

Perhaps these weren't the first attempted murders to take

place at MacGillicuddie House. Could this little girl have been the first?

And if so, had it been a *successful* murder attempt? She shuddered at the thought.

Slipping the photograph into her pocket, Ernestine heard sirens screaming toward the house for the third time in three nights.

"Wow. Mr. Sangfroid. Who would have thought it was him?" Charleston stuck his hands in his hair in shock.

"Hm," was all Ernestine would commit to. Several things about this situation bothered her, though at first she couldn't put her finger on all of them. "Charleston, do you still have that shoe I handed you?"

"Sure." Charleston had to search around on the ground for a moment, but eventually he came up with it.

Taking it in her hand, Ernestine laid it next to the one still on Mr. Sangfroid's foot.

"Look."

Charleston scrunched up his face and stared at the shoes. He nodded solemnly like he got it, too, and then asked, "What is it I'm looking at other than a pair of sparkly green shoes?"

"But that's just it. They *aren't* a pair." Ernestine pried the shoe off of Mr. Sangfroid's right foot and held it up. Both shoes were absolutely identical. "They're both for the *right* foot."

"Maybe he has two right feet?" They both looked down at Mr. Sangfroid's very gnarled, very hairy feet. They looked like he might have gotten them off of an elderly hobbit, but other than that, he had one perfectly normal right foot and one perfectly normal left foot.

"I think someone set Mr. Sangfroid up in case they were caught. I think someone knocked him out before they went into Mrs. MacGillicuddie's house. Then, on the way back out, the would-be murderer put one pair of shoes on his own feet and the other on Mr. Sangfroid's to frame him. Only that person was in a hurry and got careless, mixing up the shoes before he shoved Mr. Sangfroid into the pond to distract us and buy time to escape. Look." Ernestine pointed at the ugly goose egg growing on his forehead.

"Why didn't the murderer just kill him before he went inside to off Mrs. MacGillicuddie?" Charleston wondered. Then he blinked. "Did I just criticize the way a murderer went about trying to murder someone? Does that seem kind of weird to you?"

"Yes, it does, Charleston."

"Oh, jeez." Charleston sat down on the flagstone path in a funk. "I feel like it makes me a bad person if I can tell someone how to be a better murderer."

"You're not a bad person, Charleston, you're just really bad at school. And used to people constantly telling you how to be better at it," Ernestine comforted him. "Anyhow, since *I'm* quite good at school, I can tell you why the murderer didn't drown him before trying to murder Mrs. MacGillicuddie. Because an autopsy would have shown that Mr. Sangfroid died before her, so he couldn't have killed her. It's exactly the sort of thing that's *always* tripping up criminals on the detective shows on TV."

"Is it?" Charleston asked in surprise.

"Oh, yes." Ernestine said confidently. At least, it had been in one TV episode she'd watched. That might not exactly qualify as "always" but Ernestine figured it was close enough. "Anyhow, between that picture and the fact that the would-be murderer wanted him dead, I bet Mr. Sangfroid knows something about whoever is doing this. I think it has something to do with this little girl and something that happened in MacGillicuddie House a long time ago."

"Wow. That sounds evil. Like, eviler-than-zombies evil."

"Oh, there are plenty of people who are eviler than zombies," Ernestine said darkly. "Believe me, I've met some of them."

"Like who?"

"Like *none of your business*," Ernestine snapped. Turning her back on him, she refused to speak to her stepbrother again until Detective Kim got there a short time later.

Ernestine showed the detective the shoes but kept the picture to herself as the paramedics loaded Mr. Sangfroid into the back of an ambulance. He was already groaning a bit and complaining about their carelessness, so she suspected he was going to be just fine. Well, aside from the fact that he was probably going to be arrested for murder—maybe wrongly.

"Mother!" Rodney bellowed, making a dramatic entrance through the alleyway gate, followed by Aurora Borealis and Lyndon. Various newspaper reporters shouted questions at Detective Kim, Rodney, and Mrs. MacGillicuddie from outside the gate.

To Ernestine's great annoyance, no one tried to interview *her*. If there was anyone they should be talking to, it was her. Not only did she have the inside scoop on the murder attempts, she knew all about the coming zombie apocalypse. Which, honestly, was what they should be focusing on. Why report on a couple of would-be murders when you could report on the possible extinction of the entire human race? Surely that should be a much bigger scoop.

"Mother! This is the last straw!" Rodney shouted as a reporter managed to wriggle her way in far enough to shove a microphone in his face and ask him how he felt about his mother almost being murdered twice within twenty-four hours (Ernestine could have answered that one:

disappointed). "This neighborhood is infested with criminals! It is no longer safe for you to live here!"

"Took you long enough to get here. I'd be dead a hundred times over if I had to rely on you to save me!" Mrs. MacGillicuddie snapped, clearly not in the mood. Wrapped in her mink coat, she stood on the porch, trying to look as elegant as possible as the reporters held their cameras over the fence to snap her picture.

"The neighborhood is infested with zombies, not criminals," Ernestine corrected, irritated that once again everyone seemed to be overlooking the most important detail. "As far as we know, there's just one murderer wandering about and possibly two zombies."

"Oh, not that again!" Aurora Borealis rolled her eyes as she posed for the reporters in her short skirt and sparkly white stiletto heels. Stiletto heels that had recently belonged to the Swanson twins, Ernestine realized, recalling how Mrs. MacGillicuddie's granddaughter had stolen them the other night. Just like she had the earring and the Fabergé egg.

The question was, what else had she stolen? Perhaps a pair or two of iridescent green heels like those used to make Mr. Sangfroid look guilty?

"Oh, yes, *that* again!" Ernestine shot right back, waving about the zombie's scalp. "What's the point of surviving a murder attempt only to get eaten by a horde of ravenous zombies? We need a game plan, people!"

"And Ernestine seems to have a better track record of stopping murders than *you* do, Aurora Borealis!" Turning around, Mrs. MacGillicuddie marched into the house, her mink coat flowing about her like a cloak. Detective Kim tried to give her a hand, but she slapped his hands smartly out of the way as they all trailed her into the grand foyer.

She stopped at the base of the cherrywood staircase. Enormous wooden cupids held up decorative balls at the bottom of the stairs, while leaves and flowers curled around the banister as it soared up three stories above. Mrs. MacGillicuddie went over to one of the cupids and yanked it downward, causing the cherub to swivel at the waist. Everyone yelped and jumped backward as dust filled the air and a panel snapped forward on the third step.

Then everyone peered forward to see a huge stash of cash, all wrapped up and stacked neatly inside the secret compartment.

"Cool!" Charleston gasped, impressed.

"Mother, you never told me that was there!" Rodney swelled up with outrage.

"What, so you could steal it from me, you ungrateful brat?" Mrs. MacGillicuddie fished out one of the bundles of cash and tossed it to Charleston. He snatched at it, almost dropped it, caught it, almost dropped it again, and then clutched it to his chest like he thought it might try to wriggle free. With a sigh, Mrs. MacGillicuddie just handed the second bundle to Ernestine.

"For saving my life again, darling. I should have given it to you last night, but I've been too distraught over planning poor Fluffy-Wuffy-Kins's funeral." She sniffled delicately. "It's going to be a grand affair, you know. I've contacted the pope to see if he could preside."

"Mother! I refuse to let you give away the family fortune!" Rodney shouted indignantly, with Aurora Borealis and even Lyndon chiming in. In fact, Lyndon was salivating so much he was practically drooling as he looked at all of that cash, and Ernestine was reminded once again that he stood to benefit as much as anybody if Mrs. MacGillicuddie died. At least Aurora Borealis and Rodney were already wealthy; they just wanted to be wealth*ier*.

"Oh, put a sock in it, you greedy fools!" Mrs. MacGillicuddie shouted right back as the reporters pressed their faces against the stained-glass windows on either side of the front door, trying to get a good look inside. The detectives surged all around them, clearly alarmed that they might have to bring in body bags to go along with all of those evidence bags.

"Let's go, dearies," Mrs. Talmadge whispered, appearing out of nowhere. She had a very contrite-looking Mr. Talmadge by the ear and was dragging him up the stairs. At the top, the Swanson twins glared down at him with their arms crossed. If looks could kill, then these would have caused a massacre. In fact, Ernestine was fairly certain that they'd be able to stop an entire zombie army with one disapproving squint of their eyes.

To the twins, Mrs. Talmadge murmured, "Thank you for bringing him home. Give Dill our apologies, will you?"

Without another word, they marched back to their apartment and slammed the door shut behind them. For once, they weren't wearing their usual fancy costumes. Instead, they had on the black yoga tights and shirts they'd been wearing the other morning in the garden.

Adding to this new mystery, Mr. Talmadge was holding a can of black spray paint. Following Ernestine's gaze, an exasperated Mrs. Talmadge took it from him.

"What happened to you?" Charleston asked, nonplussed, as they followed the Talmadges into their apartment.

"What happened to him? What happened to him?" Mrs. Talmadge shoved Mr. Talmadge down onto the couch. The various nuts and bolts in her ears shivered with rage as she bellowed, *"He got caught, that's what happened!"*

"Now, Pansy, dear." Mr. Talmadge hunched his shoulders sheepishly. "It was just a bit of fun, pet. Like back in the old days."

"You didn't get caught back in the old days!"

"Um, maybe we should leave," Charleston whispered to Ernestine.

"Are you kidding me? I think she might shank him with a paring knife." If Mrs. MacGillicuddie and Eduardo had been there to take bets, Ernestine definitely would put her new stack of fifties on Mrs. Talmadge. In fact, she was pretty sure the elderly, pink-haired chef could fillet an entire army of the undead without breaking a sweat.

"And what has that poor boy done other than open a successful business?" Mrs. Talmadge demanded, clueing Ernestine in that they were probably talking about Dill. "Just because you both want to open a restaurant in the same space, you're determined to have a ridiculous feud with him!"

"Successful business! Bunch of vegetable garbage, that's what his food is! We called it 'compost' back in my day, and now he's selling it for twenty dollars a plate!"

"Well, I happen to like it." Mrs. Talmadge crossed her arms as Mr. Talmadge slowly raised his head in horror from where he had been holding it in his hands.

"Pansy, say it isn't so!" he gasped.

"It is, and furthermore, I'm the one who told Mrs. MacGillicuddie not to give you your inheritance early! She was all set on it, you know!"

"*What?*" Furious, Mr. Talmadge rose up off the couch.

Mrs. Talmadge grabbed a frying pan off the rack in the kitchen and flung it at the wall.

"That's right, it was me, you old codger, you!"

Yelping, Ernestine and Charleston dove under the kitchen table for cover.

"How dare you!" Mr. Talmadge snatched up a butcher knife and buried it into the counter.

"Because you're seventy and have had two heart attacks already! You don't need more stress!" Dishes hit the floor.

"Well, they brought me back both times, didn't they?" A meat mallet hit the table, making it shake violently. Already feeling claustrophobic, Ernestine shot out from underneath it just in time to have a teacup go whizzing past her nose and smash against a cupboard door.

Charleston yanked her back under again.

"I didn't want to find out if a third time was going to be the charm!" An entire drawer full of cutlery clattered down onto the floor like it was raining all about the table. Ernestine desperately wanted to get out from the dark, confined space, but Charleston kept a tight grip on her for someone so tiny.

"I'm not past it yet, Pansy! I could handle opening a new restaurant at my age!"

"Like you could handle spray-painting graffiti all over poor Dill's storefront?" More dishes smashed against the walls. "What if it had been the police who caught you instead of the Swanson twins?"

"Aw, Pansy. We've had to bail each other out of prison plenty of times, luv!" Mr. Talmadge's voice softened as he said it. Things finally stopped breaking all around them. "Remember that time I had to bail you out for lobbing a tea cake at Margaret Thatcher's hat?"

"It was her nose I was aiming for. It landed in her hat by accident," Mrs. Talmadge said mistily. "Those were the days, weren't they, Rupert?"

"They were, luv, weren't they?"

"Rupert, I'm not done having days. And I'd like to have you there with me when I have them. Opening a new restaurant would kill you."

"Aw, luv." Now their feet moved closer together. As Mrs. Talmadge lifted up one foot, the sounds coming from above the table clearly indicated they were kissing passionately, completely having forgotten the children in their apartment.

Ernestine made a *let's go* gesture to Charleston, and the two of them crawled out from beneath the cramped table.

"Now I wish I hadn't done what I did to Mrs. MacGillicuddie," Mr. Talmadge admitted.

Both Ernestine and Charleston froze, still on their hands and knees.

"No harm done in the end," Mrs. Talmadge whispered. "And she'll never know it was you."

Charleston opened his mouth, but Ernestine quickly clapped her hand over it and shoved him out the door.

Forget about being eaten by the ravenous undead.

Now they had to worry about ending up as the main course for two unscrupulous chefs.

Chapter Ten
Zombies Found and Lost

THURSDAY, 3 AM

Before Ernestine and Charleston could make their getaway, Maya pounced on them.

"What on earth is going on?" she demanded, her lovely wiry curls shaking with fury as she stood in a pair of batik-print pajamas.

"We think we've just figured that out," Charleston said helpfully as Ernestine crossed her arms and pressed her lips together defiantly.

"I told you both not to go roaming around while there's a murderer about!" Maya propelled them toward the steps. Rarely did she give Ernestine a good talking-to, but when she did, Maya's tone could be every bit as impressive as her own mother's, whom Maya had once described as being like Miss Trunchbull from *Matilda*, only more rigid and less cuddly. "Do I have to lock you both in the attic? Every time I turn my back, the two of you are sneaking out someplace! I don't force a lot of rules on you two, but I do ask that you tell me where you're going!"

"You sound exactly like your mother." Ernestine knew exactly where to stick the dagger.

Maya froze. Turning to look at her daughter, she said, "That was low."

Before Ernestine could say anything back, a hideous scream split the air in two.

"Now what?" Maya cried. She tried to push Ernestine up the stairs to safety, but Ernestine nimbly jumped around her and headed in the opposite direction, toward the screaming.

"Probably another person getting murdered!" she called back cheerfully. If it was, Ernestine wasn't about to miss it. As she passed by Mr. Theda and Mr. Bara's apartment, Mr. Theda stuck his head out the door, looked wildly about as though expecting to see the zombie hordes massed in the hallway, and then returned to his apartment when it became clear there was probably nothing more interesting going on than yet another murder attempt. At least he had the sense to bolt his door after he shut it.

The real reason for Mr. Theda both looking out into the hallway and then double-locking his door became clear when Ernestine arrived in Mrs. MacGillicuddie's apartment to find her landlady still screaming.

"They're gone!" Mrs. MacGillicuddie waved her hand dramatically toward the cabinet that had stored all of the videos of Mr. Theda's old soap opera, *Torrid Dilemmas*.

"What's gone?" Detective Kim demanded, racing back to her apartment from the back garden as Mrs. MacGillicuddie collapsed onto her couch.

For a moment, Ernestine thought her landlady was going to give Mr. Theda away. Instead, she laid back limply on the settee. "The zombies, darling. It's *such* a relief. Go back to fingerprinting my koi pond or whatever it is you need to do to catch that *awful* zombie impersonator who tried to kill *darling* little Mr. Sangfroid, the sweet old thing."

"We haven't actually ruled Mr. Sangfroid out as a suspect," Detective Kim pointed out.

"Then you should probably run along and do so, darling. Go on, I'm fine."

Peeping out from beneath her one hand, she made sure Detective Kim left as she waved him off with the fingers of the other. Then she hopped up and fished the shotgun out of the umbrella stand where Ernestine had deposited it earlier in the day. In a no-nonsense voice very different from her usual drawl, she said, "Right. I'll fix him. There's one person in this house who knows how to commit a proper murder."

"Mrs. MacGillicuddie!" Ernestine grabbed her by the nightgown to keep her from marching out of the apartment with her weapon, giving her mother enough time to snatch it out of their landlady's hands.

"Maya Montgomery! You give that back to me this instant!" Mrs. MacGillicuddie tried unsuccessfully to swipe it back, but Maya managed to hold her off. Not knowing what else to do with it, she dumped it back into the umbrella stand right before the Talmadges burst through the door.

"What is it? What's going on?" Mrs. Talmadge gasped.

"*Murderer!*" Ernestine shrieked as dramatically as she could, being sure to hop up onto the ottoman so everyone could see her. Eduardo had just walked into the room, but upon hearing her accusation, he rolled his eyes and walked back out again.

Mr. and Mrs. Talmadge clutched each other. In a quavering voice, Mrs. Talmadge asked, "W-w-w-what do you mean?"

Detective Kim ran back into the room, panting. For such a young guy, he really needed to get into better shape or he'd never be able to outrun the zombie masses, in Ernestine's opinion. Of course, she supposed that would at least give everyone else time to escape. Maybe Detective Kim was just an especially dedicated public servant, one willing to get eaten for the greater good.

"Arrest them!" she declared, still pointing at the Talmadges. "They're the ones who've been trying to off Mrs. MacGillicuddie!"

"Rupert!" This time Mrs. MacGillicuddie really did collapse onto the settee. Charleston rushed to her side as she added, "Pansy!"

"It wasn't us!" Mrs. Talmadge cried as Mrs. MacGillicuddie thrust Charleston aside and reached into the umbrella stand. *"No!"*

However, instead of a shotgun, Mrs. MacGillicuddie tried to shoot them with an actual umbrella. It popped open impressively but did no worse damage than causing Mrs. Talmadge to throw herself protectively (and rather sweetly) in front of her husband just as he tried to throw himself in front of her. Instead, they both collided together and fell to the floor.

"Oh, drat." Mrs. MacGillicuddie tossed the umbrella away, but before she could get to the shotgun, Detective Kim stepped in between her and the Talmadges, helping them up.

"What's this all about?" he demanded.

Grabbing Charleston by the hand, Ernestine yanked him

up onto the ottoman. "We heard them, didn't we, Charleston? Confessing to the murder."

"Yup," Charleston agreed, well, agreeably.

"We never said any such thing!" Mrs. Talmadge gasped.

"You did," Ernestine argued back. Pointing at first to Mr. Talmadge and then Mrs. Talmadge, Ernestine said, "*You* said you wished you hadn't done what you did to Mrs. MacGillicuddie. And then *you* said that she'd never know it was you."

"Oh. That." Mr. Talmadge flushed in shame.

"Oh, dear." Mrs. Talmadge closed her eyes as though developing the same headache that seemed to lurk between Detective Kim's brows when Ernestine was around. "You'd better tell them, Rupert."

Mr. Talmadge muttered something unintelligible.

"What's that?" everyone asked at the same time.

Heaving a sigh, Mr. Talmadge said more clearly, "I said that I've been using real cream and butter in all of her low-fat dishes for the past week now."

"Come again?" Detective Kim blinked.

Ernestine grabbed Charleston and yanked him down onto the floor as their landlady sailed over the ottoman in a murderous rage.

Wielding the umbrella, she whacked Mr. Talmadge about the head and shoulders with it. "You monster! That's why I've gained five pounds! I'll never forgive you for this, you beast!"

Detective Kim and his officers swarmed them. By that time, Mrs. Talmadge had gone after Mrs. MacGillicuddie with the golf putter also tucked inexplicably into the umbrella stand. Thankfully, no one thought to grab the shotgun as Maya hustled both Ernestine and Charleston out of the room and back up to the attic:

"But I still have a ton of questions I need to ask everybody!" Ernestine protested. "Where was everyone tonight? Do they all have alibis? What were the Swanson twins doing over by Dill's store? Was Mr. Theda the zombie? He certainly took advantage of the murder attempt to get his videotapes back! And where was Eduardo? Do we know for sure he was poisoned? Maybe he was faking!"

"Ernestine, you're babbling," her mother said firmly, shutting and locking the door. Then she pointed at their bedroom and plunked herself down on the couch to make it clear there would be no more sneaking out. "I'm calling you both into school sick tomorrow. Neither one of you has gotten a decent night's sleep in almost three days! You need your rest or you'll both end up in the hospital with pneumonia from all this wandering about in the cold."

Under normal circumstance, Ernestine would have been

outraged by this speech of her mom's. She hadn't missed a day of school since kindergarten and all of that...unpleasantness with Rocco. Even then, she had only missed one day so she could give a rousing speech encouraging the jury to execute him. Well, technically, she was only supposed to testify against him, but Ernestine was never one to give up the opportunity to make a rousing speech.

Anyhow, Maya had a point about their lack of sleep. Plus, if she stayed home from school, she'd be able to grill the residents of MacGillicuddie House to see which one of them was the would-be murderer. Assuming, of course, that it wasn't one of Mrs. MacGillicuddie's family members, which was personally where Ernestine was placing her money.

Speaking of money, she snuggled up in her top bunk with her big wad of cash in one hand and baseball bat in the other, and fell almost instantly to sleep. If zombies were going to attack tonight, someone else would just have to deal with it for once.

In the morning, she slept until quite late, not hopping out of bed until the sun was high in the sky. Charleston still lay in the bottom bunk, his glasses askew and a little smile on his lips. He, too, clutched his money like it was a teddy bear, but at least his baseball bat was close at hand. Letting him sleep, Ernestine went out to the kitchen. On the counter, she found a bowl filled with pancake batter but no pancakes. The egg carton was still out, as was the bag of flour, and she could hear music over in her mom's studio. Apparently, she'd gotten distracted before actually making Ernestine pancakes.

Which was fine because she shouldn't have even been making pancakes in the first place. What she *should* have been making was a birthday cake, Ernestine thought grumpily. Stupid gallery opening.

After cleaning up the mess from the almost-breakfast, Ernestine took a very long, very hot bubble bath. As she soaked, she took out her notebook and made a list of suspects:

MR. TALMADGE – Would inherit enough money to open his restaurant if Mrs. MacGillicuddie died. Caught spray painting Dill's store shortly after the murder attempt but could have been establishing an alibi. Likelihood of guilt: MEDIUM.

MRS. TALMADGE – Would prefer not to see Mr. Talmadge inherit and open the restaurant, so has nothing to gain from Mrs. MacGillicuddie's death. Likelihood of guilt: EXTREMELY LOW.

MR. THEDA – Would inherit Mrs. MacGillicuddie's incriminating tapes if she died. But clearly stole them from her tonight. So no need to murder her for his inheritance after all? (of course, she could always get them back.) Likelihood of guilt: ??????

MR. BARA – Would do anything for Mr. Theda. Likelihood of guilt: ALSO ??????

EDUARDO – Stands to inherit quite a bit of money when Mrs. MacGillicuddie dies but sick in bed at time of murder attempt. Of course, could all be a ruse. Maybe he never really drank the poison and only pretended to be sick. Likelihood of guilt: ??????

RODNEY – Hates his mother and wants her money. Likelihood of guilt: EXTREMELY HIGH.

AURORA BOREALIS – Hates her grandmother and wants her money but extremely lazy. Likelihood of guilt: MEDIUM.

LYNDON – Likes his aunt but wants her money. Completely incompetent. Likelihood of wanting to kill someone: HIGH. Likelihood of being even sort of successful at it: EXTREMELY LOW. Overall likelihood of guilt: LOW.

MR. SANGFROID – Stands to inherit some very valuable paintings when Mrs. MacGillicuddie dies. Hates her and everyone else. Found at scene of the crime but might have been framed. Likelihood of guilt: ??????

Ernestine tapped her lip with her pen. It was quite a long list, but it occurred to her that there were two more names she should add to it, though they only required one additional entry:

THE SWANSON TWINS - What were they doing over by Dill's store at 12:30 in the morning? Likelihood of guilt: ??????

Hm. Too many questions marks and also too many suspects to deal with in one day. So Ernestine decided to scratch off the least likely suspects as well as the one still stuck in the hospital and therefore unavailable to be grilled. That left her with:

MR. TALMADGE

MR. THEDA

MR. BARA

EDUARDO

RODNEY

AURORA BOREALIS

THE SWANSON TWINS

Getting out of the tub, Ernestine dried herself off. Looking in the mirror, she grimaced at the mess that was her hair, then shrugged and pulled it up into the neatest bun she could. After tidying up in the bathroom, she headed out to the kitchen to find Charleston giving Maya lessons on how to make pancakes.

"You see," Charleston explained, glasses askew and hair a

mess, "the lemon zest helps bring out the fruitiness of the blueberries."

As Maya watched with interest, he poured the batter onto the griddle.

"Where did you learn that?" Maya asked, impressed.

"Tllmdgs," Charleston mumbled, taking a bite of bacon. Ernestine took that to mean either "Talmadges" or else "Tall midgets."

When the pancakes finished cooking, Charleston whisked them onto the plate, dusted each one with powdered sugar, and then served them up as the rest of the family sat down at the table.

"I need the two of you to deposit this for us today." Ernestine brought out the two stacks of cash Mrs. MacGillicuddie had given them last night. She also took out the stack Mrs. MacGillicuddie had given her earlier and divided it evenly between herself and her stepbrother.

"Wow! You're giving me half of that, too?" Charleston missed his mouth with his fork, delivering the bite of pancake it was carrying to his ear.

"Of course. I wouldn't have even been there to save Mrs. MacGillicuddie if you weren't helping me start the apocalypse."

"There's an apocalypse about?" Frank set down his cup

of coffee and blinked about with interest, trying to spot it. "Why didn't anyone tell me?"

"I'll let you know when it gets here." Maya laid her hand reassuringly on her husband's.

He smiled at her and then seemed to notice all of the money on the table for the first time. "Where did all of this come from? Have we sold something and I've forgotten about it?"

"No, the kids keep sneaking out and saving people from certain death," Maya sighed.

"Wow! Like superheroes? Righteous, man!" Frank beamed approvingly, causing Maya to sigh again and Charleston to smile and sit up straighter.

Ernestine, too, liked his way of looking at things. Superheroes of the Apocalypse. Yes, she definitely could get used to being called that. It would lead well into: *Montgomery for President: Superhero of the Apocalypse, Leader of the Free World.*

After breakfast, they all divided up the day's maintenance work. Ernestine immediately claimed the mouse problem in Mr. Theda and Mr. Bara's apartment, while Charleston chose feeding the various chickens, swans, peacocks, and other fowl that lived in the carriage house when the Swanson twins weren't using them for their act.

"If you see the Swanson twins, keep an eye on them," she warned in a low voice as they headed out of the apartment.

"Why?"

"They might try to murder you." Technically, Ernestine supposed anyone *might* murder anyone else at any given time. You never could tell what was going through someone else's head. Still, if the twins were murderers, then Ernestine figured there was an above average chance they might murder someone asking questions about the first murder. Murders were probably like lies. As soon as you did it once, you had to keep on doing it to cover up the first one.

Leaving Charleston behind with his mouth hanging open, Ernestine went to her first stop. Which was actually neither Mr. Theda and Mr. Bara's apartment, nor was it in MacGillicuddie House at all.

No, her first stop was at the police station four blocks away. Well, to be technical again, her first stop was actually at Mitzy's Coffee Shop for a coffee and an éclair. These she presented to a very weary Detective Kim as he peered at his computer, trying—and failing—to summarize the night's events in a believable way.

"I brought you some coffee because I thought you'd be tired after last night." Ernestine handed him the cup and the bag with the éclair in it. She had put on her school blazer and navy skirt to make her look more professional.

"That was very nice of you." Surprised, he accepted them

gratefully, tearing the lid off the cup so he could guzzle the scalding liquid as though impervious to burns. "Wait, shouldn't you be in school?"

"I'm out sick due to psychological trauma," Ernestine bragged, actually quite pleased to have such an interesting injury. "Also, I have some questions."

"Of course you do." Detective Kim set the éclair down just as he had picked it up. Looking around to see if anyone was listening, he whispered, "Look, I'll answer what I can." In a much louder voice, he announced, "OF COURSE, I CAN'T SHARE CONFIDENTIAL POLICE INFORMATION WITH YOU."

"I UNDERSTAND," Ernestine replied loudly and, she felt, convincingly. Then she plunked herself down in the chair next to his and said in a low voice, "How's Mr. Sangfroid doing? Have you been able to question him?"

"Not yet," Detective Kim admitted ruefully. "The doctors say he's going to be fine, but he's had quite an injury to his head. He's not exactly coherent yet. He keeps babbling about his cat, Tiddlywinks, and dancing the tango with Libby Swanson down in Brazil. None of it makes a lot of sense yet, to be honest."

"Do you think he did it?" Ernestine asked.

"I don't know," Detective Kim sighed. "It doesn't look

good for him, but it also looks a little too convenient to me. Let's just say I'm not ready to arrest him, and I'm not ready to rule him out."

This all sounded very sensible to Ernestine, who was beginning to think that Detective Kim would do just fine in the apocalypse. He seemed like he knew how to keep his head about him.

"Okay, have you confirmed Mr. Talmadge's alibi? Could he have tried to murder Mrs. MacGillicuddie, then run over to Dill's store just in time to be caught by the Swanson twins?"

"Definitely not." Detective Kim clicked around on his computer and pulled up video of Mr. Talmadge skulking around outside Dill's store before pulling out his can and spraying paint onto the bricks below the camera. "Dill turned the video over to us this morning. If you look at the times, you can clearly see he arrives around midnight and doesn't get caught until the Swanson twins walk up at 12:25 on their way back from practicing at the Palace Theater. Since you caught the zombie attacking Mrs. MacGillicuddie at 12:17, he's accountable for until eight minutes after the attack."

He fast forwarded to that part, showing the twins coming out the theater's front door across the street and marching up to Mr. Talmadge. Outraged, one of them put him into a pretty good headlock while the other removed the can from his hand while giving him what looked like the scolding of his life. Even through the camera, she made Ernestine sit up straighter and uncross her legs.

"Do we know what time they arrived at the theater?" Ernestine tapped her lip thoughtfully.

"You think just like a detective." Detective Kim grinned at her. Ernestine beamed in response. She did so love to have her intellect appreciated. "The janitor said they arrived at eleven, just like they always do as he's leaving for the night."

"Hm." Ernestine tapped her lip with her pen. "What about Rodney, Lyndon, and Aurora Borealis? Do they have alibis?".

Detective Kim shook his head. "They say they were all home asleep at the time of the attack, but none of them can prove it."

"What about Eduardo? Could he have faked his earlier poisoning and then attacked Mrs. MacGillicuddie?"

"Faked? No. The doctor's report came back, and he was definitely poisoned. But I suppose it's always possible that he did so deliberately to throw suspicion away from himself. Heck of a way to do it, though."

Maybe he poisoned himself with the intent of coming back as a zombie. Though, like Detective Kim, Ernestine rather doubted it. She thanked Detective Kim and headed out. On her way, she pulled out her list and crossed off two names:

For now, Ernestine decided to leave both Eduardo and Mr. Sangfroid on the list. As she walked, she looked for signs of either one of her zombies, Herbert and Ella, but came across nothing other than her own **MISSING ZOMBIE** posters. From the people she passed, everyone seemed to think the flyers were just part of Mr. Theda's upcoming appearance at the Palace Theater. The marquee advertised both him reenacting scenes from his most famous movies and the Swanson twins doing a death-defying act beforehand.

As she continued toward MacGillicuddie House, she passed Dill's store. Spotting her through the plate glass window, he raced out the door and brandished one of the flyers at her. "Is this yours?"

"Er, yes?" Ernestine wasn't sure if he meant the zombie or the flyer, but either way, she supposed the answer would still be yes.

"He was in yesterday, eating some of the tulip bulbs I'd just gotten in! Shuffled off without even paying for them! Just grunted when I tried to stop him." The skinny vegan grocer glared at her with his hands on his hips, jaw thrust out like he wanted to know what she was going to do about it.

Ernestine just blinked at him before finally admitting, "I don't even know what to say to that."

In answer, Dill thrust out his hand, palm open.

Sighing, Ernestine dug into her pocket for change. "How much were they?"

"Twenty dollars!"

"For *tulip* bulbs?"

"They're vegan." Taking the money, Dill crossed his arms, clearly still unhappy with her. "He's not going to be back, is he?"

"They always come back," Ernestine warned in her most foreboding voice.

"Huh. Well, tell them to bring cash when they do." Dill turned to go, but Ernestine grabbed him by his grocer's apron and refused to let go.

"Hey, that twenty dollars doesn't just cover the cost of the tulip bulbs. I want some information, too." Now it was her turn to thrust out her chin to let him know she meant business.

"What kind of information?" Jerking his apron free from her grip, Dill suddenly looked as hunted as a rabbit, a reaction Ernestine found both unexpected and very, very interesting.

"I want to know why the Swanson twins would be coming to see you at 12:30 in the morning." That they were coming to visit him was just a wild guess. Well, not entirely wild. Based on the video footage Detective Kim had shown her, the Swanson twins had seemed disproportionately angry at Mr. Talmadge's vandalism. It was the sort of outrage Ernestine would have shown if she'd caught someone messing around with MacGillicuddie House.

"They weren't coming to see me." Suddenly, Dill's skin color didn't look so good. His eyes twitched this way and that, as though to see who else might be listening.

"Liar."

"I am not. *You're* the liar." Dill tried to scoot back in through the door, but Ernestine quickly threw herself in front of it.

Spreading her arms and legs out wide, she said, "If you don't tell me, *I'll* go tell Detective Kim there's something fishy about you, and then *he'll* start wondering if you had anything to do with Mrs. MacGillicuddie's attempted murders. And then *she* won't let you cater any more of her parties, *if* you're lucky. If you aren't, Eduardo and I won't be able to get the shotgun out of her hands in time."

Dill gulped. He clutched the twenty she had given him to his chest like he could use it to deflect the imaginary bullets when they started flying. Glancing around to confirm that he wasn't being stalked by an angry old woman in a sequined dress and tiara, he hissed, "Shhhh! Keep your voice down, will you?"

"I will if you'll tell me what's going on." Ernestine

stiffened her arms when he tried to push them down so he could get inside.

"There's nothing going on!" Dill slapped his face. "Look, Mora's my mom, okay?"

That was the second time within a few minutes that he'd left Ernestine completely flabbergasted. "Say what now?"

This time Dill was successful in pushing her out of the way, but he didn't go inside. Instead, he repeated, "My mom is Mora Swanson. Don't tell anyone, though. I promised her I wouldn't say anything when she moved in. She doesn't want anyone to know that she's old enough to have a grown-up son."

"Um, okay." Ernestine was fairly confident that people could guess she was that old anyhow, but she wasn't about to point that out right now. "So what was she doing here last night?"

"Well, they would have been coming by to see me, if they hadn't run into that nutjob Talmadge. They stop by every night after they finish practicing over at the Palace." Dill waved down the street at the fancy old movie theater. He continued on, "What a lunatic *that* guy is! And Mom and Aunt Libby had even been trying to make things better between us ever since they found out he wanted to open a restaurant in the same space I did. They even convinced Mrs. MacGillicuddie to let me cater her party, thinking he might be in a good enough mood to at least give my food a try. Maybe let a young, new guy have a go at success since he already had his. It, uh, didn't exactly work out that way."

"So I noticed," Ernestine said dryly, remembering the fight about to take place right before the chandelier put a stop to things. "Why do your mom and aunt care if you and Mr. Talmadge get along, anyhow?"

"They're concerned he might make things difficult for my restaurant if we don't. Tell people that there's really chicken in my tofu tacos or hamburger in my meatless lasagna. That sort of thing." Dill shuddered at the very thought.

Well, that certainly explained what the Swanson twins were doing here last night and what they had been doing while the zombie was off trying to murder Mrs. MacGillicuddie.

With a rodent problem to take care of and a murderer to ferret out, Ernestine returned to MacGillicuddie House around noon. That put her just in time to witness Aurora Borealis scuffling with both Swanson twins outside over an absolutely enormous bouquet of red roses. It was so humongous that Ernestine's first reaction was to wonder who had died. Her second reaction, of course, was to wonder whether she'd have more success raising a zombie from *that* corpse, it being really fresh and all, than with Herbert or Ella.

"They're mine!" one of the Swanson twins cried from the other side of about a hundred blooms. "It clearly says 'Mora'!"

"It does not!" Bracing her stiletto heels into a crack in the garden path, Aurora Borealis tried to wrench the bush free of the other two. "It says 'Aurora'!"

Charleston huddled nearby under a sculpture of a rhinoceros made out of old game systems. Red flower petals decorated his hair. As Ernestine approached, he warned, "Don't try breaking them up. I did, and they all beat me with roses. I've still got thorns stuck in my scalp."

Not one to run away from a confrontation, especially one that promised to be interesting, Ernestine was just about to turn the hose on them and freeze them into decorative sculptures when she noticed Aurora Borealis's phone lying on the ground.

Snatching it up, she cried, "Selfie!"

Aurora Borealis instinctively stopped what she was doing and posed with her hand on one hip and her lips puffed out in a pout.

That allowed the Swansons enough time to jerk the giant-sized bouquet free and shout, *"Ha!"* before staggering backward under the weight of all those flowers. Before one of them could be impaled by the Nintendo rhinoceros horn, Charleston shot gallantly forward and steadied them. Ernestine snatched the card off the bouquet and read it. In snowflake-smudged handwriting, it read: *Morora.* Or possibly: *Aumora.*

Goodness. Whoever wrote the name out had terrible handwriting.

"Yeah, I've got no idea." Before the squabbling could start up again, Ernestine yanked the bouquet apart. She shoved about fifty roses into Aurora Borealis's arms and about fifty more into Mora's arms. "There, each of you gets half. And there better be no complaints, or I'm going to give them all to Charleston for getting thorns in his head. Then you'll just have to complain to Mrs. MacGillicuddie if you don't like it."

"I'm going to tell my daddy on you!" Aurora Borealis whined, clearly not pleased to be receiving a mere two hundred dollars' worth of roses.

"Oh, don't be such a crybaby," Libby said sourly. "And give us back our shoes!"

Aurora Borealis went pale and skittered backward. She glanced guiltily down at her feet, where a pair of high, white shoes covered in crystals glittered up at them all.

The shoes she'd stolen from the Swanson twins the night the chandelier fell.

"I don't know what you're talking about." Sticking her nose up in the air, she marched up to the house, dumping her flowers in the garbage can sitting out on the front porch.

"What an awful girl," Libby muttered, staring after her.

"She can afford thousands of pairs of shoes of her own. Why does she have to keep stealing ours?"

"She's stolen more than one pair?" Ernestine sucked at the various cuts the thorns had made in her hands, trying to get them to stop bleeding.

"Well, someone has! If not her, then who?"

That was an excellent question. Aurora Borealis was, indeed, an awful girl. The question was, had she stolen the green iridescent shoe found on Mr. Sangfroid? Had it once belonged to the Swanson twins or had it come from somewhere else?

Wherever it had come from, had the would-be murderer stolen it from Aurora Borealis?

Or was she a budding murderer as well as a thief?

Chapter Eleven
Mice and Missing Children

THURSDAY, 12:56 PM

Before she left the Swanson twins behind to fish the flowers out of the dumpster, Ernestine showed them the picture of the little girl that she had found clutched in Mr. Sangfroid's hand the night before.

"Do either one of you recognize this kid?" she asked.

Libby's eyes widened in recognition and Ernestine's heart leaped in elation. Finally! A lead!

"Oh, look, Mora! It's that darling little girl from *The Addams Family*!" Libby cried, and Ernestine's heart immediately sank back down again.

"What?" Mora dug a pair of spectacles out of her purse.

Pinching them on her nose, she peered down at the picture. "That's not Wednesday Addams, you goose!"

"It isn't?" Libby took the spectacles from her sister and squinted closer at the picture. "Oh dear, it isn't, is it?"

"No, it's not."

Making a face, Libby handed it back to Ernestine. "Sorry, dearie."

"That's okay." Ernestine had to admit that the girl *did* sort of look like a toddler Wednesday Addams. Which might explain what was so unsettling about the photo. However, that hardly explained, either, why it was in a MacGillicuddie photo album or why Mr. Sangfroid had been carrying it around.

Feeling no closer than ever to solving who was behind the false zombies and the murder attempts, Ernestine and Charleston went off to apply disinfectant to the spots where the roses had mauled them.

"Maybe it's a picture of Mrs. MacGillicuddie when she was a kid," Charleston suggested as they daubed their wounds. "Maybe Mr. Sangfroid has — or had — a crush on her. Maybe that's why he stole the album and was carrying the picture around. The Talmadges said love makes people do crazy things."

"But *she* wasn't born into the MacGillicuddie family, she married into it," Ernestine countered, handing him a bandage. "And that picture was definitely taken at MacGillicuddie House, remember? It's written on the back, *and* I saw the mirror frame down in the basement. No, I think it had something to do with the secret he was threatening to reveal—and maybe why he tried to murder Mrs. MacGillicuddie, if it *was* him."

Their wounds covered, they went off to deal with Mr. Theda and Mr. Bara's mouse problem.

"Thank goodness you've arrived!" Throwing an arm across his forehead, Mr. Theda collapsed into a tall wingback chair next to the fireplace as Mr. Bara let Ernestine and Charleston into the apartment. The former horror movie star wore a cravat and an elegant silk smoking jacket. "It's been horrendous! Just dreadful! I didn't know how much longer I could go on!"

"Don't be so dramatic," Mr. Bara sighed, shutting the door and stepping onto a footstool made out of a crocodile (possibly fake, possibly not). He held a feather duster in his hand to clean an array of skulls, candelabras, and stuffed ravens. "It's just a mouse."

"It's *vermin*." Mr. Theda cringed in his chair as though about to be devoured. Unless it was zombie vermin, Ernestine didn't know what he was so worried about.

"It's fuzzy wuzzy," Ernestine pointed out as Charleston

squatted down next to the mouse caught in the no-kill trap by a suit of armor that had been a prop in a movie called *The Knight It Came Alive!*

"It has fangs," Mr. Theda said sulkily, straightening up in his chair and smoothing out his smoking jacket while Mr. Bara rolled his eyes and wiped off a two-headed cobra posed as though about to strike.

"They're called teeth," Mr. Bara said, "and it's using them to eat a hunk of Muenster."

"Just get it out of here," Mr. Theda snapped, dropping the dramatic act and sounding quite practical.

"Okey-dokey." Ernestine took the mouse out of the trap and popped it into the cage she'd brought along, wondering what on earth she'd do with it. She supposed she'd have to kill it but felt sort of bad about the thought. Maybe she could bring it back as a zombie afterward?

"Goodness, what a morning!" Mr. Theda fidgeted with his cuff links. To Ernestine's surprise, the onyx stone set in the cufflink fell back to reveal a compartment beneath. Out of this, Mr. Theda popped two aspirin and swallowed them with a glass of water.

"Nifty cuff links," Ernestine observed, impressed.

"You like them?" Mr. Theda beamed with pride. "Mrs. MacGillicuddie gave them to me. They belonged to her ex-husband. Apparently, the Duke of Wibblington once used them to poison a political rival."

"Gosh! That's terrible!" Now Ernestine was even more impressed. Not least because it seemed that Mr. Theda had the perfect means for storing the poison that had been slipped into Mrs. MacGillicuddie's bottle of bourbon.

"Well, it saved the Duke the bother of having to frame him for a crime and executing him legally. Courts can take a terribly long time to get around to that sort of thing, you know."

"I'll keep that in mind." Ernestine really would. When you were planning the apocalypse, you never knew what sort of legal trouble you might get into. "Say, Mr. Bara, could you take a look at this, please?"

She took out the bag with its zombie body part and handed it to him. Mr. Bara took the bag and smiled fondly. "Ah, these bring back memories."

"Body parts bring back memories?" Charleston asked as he fed the mouse a wedge of Muenster.

"It's not a body part. It's a fake zombie wound. I have a whole drawer full of them."

He waved toward a spiky, elaborately carved cabinet that looked like it either belonged in a Victorian parlor or else maybe a torture chamber. With Mr. Theda and Mr. Bara, you never knew which set they'd taken their furniture from. Ernestine opened it gingerly in case she was right about the torture chamber and doing so would trigger a trap to dismember her. Nothing did, which was both good and faintly disappointing. More exciting, it *did* contain all sorts of realistic-looking severed hands, eyeballs, shrunken heads, and a pickled brain. Just as Mr. Bara promised, there was also a whole drawer full of fake wounds and scabs, plus stuff to make them ooze.

Ernestine stared into the jar with the pickled brain. Where on earth did you buy a pickled brain, she wondered? Or was that more of a do-it-yourself sort of thing?

"You know, I think this is one of mine, actually." Mr. Bara used the feather duster to clean it up a bit. "Whoever has been trying to kill Mrs. MacGillicuddie must have taken it when they also stole that prop wig."

"That was yours, too?" Charleston asked, taking a bite off the hunk of Muenster before handing it back to the mouse again.

"Of course it was ours. Who else has a large collection of zombie costumes just lying around?" Mr. Theda snorted scathingly, then stopped to think about it for a moment. "Well, aside from all of our fans, I mean. So I suppose millions of people, really."

As Mr. Bara got down off of his crocodile and gently pushed Ernestine out of the way so he could take stock of his body part collection, Ernestine decided this was the perfect opening to grill Mr. Theda. Especially now that she knew about his possibly-poison-storing cuff links. "Yes, you have a lot more fans now than you did back when you were on *Torrid Dilemmas*, don't you, *Frankie Nelson?*"

Gasping, Mr. Theda recoiled in horror from her as though she was one of the monsters he usually unleashed in his movies. Mr. Bara closed his eyes like he'd just developed a very bad headache.

"How—how—how—did you—" Mr. Theda stuttered before trying the same tactic both Dill and Aurora Borealis had used. He drew himself up and said haughtily, "I don't know what you're talking about."

"Oh, really?" Ernestine marched over to Mr. Bara's computer and pulled up the picture of Mr. Theda as Frankie Nelson. Turning around, she crossed her arms smugly and dared him to deny it.

"Oh, *farts*," Mr. Theda swore, crossing his arms sulkily.

"Um, Ernestine? Maybe we shouldn't provoke the potential murder suspects while in a room filled with weapons?" Charleston glanced around at the various axes, maces, and swords. To say nothing of the chandelier made out of all the prop knives that had ever appeared in Mr. Theda's movies.

Getting up from the cabinet with a handful of spare body parts, Mr. Bara said, "I had our legal team contact that website months ago, telling them to take it down! Well, looks like I'll have to hack it instead."

Dumping the fake body parts into Ernestine's hands, he sat down in a chair made out of a leftover medieval throne from *Mutilated Medieval Misanthropes* to type complicated things in code.

Dumping the various ears, fingers, and eyeballs onto the floor, Ernestine snatched up a mace for protection. "Were either one of *you* the zombie last night? Did you break into Mrs. MacGillicuddie's suite to steal those old VCR tapes?"

"No!" Mr. Theda cried in shock. Then, wringing his hands, he added, "But also, yes."

"I'm confused." Deciding it was best to be prepared, Charleston grabbed the axe off the mantel and brandished it about, ready to defend himself and his new fuzzy friend.

"You know that's rubber, right?" Mr. Bara took the mace from Ernestine's hand and whacked himself over the head with it. Rather than caving his skull in, it just bounced off like a basketball.

"That, too. Though it's lovely for slicing cheese with." Mr. Theda took the axe from Charleston and used it to carve himself off a hunk of the Muenster to nibble.

"I think you'd better tell them, Sterling," Mr. Bara said to Mr. Theda. "I'm missing quite a bit of zombie makeup from my cupboard. If the police come asking questions, it will all come out, anyhow."

"Oh, *all right*." Still munching sourly on his cheese, Mr. Theda did just that. "Yes, I was Frankie Nelson, but after that laughably awful soap, I couldn't get any work under that name. So I became Sterling Theda."

"It was my suggestion that he try out for the horror movies I was working on," Mr. Bara explained, still tapping away at the keyboard. "They didn't pay much, but each one was filmed so quickly that he could make dozens of them each year."

"Soon, I had hundreds of credits to my name and no one at all remembered Frankie Nelson or *Torrid Dilemmas*." Mr. Theda wrung his hands some more. "Except that blasted woman. She'd taped every single episode."

"If you'll recall, the reason she invited us to live here was because she loved you in that soap opera," Mr. Bara pointed out just as the old photo of Mr. Theda vanished from the website.

"She promised never to reveal my secret to anyone! I'm to inherit the tapes when she dies so I can finally destroy the last evidence of that—*unfortunate*—period in my career. But I know she still watches them every night! And with all of those parties she throws, how could I be sure someone wouldn't stumble across them?"

"But neither one of us would ever harm Mrs. MacGillicuddie," Mr. Bara said firmly, closing the lid on the laptop. "She's been a good friend to us both, even if those tapes make Sterling a little…anxious."

Mr. Bara, Ernestine, and Charleston all turned to look at Mr. Theda. Who, by now, had wilted halfway out of his wingback chair, murmuring over and over again, "The horror…the horror…"

Tugging him upright, Mr. Bara explained, "We were in our apartment when we heard the commotion downstairs. Sterling took advantage of it to retrieve what he felt should rightly be his. So, yes, he did break in, but neither one of us was the zombie. However, someone *has* stolen quite a bit of my prop makeup."

"Do you know who it could be?" Ernestine asked.

"I don't." Mr. Bara shook his head. "Though the night after Mrs. MacGillicuddie's Mardi Gras party, I came home to find a window open."

"*I* could guess." Straightening up, Mr. Theda made a face. "I caught that ridiculous granddaughter of Mrs. MacGillicuddie's in here the night of the party, trying to steal the jeweled collar off that fake mummy over there. She was getting ready to toss it out that open window and down into the bushes below. No doubt so she could retrieve it later, the thieving little brat. She probably came back the next night."

He waved his hand toward the open sarcophagus propped between the living room and dining room.

Aurora Borealis. Who had stolen at least one pair of the twins' shoes. Who would need to pry a window open with a crowbar to attack her aunt because she didn't have a key to the building. Who would have had ample opportunity to saw apart her grandmother's floorboard and sneak poison into her bourbon.

Aurora Borealis, who had a lot to gain if her grandmother died.

Which, of course, would also make her the perfect person to frame for the crime.

"One last question." Not ready to jump to any conclusions just yet, Ernestine showed them the picture of the little girl looking in the mirror. "Do you know who this is?"

Both gentleman looked at the picture, but once again, they shook their heads. However, Mr. Theda flipped it over and read the notation on the back about MacGillicuddie House. "Perhaps it was Mr. MacGillicuddie's sister? Lyndon's mother?"

"Hm. I never thought of that." Actually, Ernestine had

completely forgotten that Mr. MacGillicuddie even had a sister, though obviously Lyndon had to have come from somewhere.

"There *is* something unusual about this photo, though, isn't there?" Mr. Bara continued to study it, frowning. "Something's wrong with it, but I can't quite put my finger on what."

"Is it that she looks like Wednesday Addams?"

"Ah, it could be that, yes."

As Mr. Bara shut the door behind them, Charleston took the mouse out of the cage so he could pet it. Ernestine took out her list and scratched off two more names:

MR. THEDA

MR. BARA

That pretty much left her with:

EDUARDO

RODNEY

AURORA BOREALIS

She couldn't rule out Mr. Sangfroid and Lyndon yet, and things weren't looking good for Aurora Borealis, but after mistakenly accusing Mr. Talmadge, Ernestine wanted hard evidence before she claimed anyone else did it. Anyone could make one false accusation of murder, but two just started to look sloppy.

Deciding it was time to talk to Mrs. MacGillicuddie, Ernestine and Charleston went downstairs. They found her with an improving Eduardo on his phone, speaking with the Vatican about arrangements for Fluffy-Wuffy-Kins's funeral.

"I want five thousand white roses," Mrs. MacGillicuddie declared into the old-fashioned, fancy gold phone as she gestured with her teacup, slopping what Ernestine suspected wasn't tea all over the oriental carpeting. "*I* don't care how you do it, darling. Fly them in from Ecuador, if you have to. *Yes,* I understand that's expensive. That's the whole point, isn't it? Why on earth would I be ordering five thousand white roses if I didn't think it would look expensive, you ridiculous creature. Oh, thank heavens. Here's someone who knows how to get things done!"

Slamming down the phone, Mrs. MacGillicuddie peered at the mouse in Charleston's hands.

"What on earth is that?" she asked.

Charleston looked down in his hands to confirm he was, in fact, still holding a mouse. "It's a mouse."

"Yes, I know *that*, darling. Why are you bringing it into my suite?"

"It seemed better than returning him to Mr. Theda's apartment?"

"Oh, *that man*." Mrs. MacGillicuddie narrowed her eyes murderously as Eduardo spotted the mouse. Holding his own phone against his ear with his shoulder, he dumped out the remains of the teapot into a nearby lemon tree and popped the mouse into it as means to ensure that it couldn't escape. To keep it happy, Ernestine dropped the last of the cheese in after it. "If he doesn't give me my videos back, I'll release a whole colony of cobras in his apartment, that's what *I'll* do!"

Mentally, Ernestine made a note to get the videos back from Mr. Theda. The last thing she needed to deal with on top of an escaped zombie was a bunch of venomous snakes roaming about the house, clogging up the pipes.

"There will be five thousand white candles set up out in the garden by tomorrow evening," Eduardo murmured to Mrs. MacGillicuddie with a bow. "A thousand for each year of Fluffy's life. And the bishop himself will preside."

"The pope wasn't available?" Mrs. MacGillicuddie's face fell.

"Not on such short notice, no. I'm also afraid that I couldn't get the permits necessary to release five thousand white doves in the middle of winter either."

"Oh, it won't be the grand affair Fluffy-Wuffy-Kins deserved, but I suppose it will have to do." Sighing, Mrs. MacGillicuddie forgot about the mouse in the teapot and tried to pour herself another cup. She blinked at the pink tail that curled out of the spout rather than the stream of liquid she had expected. Though Ernestine supposed it would have been worse if a stream of liquid *had* poured out of it.

"Mrs. MacGillicuddie." Ernestine settled herself down in the least elaborate chair she could find. "I'm very sorry for your loss, but I need to ask you some uncomfortable questions."

"Oooh! That sounds exciting!" Her landlady perked up, and so did Eduardo. They both leaned in with teacups in their hands as though preparing to hear a particularly juicy story.

"Do you have any idea what scandalous things Mr. Sangfroid knows about the MacGillicuddie family?"

"Heavens!" Mrs. MacGillicuddie blinked, rather surprised. She collapsed backward onto the fainting couch as though exhausted. "There are so many of them, I couldn't even begin to know which ones *he* knows."

"There's the fact that Mr. MacGillicuddie's grandfather accidentally started the Great Depression," Eduardo suggested helpfully.

"True, it could be that," Mrs. MacGillicuddie agreed. "Or

it could be that unfortunate cigarette his second cousin Perpetua lit aboard the *Hindenburg*."

"Yes, or the fact that his Great-Great-Uncle Phineas distracted the captain of the *Titanic* by doing the can-can on the railing. If only he'd chosen to do it on the *other* side of the ship, perhaps things would have turned out a bit differently that night."

"And then there was his great-great-great-great-great-grandfather who had a bit too much to drink and then started tossing all of that tea in the harbor, thinking he was brewing the world's largest cup of tea. Strange family."

Ernestine and Charleston's heads whipped back and forth from one to the other as they each tossed out these possibilities, not quite sure whether to believe them.

Then both Mrs. MacGillicuddie and Eduardo went silent, raising their teacups to their lips. Realizing hers was still empty, their landlady sighed and set it down. "They were all a bit mad, you know, but not in a good way. Well, Uncle Phineas seemed to be crazy in a good sort of way, but *he* ended up as an ice cube long before I could meet him. The rest of them were *horribly* uptight and proper. Awful people, really. Don't know what I was thinking marrying into them. Ah, yes, now I remember. They had money. Lots and lots *and lots* of lovely money."

"Do you know who this girl is? Mr. Sangfroid stole one

of the MacGillicuddie photo albums that contained this picture the night of the party, and he was still carrying it around when he was attacked." Ernestine handed her the photo. "Charleston thought it might be you, but it was taken at MacGillicuddie House. Could it be Lyndon's mother?"

Eduardo gallantly held a pair of glasses between Mrs. MacGillicuddie's nose and the picture so that she couldn't technically be said to be wearing them and could therefore honestly claim that she "didn't wear glasses."

"Heavens, darling! I was born *many decades* after 1952! And no, that's not Patricia, Lyndon's mother. *She* was a blonde and this girl is a brunette. Plus, Patricia was as skinny as a string bean, not all adorable and chubby like this little girl. I don't know who this is, though I wonder…"

Waving the glasses away from her face, Mrs. MacGillicuddie trailed off. Now Ernestine and Charleston leaned forward, suspecting they were about to hear something good.

"Of course, there *was* another sister they made disappear."

"*What?*" Ernestine and Charleston cried together.

"*¿Que?*" Eduardo cried on his own.

"Disappear?" Ernestine sputtered. "What? How? Did they murder her?"

"*I* don't know! *I* didn't do it! I just know that soon after she was born, the MacGillicuddies shut the house up and stopped socializing with *everyone*. No one minded that much, of course, because no one much liked them. As I said before, *dreadful* lot." Mrs. MacGillicuddie smoothed her poofy black hair and adjusted the flow of her silver gown before continuing, "Of course, people tried to bribe the servants to find out what was going on, but no one wanted to risk their jobs by talking. There were rumors that the MacGillicuddies considered the little girl some sort of monster, but no one could ever figure out why. Mind you, the MacGillicuddies were such snobs that they would have considered her a monster for burping after taking her bottle, so who knows what was really wrong with her? Anyhow, they moved down to Rio de Janeiro around the time the girl would have been two or three, and there they stayed for years and years until they suddenly moved back to Mac-Gillicuddie House around the time I had my debutante ball. Wouldn't say a word about their time down in Brazil, but not long after I married Mr. MacGillicuddie, I stumbled across a couple of pairs of baby booties in an old trunk. I brought them down to dinner to ask my mother-in-law about them, and the whole family went crazy! Mother MacGillicuddie threw them in the fire and Father MacGillicuddie swore that he'd have me committed to an insane asylum if I ever brought it up again."

"So you didn't?" Charleston asked, eyes large.

"Don't be ridiculous, darling. I had *him* committed to

an insane asylum instead. Mr. Sangfroid, who was an art critic, remember, was *ever* so helpful with that, you know. Convinced the judge that Father MacGillicuddie had an unhealthy obsession with Stubbs's paintings of horses. Well, it didn't hurt that Father MacGillicuddie had become convinced that his real calling in life was to become the world's oldest jockey. Anyhow, once *he* was gone, I shipped Mother MacGillicuddie off to a commune in California where she lived out her life happily making papier-mâché flowers and selling them in airports. With them conveniently out of the way, I was free to help myself to their fortune." Mrs. MacGillicuddie and Eduardo both chuckled at the ridiculousness of anyone intimidating her. "I also made some inquiries down in Rio, but all I could come up with were some vague sightings of a little girl the family considered a monster. I never could find out why, but apparently, they shipped her off to an orphanage and claimed there never had been a third child. Horrible people. Rodney, Lyndon, and Aurora Borealis have all turned out quite well, really. They might be ungrateful, dreadful wretches, but if *they've* made anyone disappear, they've at least had the good sense to hide it from me."

"Unless they're trying to make *you* disappear," Ernestine pointed out.

"Yes, well, there *is* that. But I *am* rich, so you can't blame them for trying, really," Mrs. MacGillicuddie said without resentment. "I tried a few times with Father and Mother MacGillicuddie, but it was so much less complicated to just ship them off someplace where they couldn't bother me. Now do scoot, darlings. I have a funeral to plan."

Getting up, Eduardo led them out, leaning heavily on the cane Mrs. MacGillicuddie had lent him.

"What about *you*, Eduardo?" Ernestine crossed her arms and looked defiantly at him once they were out of Mrs. MacGillicuddie's hearing. "You stand to gain a lot from Mrs. MacGillicuddie's death."

"*¿Yo?*" Eduardo pressed a hand against his chest in shock. "But I was poisoned! I could have died, too!"

"Which is just the sort of thing a smart, organized person like you would do to throw suspicion away from yourself," Ernestine noted.

In spite of himself, Eduardo preened, flattered. Then, having smoothed his hair back down, he turned serious. "When Mrs. MacGillicuddie dies, I will lose the best friend I've ever had. No amount of money I will inherit will ever replace that."

He shut the door on them, leaving Ernestine and Charleston to take both the mouse and the teapot back upstairs. As they went, Ernestine looked down at the remaining names on her list:

EDUARDO

RODNEY

AURORA BOREALIS

Eduardo had seemed sincere when he said that no one could replace Mrs. MacGillicuddie in his life. Still, maybe he had some money problems Ernestine didn't know anything about? Maybe he'd regret Mrs. MacGillicuddie's death but still feel he had no choice but to murder her. Reluctantly, Ernestine left his name on the list.

What about Mrs. MacGillicuddie's son and granddaughter? Could one of them know something about their mysterious, monstrous relative? The one who had disappeared so many years before? Or did this have nothing at all to do with the picture?

And still, there were Mr. Sangfroid and Lyndon. Maybe Mr. Sangfroid *had* tried to kill Mrs. MacGillicuddie, only to accidentally trip and knock himself out.

Or maybe for once in his life, Lyndon was actually managing to pull off some crazy plan somewhat successfully.

If Mr. Sangfroid was the guilty party, then Mrs. MacGillicuddie was safe until he got out of the hospital. If it was anyone else, then she was still in danger.

And the killer could strike again at any time.

Chapter Twelve
In Loving Memory of Fluffy-Wuffy-Kins

FRIDAY, 7 PM

No one got eaten or murdered Thursday night, so both Ernestine and Charleston managed to sleep well for once. After school on Friday, Ernestine's animal problems temporarily overrode both her zombie and murder problems. Aside from the growing list of maintenance work her mom and stepdad had been ignoring because of tomorrow's stupid gallery opening, she had a mouse to exterminate and a dead cat to bury. Most kids looked forward to the weekends. Personally, Ernestine found school to be a much-needed break from the responsibilities of her home life.

It turned out that murdering an innocent mouse wasn't as easy as you might think. They tended to stare pleadingly up at you with big black eyes and trembling whiskers. Ernestine discovered that she much preferred returning the undead to life than she did removing the living from it. So she reluctantly went to the bank and took out two hundred dollars of Mrs. MacGillicuddie's money. With it, she bought the newly named Mr. Whiskers the poshest cage-and-tunnel-set the pet store owned. The tubes ran all around the attic and it took her and Charleston forever to set it up.

Around seven, they changed back into their school uniforms and joined Maya and Frank downstairs in the garden. Mr. Ellington and the Hep Cats dolefully played the blues beneath the frozen pergola, which had been decorated with white roses and white Christmas lights. Candles filled the veranda and gardens, even floating in the half-frozen koi pond. Honestly, it looked more like someone was going to get married than buried, but it certainly was pretty.

Most impressive of all, the Swanson twins sat on swings suspended high above the garden from the branches of a giant old oak tree. They wore angel costumes. Well, they were actually the swan costumes they had worn to Mrs.

MacGillicuddie's party earlier in the week. They'd just grabbed small harps and added halos to their heads and were busy adjusting them so that they'd be mirror images of each other, though that seemed to be leading to some unusual disagreement among the twins.

"No, Libby, I want my halo on the right! *I'm* the one that's right-handed, after all!" Mora cocked the sparkly foil ring above her head off to the right.

"What does being right-handed have to do with it? I look better with mine on the right. *Yours* should be on the left. That's your better side!"

"We're twins, you fool! We both have the same better side!"

"Which is the right." Pressing her lips together with determination, Libby adjusted her halo to the right as well.

"Can't you both wear them on the right?" Ernestine called up as she passed beneath them.

"Hello, dearie!" They wiggled their fingers down at Ernestine. Then Mora remembered that she was mad and huffed. "Don't be ridiculous! The point is for us to be mirror images of each other!"

"Which we will be, if Mora would just put her halo *off to the left!*"

Shrugging, Ernestine went to find her landlady.

Standing next to the cat-sized coffin, Mrs. MacGillicuddie wore a black sequined dress, fur coat, long black gloves, a veil, and enormous sunglasses that seemed rather unnecessary given that it was both night and she was already wearing the veil. Ernestine went up to give her condolences, only to have Mrs. MacGillicuddie grab her and drag her behind a massive hydrangea bush.

"This funeral is going to be a disaster!" her landlady hissed, throwing up her veil and tearing off her sunglasses to reveal her elaborately made-up face. "No pope! Only a bishop! No white doves to release, only pigeons! Just four thousand roses when I specifically ordered five! I bet they thought I wouldn't count!"

"I'm sure Fluffy would approve of how miserable Rodney and Aurora Borealis look out there," Ernestine said encouragingly. "Would you like me to sneak Fluffy's favorite pillow under Rodney when he goes to sit down? That way he could cover his suit in white cat hair one last time."

"No, Eduardo already has that under control. What I need *you* to do is cause a scene. Something that will make the eleven o'clock news. Or get retwitted on Snoopchat or whatever on earth it is you crazy kids do these days."

"What?" Ernestine exclaimed as Mrs. MacGillicuddie shoved her back out from behind the bush.

"Go accuse someone of murder! That always causes a sensation!"

"But I don't know who tried to do all of the murdering yet!" Ernestine had no problem at all causing a scene. She was more than happy to cause a scene if it meant she got to be the center of attention while it happened. However, if she was going to accuse someone of murder, she'd prefer it be the correct person, and she *still* couldn't decide whether it was Aurora Borealis or Rodney framing Aurora Borealis. Without further evidence, it could be either one of them. Or Lyndon or Mr. Sangfroid or Eduardo.

"*I* don't care! We can always bail them out tomorrow morning if you're wrong! Just pick someone. Preferably my son. I think Fluffy-Wuffy-Kins would have liked it that way."

"Oh, all right." Jerking her arm away, Ernestine smoothed down her coat and looked around for someone to accuse.

Rodney now stood next to the tiny pink coffin that held Fluffy-Wuffy-Kins's earthly remains. He sneered down at it in disgust, clearly revolted by all of the money being thrown into mourning the feline. Money he probably felt *he* should be able to spend instead. Probably on awful skyscrapers with his name on them or possibly a casino or two.

Ernestine supposed he *could* be the would-be murderer,

but then her eyes fell on Aurora Borealis standing right next to him in a pair of bright pink stiletto heels.

Heels Ernestine recognized as being part of the flamingo costumes the Swanson twins had worn to Mrs. MacGillicuddie's New Year's Eve party a few weeks before.

The twins had been right. She had stolen more than one pair of shoes from them.

Just like she'd broken in and stolen the zombie makeup from Mr. Bara.

As Aurora Borealis lifted her phone up to take a selfie with the coffin, a loose coat sleeve fell backward, revealing red scratches crisscrossing the skin of her forearm.

Scratches that couldn't possibly have been made by the diamond bracelet on her wrist.

Scratches that could, however, have been made by the claws and beaks of several very angry chickens.

Perhaps Mr. Sangfroid's photo of the girl had nothing to do with the murder attempts after all. Perhaps Mr. Sangfroid had been on his way to threaten Mrs. MacGillicuddie with the revelation of a missing MacGillicuddie sibling when Aurora Borealis had run into him while escaping Ernestine and her fighting chickens. Maybe knocking him out and thrusting the shoe on his foot had been a spur-of-the-moment attempt to throw suspicion on someone else.

Detective Kim arrived, taking up residence toward the back of the crowd, and then the service started. Facing each other and moving together in perfect time as though puppets controlled by the same string, the Swanson twins descended midway down toward the standing crowd, strumming their harps and softly singing "Ave Maria." They would have been the mirror images of each other, if they hadn't both had their halos cocked off to the right, which somewhat ruined the effect.

The bishop prayed for God to welcome Fluffy-Wuffy-Kins's soul to heaven, preferably right onto His lap. Mrs. MacGillicuddie wept daintily, dabbing at her eyes with lace-trimmed handkerchiefs from the stack Charleston thoughtfully held out for her. He also held her flask until Ernestine glared at him. Then he hastily passed it off to Mr. Ellington, who took a swig and then tucked it into his saxophone.

When the bishop finished, Ernestine stepped up to the podium. As the Swanson twins continued to swing overhead and strum their harps, she looked out over the crowd and wished she had a microphone. This was her big moment, and she wanted to be sure that everyone could hear her.

"Murder," she began, gesturing at the rose-covered coffin, "is a dreadful business. Not, perhaps, as dreadful as forgetting someone's birthday, but dreadful just the same. That should seem obvious, should it not? Yet here we all stand because to someone it was not obvious at all. To that someone, what was obvious was that murder would be the perfect solution to any number of problems.

"While the most logical explanation might *seem* to be that these murder attempts are the work of zombies, the most logical explanation in this case is not true. What is true *is* that *a member of Mrs. MacGillicuddie's own family has been trying to murder her!*"

With dramatic flair, Ernestine pointed her finger at the family in question, all of whom recoiled in horror.

"The child is mad!" Rodney cried, flinging his arms around Aurora Borealis while Lyndon started looking around for a way to escape in case she meant him. "What morbid nonsense!"

"Morbid, yes, but not nonsense," Ernestine shot back. Gosh, this was fun. No wonder people hung out in murder mysteries where everyone around them dropped like flies, even though the sensible thing to do would be to get the heck out of town. "You, madam, have been impersonating a zombie. You stole the costume from Mr. Theda and Mr. Bara, dressed yourself up in it to resemble the undead, and then broke into your grandmother's house to murder her!"

"No!" Mr. Theda cried and fainted dead away. Or at least pretended to. He didn't get enough chances to break out his acting skills these days, so he probably needed to warm up for next weekend's convention at the Palace. Mr. Bara, apparently expecting this, caught him before he could tumble into the open grave. What Mr. Theda was so upset about, Ernestine didn't know. It wasn't like she'd accused *him* of murder.

"You're crazy!" Aurora Borealis looked around at all of the appalled faces, her gaze finally landing on the nearby bishop, who decided to scoot away in case Ernestine was correct. "Ew, I'd never wear anything so gross as zombie scabs!"

"Yet you *would* wear shoes stolen from the Swanson twins!" The entire congregation strained to get a good look at Aurora Borealis's feet. Above them all, the Swanson twins craned their heads downward so they could see, too.

"Not another pair!" Libby cried, dropping her harp onto the drummer for the Hep Cats. Unnoticed by anyone except for Ernestine, he keeled over backward but at least avoided both the koi pond and marble bench that had been taking out so many other people lately.

"You filthy little thief!" Chucking her harp to the side, too, Mora did an impressive somersault down off of her swing and landed — very nimbly on her feet for someone sixty years old — next to Aurora Borealis.

Libby followed her sister, dropping like a heavenly ninja on the girl's other side. As Mora grabbed Aurora Borealis,

Libby tried to pry the shoes off her feet. Once again, feathers flew everywhere. As did a dozen homing pigeons dyed white.

"What? No! Ow! Get off me! You gave them to me, remember?" Aurora Borealis tried to kick away the elderly twins. In doing so, she lost her balance, knocking over Fluffy-Wuffy-Kins's pink coffin. It toppled into the hole, followed by Aurora Borealis, Libby, and Mora.

"Oh, my," Maya gasped.

"Get her, Libby! She's not getting away with another pair!"

"Give them back to me, you old biddy! They're mine!" Aurora Borealis kept a tight grip on one of the sparkly pink shoes.

"Oh, this is lovely!" Mrs. MacGillicuddie clasped her hands together. "Fluffy-Wuffy-Kins would have loved this!"

Rodney tried to pry one of the Swanson twins off his daughter, only to have her slug him. Lyndon dove out of the way, accidentally elbowing the bishop into the koi pond as he did so. Mr. Ellington's entire band sprang forward to fish the holy man out, but by then, half the residents of MacGillicuddie House were brawling with Rodney, Aurora Borealis, and Lyndon as they all tried to make their escape.

"Isn't this fun!" Mrs. Talmadge called cheerfully to Mr. Talmadge as she swung a chair at Lyndon's head, which he just managed to avoid.

"Just like old times, luv!" Mr. Talmadge chucked another

chair into the hydrangea bush Mrs. MacGillicuddie had dragged Ernestine behind earlier, which had started this whole mess. "Ah, I feel young again!"

Ernestine felt in danger of losing various body parts she was very attached to. Fortunately, Maya snatched her backward just as a very muddy, very bedraggled Aurora Borealis launched herself at Ernestine.

"*You!*" she screamed, taking a swing at Ernestine's head with the stiletto heel still in her hand.

"Leave my daughter alone!" Maya whacked her in the knees with the shovel hard enough to send her sprawling backward into the bishop just as the Hep Cats got him onto his feet. They all fell into the pond with a splash that sent frozen koi fish flying everywhere as though the universe was raining kitty treats in Fluffy-Wuffy-Kins's honor.

As Charleston ran about trying to collect the fish, Detective Kim snagged Aurora Borealis and pulled her back onto dry land. He immediately slapped handcuffs onto her wrists as Maya stuck the shovel back into the ground, apparently satisfied that she'd kept Ernestine safe.

Ernestine seized this opportunity to yank up the sleeve of Aurora Borealis's coat so everyone could see the scratch marks on her arms. "The chickens I threw at the zombie attacking

Mrs. MacGillicuddie scratched up its arms. Scratches that perfectly match *these marks!*"

The crowd gasped.

"Aurora Borealis!" Rodney cried, fighting his way through the crowd to reach her side. "Tell me it isn't true!"

"Daddy! I didn't do it!" Aurora Borealis tried unsuccessfully to tug herself free of Detective Kim. "Grammy's just being an old biddy!"

"I am *not* a biddy!" Mrs. MacGillicuddie straightened up in outrage. "And forty-five is not old!"

"You're eighty," Charleston pointed out, hands full of frozen fish.

"Hush up, darling, and let the grown-ups talk."

Rodney had gone quite white and stiff in the face. Of course, as he was always very white and stiff, most people wouldn't notice a difference, but Ernestine did. It didn't look like his usual outrage, either, which was pretty much the only emotion she'd ever actually seen him show. Ernestine was sure she must be wrong, but it almost looked like fear.

"She didn't do it! It was me!" he shouted, commanding the crowd's attention.

Charleston was so surprised, he dropped his fish right onto the heads of the Hep Cats as they struggled up out of the pond.

"What?" As one, everyone in the crowd swung their

heads from Rodney to Mrs. MacGillicuddie. She staggered backward and for support, had to grab the shovel used to dig Fluffy-Wuffy-Kins's grave. For all her casual talk of her son trying to murder her, the revelation that he actually *had* seemed to be quite a blow to her. Eduardo scooped the flask out of Mr. Ellington's saxophone, but she waved it away when he tried to hand it to her.

Rodney straightened up, smoothing down his tie. "I'm sorry, Mother, but it was me. I've squandered my inheritance from Father so I wanted to get my hands on yours. All of this ridiculous talk of zombies gave me the idea for the disguise, and I tried to frame Mr. Sangfroid by putting the shoe on his foot. But it was me all along."

The crowd went quiet.

"Daddy?" Aurora Borealis gasped, unable to believe what she was hearing.

"I'm sorry, darling. I know I haven't always been the best father, but I would truly do anything for you." For just a moment as he gazed at his daughter, Rodney didn't sound pompous or whiny. In fact, in confessing that he'd tried to murder his mother, he sounded to Ernestine the most likable she'd ever heard him to be. Then he turned to his mother and said, "Which is more than I can say for *you*, Mother."

Mrs. MacGillicuddie wavered as though his accusation

had been a terrible blow. Still soaking wet, the Hep Cats stepped forward to catch her.

Instead of falling, Mrs. MacGillicuddie picked up the shovel and ran at her son while screaming, "HIIIIIIII-YAAAAAAHHH!"

Chaos broke out again. Several police officers swarmed Mrs. MacGillicuddie before she could accomplish the week's first successful murder. Libby Swanson had to actually vault onto her sister's shoulders and then spring up into the tree to avoid being sideswiped by the shovel.

"You once left me in a department store while you went to Paris!" Rodney shrieked at his mother as Detective Kim sat on him to keep him from attacking her. This would have been impressive if it wasn't for the fact that five police officers in riot gear were still struggling to wrench the shovel out of Mrs. Mac-Gillicuddie's hands. Meanwhile, the other Swanson twin and the dripping-wet bishop had also taken refuge up in the tree.

"It was Tiffany's, and some people *dream* of being left there over a long weekend!" Mrs. MacGillicuddie managed to shake the police officer off her right elbow. However, the officer hanging on to the tip of the shovel managed to keep her from swinging it at anyone.

"I was all alone!"

"You were fifteen! And the staff knew to look after you!"

"Take a video of me being brave." Aurora Borealis shoved her phone into Charleston's hands, apparently having correctly identified him as the helpful one. Before Charleston could ask what she was planning, she took off her diamond earrings and screamed, "HIIIIIIII-YAAAAAHHH!", sounding just like her grandmother, as she tackled Detective Kim and knocked him off her father.

Rodney took off running through the garden and out the back gate, half a dozen officers pounding after him with police batons raised.

Mr. Ellington and the Hep Cats looked at each other, nodded, and packed up their instruments. He had once told Ernestine that any decent band always knew when to clear out of a place before anyone could lose a limb. If they had decided it was time to go, Ernestine felt confident the police must be just about ready to call in air support.

Quite unfazed by all of the officers hanging on to his enraged employer, Eduardo walked over to her and smoothly said, "Do remember what your plastic surgeon said about straining your facial muscles too far back."

Gasping, Mrs. MacGillicuddie instantly let go of the shovel and handed it to the police officer who had been dangling off of it.

Taking the phone from Charleston, Eduardo continued

over to where Detective Kim held a snarling Aurora Borealis. "Aurora Borealis, I believe your Instagram account just hit two million followers."

"Oooh! Gimme!" She immediately stopped struggling and snatched her phone from the butler.

"And Detective Kim, you'll find Rodney inside his limo just on the other side of the fence. The Talmadges were kind enough to slash his tires for me." With a dignified bow to the detective, Eduardo took the shovel from the police officer holding it and went to work filling in Fluffy-Wuffy-Kins's grave.

Ernestine was impressed. When the apocalypse came, Eduardo might be humanity's best hope.

"Well, I suppose I had better arrange to go bail Rodney and Aurora Borealis out," Mrs. MacGillicuddie sighed as the SWAT team helped the bishop and the Swanson twins down out of the tree.

"Bail Rodney out?" Ernestine asked in surprise. "Mrs. MacGillicuddie, you did notice how he tried to kill you, didn't you?"

"Yes, but he's family, darling. If I left him locked up, who would I have to fight with?" Mrs. MacGillicuddie waved her hand dismissively. "Besides, I'm quite certain that I can make his life far more miserable than the prison can!"

All in all, it was quite a funeral.

Ernestine liked to think that Fluffy-Wuffy-Kins would have been pleased. Well, he probably would have been more pleased by it if he hadn't been dead, but Ernestine had plans to fix that. True, her attempts to raise human zombies had been met with a few minor setbacks like not working, but perhaps that just meant she needed to start smaller.

And possibly...fluffier.

As the bishop walked past, wringing out his robes, he picked a piece of paper up off the flagstones. Handing it to Ernestine, he said, "I think you dropped this."

It was the picture of the little girl looking in the mirror. It must have fallen out of her pocket sometime during the brouhaha. Looking down at it now, Ernestine still felt quite certain there was something wrong with it.

"Did you ever figure out who it was?" one of the Swanson twins asked as she tugged her harp out of the hydrangea bush.

"No, but I suppose it doesn't really matter anymore," Ernestine reluctantly admitted. "I mean, if Rodney did it all just because he doesn't like his mother, then I guess this has nothing to do with it."

"Would you like me to take it inside to Mrs. MacGillicuddie for you?" the other Swanson twin asked. Their landlady had already gone inside for a soothing cup of tea and reassuring call to her plastic surgeon in Switzerland.

She reached for the photo, but Ernestine wouldn't let it go. "No. I want to know why Mr. Sangfroid stole it in the first place. Even if it doesn't have anything to do with all of these murder attempts, I still want to know *why*."

"Better you than me! I had enough of the old grump when I dated him all of those years ago!" Libby Swanson made a face. "Good luck!"

The twins went inside with a little wave. Detective Kim showered Ernestine with compliments for breaking the case, and Eduardo oversaw the cleanup of the backyard. The eleven o'clock news featured the brawl, which pleased everyone. As Mrs. MacGillicuddie pointed out, fame was fleeting but notoriety was forever.

Later that night after all of the fuss had finally settled down, Ernestine and Charleston dragged a goat into the graveyard to get the weekend started right.

"Ernestine, it's trying to eat me again," Charleston complained, tugging his coat free from the goat.

"Well, that's good practice for fighting off the undead. Do you really think you're going to be able to fight off zombies if you can't even get the better of a goat?"

"You know, I'm really beginning to think that maybe the

apocalypse isn't such a great idea if it might end with me as an appetizer!"

"Oh, that won't be the end of it," Ernestine said vaguely as they wandered among the tombstones, trying to find a recent one. Well, relatively speaking. Less than half a century would be recent in this graveyard. There were also a lot of elaborate mausoleums, but Ernestine wasn't about to willingly shove herself into such a small, confined space.

"What do you mean that won't be the end of it?" Charleston demanded, digging his heels into the frozen ground as he tried to drag the goat along.

"Oh—er, nothing."

"Ernestine, you're not planning on turning *me* into a zombie, are you?"

"Only if you get accidentally killed in the apocalypse. Which you won't, if you've been paying attention to everything I've been telling you! But if you do accidentally die, would you really want to spend eternity stuck down in some cramped, moldy grave? I'd much rather be up and moving about, having some fun."

"*Eating* people."

"Well, you'd be dead," Ernestine pointed out. "Your ways of having fun are sort of limited."

"I don't think I want to get eaten by a zombie. I want to

grow up and turn into an old person. All of the people around here seem to be having lots of fun. Just look at the Swanson twins. I *never* get to somersault down off of a moving swing."

"Yeah, they do make it look easy," Ernestine agreed, studying her various corpse choices.

"Did you *see* them tonight when they dropped down above the crowd?" Charleston continued, "It was like looking in the mirror!"

"Except for their halos," Ernestine chuckled. "You should have heard them before the funeral, arguing about which side of their heads — hang on."

Ernestine stopped dead in her tracks. Charleston bumped into her. And the goat bumped into Charleston.

"Ow," said Charleston.

"Oh!" said Ernestine. She reached into her pocket and pulled out the picture of the little girl. "Charleston! Oh, Charleston! I've finally figured out what was wrong with the photo of this girl! *Look at the hair ribbons!*"

"What about them?" He didn't sound very interested. Possibly because he was currently caught in a game of tug-of-war with the goat and his left-hand mitten.

Ernestine yanked the mitten out of the goat's mouth and stuffed a handful of alfalfa from Dill's store into it instead. "Charleston, *look*. If this was a girl looking in a mirror, then her hair ribbon would be reflected on the same side of her head. But *it's in a different spot on the girl's head!* That's because it's not a mirror, it's an empty picture frame. And that isn't one girl standing in the picture, it's two! *The Swanson twins!*"

"*The twins?*" In his shock, Charleston let go of the goat so he could grab the photo and take a look.

"Yes!" However, before Ernestine could continue any further, she saw a shadow speeding through the cemetery.

An ominous shadow.

A *mom*-shaped shadow.

"Ernestine Verna Montgomery!"

Ernestine winced. Never, anywhere ever, had it ended well for a child when their mother used their full name. "*What are you doing in a cemetery at this hour of the night?*"

"Using a goat to raise a zombie from the dead," Charleston said helpfully. Then, catching a glimpse at the appalled look on Ernestine's face, he asked uncertainly, "Or were we not supposed to tell people that?"

"No, Charleston, we were not."

"Well, *you've* been telling people we're raising the dead! What difference does the goat make?"

Ernestine opened her mouth to reply that it wasn't so much the goat as it was being out without permission, but Maya arrived before she could.

"*Where* did you get a goat?" Maya picked up its leash, fixing it with a stern look until it spat out Charleston's other mitten onto a frosty grave. "More importantly, *why* do you two have a goat?"

Charleston looked from Maya to Ernestine and then back again before obviously deciding there was wisdom in silence. Personally, Ernestine thought a better question would have been whether they planned on keeping the goat when they were done with it.

Craning her neck over their shoulders, Maya had one last question. "And why is there an open grave over there?"

"What?" Charleston asked in shock.

"Where?" Ernestine demanded, whipping around in excitement.

Sure enough, someone had been digging at Herbert McGovern's grave. Whether that someone had been digging up or down, Ernestine couldn't tell. Huge clumps of frozen earth sat on either side of a caved-in hole big enough for a rather large something to fit through. At the bottom of it was a splintered wooden coffin.

An *empty* splintered wooden coffin.

Maybe that really *had* been a zombie rummaging through the clothing donation bins.

Maybe it also really had been Herbert eating tulip bulbs at Dill's store.

Maybe zombies really did wake up disoriented and unsure of what to do.

Maybe it took them longer than one night to dig their way up out of the grave.

Maybe if you were going to raise one from the dead, you should stick around longer than fifteen minutes or so to see if it worked.

Ernestine had a whole lot of maybes and one definite that she didn't think about until too late. No matter what else happened in a zombie apocalypse, you should definitely not stand about gaping at the zombie's empty grave. The empty grave is never your biggest problem.

Anything standing behind you is way more dangerous.

Ernestine realized that just as she heard two dull thuds followed by the sound of two bodies hitting the ground.

Whipping around, she saw one of the Swanson twins standing over Charleston and her mother as they lay unconscious.

"You're too smart for your own good, dearie," that twin said.

Then the other one smacked her across the head from behind.

Just like that, Ernestine had a whole new set of problems.

Chapter Thirteen
Zombie Leftovers

SATURDAY, 2:47 AM

Ernestine awoke to find herself gagged as well as bound hand and foot. For a moment, she thought she was blindfolded, too, since she couldn't see a thing. Perhaps the zombie had stuffed her down into its grave. Sort of like tucking a doggie bag in the fridge for later. Just as her hysteria bubbled over into a scream, Ernestine remembered that it hadn't been a zombie who attacked her at all. It had been the Swanson twins, who had only made it look like a zombie was out and about to cover up their murderous plans. Probably, they weren't planning on eating her, and given the amount of room she had to wiggle about in, they didn't seem to have shoved her into the grave Ernestine now realized they must have dug as a distraction.

In fact, she had an entire roomful of room in which to move around. A room full of stuff that she kept banging into and bruising herself on.

Which meant she was either locked in an actual room or else this was the biggest, poshest penthouse of a coffin in the world. Since she was betting on a room, Ernestine immediately calmed down a bit.

Not all the way calmed-down, of course. She still had all sorts of problems. Like the fact that she was tied up and gagged. On the bright side, she didn't seem to be blindfolded, after all. If she could find a light switch, she might be able to find a way out of here. Which Ernestine would have liked to have done as quickly as possible before she could think too much about tight, dark places.

Now that she was fully awake and only panicking a little, Ernestine remembered that it had been the Swanson twins who'd attacked her and her family. She appeared to be sitting on some rather dank paving stones, with the cold seeping up through her coat. It was hard to tell, what with not being able to see anything, but the air had a musty chill to it that reminded Ernestine of the basement in MacGillicuddie House.

A bit of wiggling about indicated that Charleston lay

tied up on the cold stone floor next to her. At least, Ernestine assumed the small, lumpy body that groaned when she poked it was Charleston. She supposed it could be anyone really since she couldn't see, but he seemed the likeliest possibility. Where, then, was her mother?

The answer to that came when she felt someone's fingers creeping across her head before locating the ties on her gag and tugging at them. Actually, Ernestine *hoped* those fingers were her mother's. In the dark, all sorts of things seemed possible, including detached-yet-helpful hands that just happened to be wandering around the graveyard, looking for their lost body. Having been unable to find it, perhaps they had followed Ernestine here like a lost puppy.

The gag in her mouth loosened and then sagged as the fingers behind her undid the last knot. Ernestine spat it out and through a tongue that felt as fuzzy as if it had been stuffed with cotton balls, she asked, "Mom?"

Whoever it was mumbled something back through a gag of their own. Following the grunts, Ernestine scooted around, and raising up her bound hands, fumbled about until she found the back of the person's head. From the soft, springy feel of her short curls and the sharp scent of turpentine, Ernestine felt confident it was her mother.

"Ernestine!" her mom cried hoarsely as soon as her gag

fell away. "Are you all right? Is Charleston there somewhere by you?"

"I'm pretty sure Charleston's on the other side of me, but I don't think he's awake yet. As for me—well, I'm tied up and locked in a small room," Ernestine pointed out tightly, panic beginning to creep its way back into her voice. Fear always made Ernestine angry, which was fine with her. If she had to pick between being scared or mad, she'd pick mad every time.

Maya leaned forward and kissed her daughter on top of the head. Well, in the dark, she might have been aiming for Ernestine's cheek, but where her lips ended up was on her head. "I love you, Nestea." Though her hands were still tied, she lifted her fingers up to ruffle Ernestine's hair.

Ernestine collapsed against her mother's side and let herself give in—for a bit—to how good it felt to snuggle there. "I love you, too, Mom."

The body next to her made a snuffling sound as though it wanted to be hugged, too. Unless, of course, the body next to Ernestine was, in fact, Charleston turned into a zombie and he was now begging to be let loose so he could devour them both. Again, in the dark, anything seemed possible.

As Ernestine curled up in a ball, wrapping her bound hands around her knees, Maya pushed past her to untie Charleston's gag.

"Ernestine!" he gasped when he could speak.

"No, it's Maya."

"Oh." Charleston went quiet for a moment. "No offense, Maya. It's just that usually it's Ernestine who helps me."

"Well, there's nothing for me to paint right now," Maya said dryly. "Or at least, if there is, I can't see it."

To Ernestine's horror, a sob welled up in her throat. She tried to strangle it before it could get out, but that also meant she couldn't breathe, which made her even more panicky.

"Ernestine?" Her mom must have been able to feel her shivering because she raised her fingers to stroke Ernestine's hair as best as she could through the ropes. "Oh Nestea, it'll be all right. There's a birthday present for you in my pocket that will help with all of this."

"Birthday present?" Charleston asked. "It's your birthday?"

"It is," Ernestine admitted. Still feeling sore and not quite able to believe Maya hadn't forgotten after all, she said, "You remembered? I thought you forgot."

"Ernestine, I know I get distracted easily. I know I sometimes forget to buy things like milk or to pay the electric bill, but I would *never* forget the best day of my life."

Unaccountably, Ernestine let out a little snuffle, suddenly—for a moment—quite ridiculously pleased in spite of of everything.

"I'll get it." Charleston scooted past Ernestine to feel around for Maya's coat.

"I *hate* the dark." Ernestine sniffled again, her happiness of a moment before quickly swallowed up by the dark as she realized that it was Charleston taking over to get things done, not her. Her stepbrother thought she was always brave and clever, and now he was finding out he was only half right. "I *hate* small places. I can't imagine anything worse than being stuck down in the ground in some tight little coffin!"

"I'm sorry, baby." Her mom hugged her as best as she could. "It's my job to protect you, and this is the second time I've failed you, isn't it?"

"What do you mean?" Charleston asked, still rooting around in Maya's pocket. In the dark, it felt a bit like a very helpful golden retriever was trying to wiggle between Ernestine and her mom. He'd found the package but seemed to be having a hard time yanking it free.

Normally, when Maya brought up the past and Charleston wanted to know about it, Ernestine shut him down. Now, in the dark, the words fell out of her mouth whether she wanted them to or not, and it helped that she couldn't see where they landed. "Mom had this boyfriend named Rocco when I was in kindergarten. He was really awful, but *she* didn't know because he was only ever awful when she wasn't around. He used to shut me up in a really tiny trunk down in the basement when he got mad at me, which was pretty much all the time she wasn't there."

"That's terrible!" Charleston stopped pulling at the package and found Ernestine's fingers, pressing them like he was trying to squeeze all of the bad memories out like toothpaste out of a tube.

"Ernestine, I'm so sorry," her mom said for what had to be about the thousandth time. "I didn't understand. When you told me he was shutting you in, I thought you meant he was giving you a timeout in your room."

"I tried to tell you!" Ernestine tensed up. If she had been a porcupine, all her quills would have popped out, but to her relief, Maya didn't stop hugging her. "I told you it was a really small space!"

"Baby, I'm sorry. I wish that I had asked more questions, but I didn't," her mom said gently.

"Getting shut in there *one* time was enough," Ernestine continued. "So after a few times I hid a fork down in the bottom of the trunk, and the next time he tried to push me in there…I jammed it right up his nose."

"Ernestine!" Charleston cried out, apparently tumbling over backward as he finally tore Ernestine's birthday present free of Maya's pocket. At least, Ernestine assumed that was why one of his sneakers whacked her chin. "You didn't!"

"Oh, yes, she did," her mom said grimly, her arms tightening around her daughter. "And then she jammed it into his leg."

"For future reference during the apocalypse," Ernestine said proudly, beginning to feel a bit better as she remembered the way Rocco had tried, unsuccessfully, to tug the fork out again as he hopped along after her, "it's *very* hard to walk when you have a fork sticking out of your thigh. I ran all the way to the library five blocks away and had the librarian call the police."

"Wow." Charleston was silent for a really long time before saying, "I'm really sorry, Ernestine."

"For what?" Maya asked, working hard to sound brave. "You shouldn't feel bad for Ernestine, Charleston. You should feel *proud* of her. She made a plan, and it was successful. My daughter can do anything, when she puts her mind to it."

"Why do you always say things like that, Mom?" In exasperation, Ernestine wiggled out from underneath her mother's arms, accidentally knocking Charleston over just as he was getting up.

"Oh, *heck*," he muttered. "I dropped the package. It's gotta be here somewhere though, right?"

Pushing themselves onto their hands and knees,

Ernestine and Maya helped him feel about for it on the floor, but Ernestine wasn't about to let up on her mother. "You're always talking about how proud of me you are! Shouldn't you be scared for me?"

"No," Maya said flatly and practically. Ernestine normally thought of her mom as being sort of artsy and oblivious, so it always surprised her how direct she could sometimes be. "Because the important part isn't that something bad happened to you. The important part is that you were able to do something about it. I don't want what other people did to define who you are, Ernestine. I want what *you* do to define you."

Unaccountably, Ernestine felt a glow of pride. Perhaps it was crazy to feel that way right then, considering they were still tied up and locked someplace deep and dark. But Ernestine felt it just the same. They hadn't talked about any of this in years, and so Ernestine had come to think her mom just didn't care.

That hadn't been the case at all. Her mom believed in her. Believed in her strength, her ability to do anything.

As Ernestine realized this, her fingertips encountered something that felt like a brick wrapped in a crinkly paper sack. "I think I found my present. Mom, did you forget my birthday until the last minute and then get me a brick?"

"Ernestine, I would never forget your birthday. We all

decided to surprise you, though this wasn't exactly what we had in mind. Go on and open it."

She tore off the paper sack and ran her fingers over the object inside. It appeared to be made of heavy, durable plastic with both smooth and ridged parts. She could also feel a switch, which, when she pressed it, shone a beam of light directly into Charleston's eyes.

"Ow!" Still tied hand and foot, he keeled over in surprise, scrunching his eyes shut to block out the sudden beam of light.

"Mom! You got me a flashlight!" Ernestine blinked about in a daze, her eyes slowly adjusting to the light.

Maya squinted, too. "I was on the way back from getting it at that twitchy guy's army supply store around the corner when I spotted you two. I'd say that he keeps strange business hours, but given that I have a daughter and stepson who were dragging a goat around a graveyard at eleven o'clock at night, I'm not sure I'm in any position to judge."

"Oh, hey. I hope the goat's all right." Charleston rubbed at his eyes with his bound hands. "Did you see that open grave? I'm not sure the Swanson twins are the only problem we've got. What if our zombie starts eating people?"

"Then at least the goat should be safe."

Shining the flashlight around, Ernestine could see they were definitely stuck in the basement of MacGillicuddie

House, inside the storage compartment belonging to the Swanson twins. Dozens of feathery costumes surrounded them, each one done in duplicate: the two flamingo costumes the Swanson twins had worn on New Year's Eve, two sparkly phoenix costumes, two silky black raven costumes, two birds of paradise costumes, etc. There were also posters advertising the twins' act all over South America, Europe, Africa, and Asia. They seemed to have started dancing and doing acrobatics quite young, as there were also framed pictures of them dancing together from the time they were about three years old.

The girls in those pictures were most definitely the same girls as in the picture Mr. Sangfroid had been carrying around in his pocket.

Ernestine scowled at them before returning her attention to her mom, a big smile erasing her glare. "This is great, Mom. You shouldn't have!"

"Clearly, I should have," Maya said dryly. "If you look in the base of the compartment, you'll find a little survival kit."

As her vision returned, Ernestine popped the bottom off of the flashlight. No wonder it was so much bigger and heavier than an ordinary flashlight. Inside a little drawer, she found a compass, a small pair of binoculars, and a Swiss Army knife.

"I suggested it," Charleston said proudly, scooting upright again. "I thought you might need them in the coming zombie war."

"Mom, Charleston, you're geniuses, both of you!" Ernestine wished she could hug them both. Of all the moms and stepbrothers in the whole wide world, there weren't any others with whom she'd want to face either twin murderers *or* the apocalypse.

As Ernestine used the knife to saw through her mother's ropes, Maya said, "What I don't understand is why Libby and Mora attacked us to begin with."

"Oh, that's easy." As her mother's ropes fell apart, Ernestine handed her the knife so Maya could cut through Ernestine's bonds. "They're trying to murder Mrs. MacGillicuddie, of course. They've also been making it seem like there was a zombie wandering around the neighborhood, too."

"What?" Appalled, Maya stopped sawing at Ernestine's ropes. "Why?"

"Well, they're impersonating a zombie to make it easier to sneak around and get away with murder."

"Yes, well, I did mean the murdering part when I asked why," Maya said dryly, resuming her work.

"Oh." Personally, Ernestine was quite offended by the zombie part, given they'd gotten her hopes up that she'd actually managed to raise one. The ropes had frayed enough for Ernestine to finish freeing her hands by yanking them apart. She fished Mr. Sangfroid's photo out of his pocket. "They're trying to murder Mrs. MacGillicuddie because *they're* the lost MacGillicuddie heiresses!"

Ernestine's deduction did not meet with the astonished gasps she felt it deserved.

Instead, Maya finished untying the ropes around her feet before taking the photo from her daughter and raising a skeptical eyebrow. "The what now?"

As she untied her own feet, Ernestine quickly filled Maya in on Mrs. MacGillicuddie's story about her husband's mysterious sister who had gone missing as a child down in Rio de Janeiro. The one the MacGillicuddie family had thought was a monster.

"Only there wasn't one little girl, there were two!" Ernestine explained, pointing at the ribbons. "See, these are in the wrong places to be reflections! The mirror must have broken, and after they took out the glass, someone must have thought it would be funny to position them so that they're looking at each other."

"I think you're right about the girls," Maya agreed, "but what could possibly have been so monstrous about them that the MacGillicuddie family would abandon them?"

"Um, a little help over here?" Charleston raised his hands to remind them that they were still tied together.

"Oh, sorry." Embarrassed, Ernestine turned her attention to freeing him. In the zombie apocalypse, it was very important not to leave your friends tied up unless you were planning on using them as zombie bait because you needed a distraction.

Hmmm.

Ernestine looked at Charleston. Charleston looked at her looking at him and clearly didn't like what he saw. "Hey, why are you looking at me like that?"

Ernestine glanced down at the knife in her hands. Then she sat back down on her heels.

In rising alarm, Charleston demanded, "Why are you looking at me like that? Maya, why is she looking at me like that?"

"I'm sorry, Charleston." With a truly apologetic grimace, Ernestine tucked the knife back into the compartment in the flashlight's base. "But we need a distraction."

"What do you mean, you need a distraction!" Charleston's voice continued to spiral upward with hysteria. Diving forward, Ernestine clapped a hand over his mouth.

"Did you hear that?" she hissed.

All three of them went very still. In the distance, a rusty

scraping sound warned that someone had opened and shut the basement door far away on the other side of the house.

Going very still, Ernestine listened. In the silence, she heard high heeled shoes tap-tap-tap toward them.

Ernestine stuffed the gag back into Charleston's mouth before he could protest further.

"I'm *really* sorry, Charleston," she whispered as he tried to call her names through the cloth in his mouth. "But I need them to think for a second that we're all still tied up. And if they see *you* there, they might think *we've* just wiggled off to the side. Which we sort of will be."

Shoving the flashlight into her mom's startled hands, Ernestine snatched up one of the Swanson twins' stiletto heels for protection.

"Ernestine! What are you planning on doing?" her mom asked in a low, urgent voice.

"Turn off the light, then hide on one side of the door, and I'll hide on the other." Ernestine pushed her mom toward the door. "When they open it, they'll see Charleston, and it will take them a second to realize what's going on. While they're looking at you, *we* attack."

"Oh, this sounds like a very bad idea." However, Maya must not have been able to come up with anything better because she did as Ernestine said and snapped off the light.

The door flew open, haloing one of the Swanson twins with the dull light from the single bulb outside.

"What—" she began, her eyes widening in shock as she took in Charleston.

Whatever else she was going to say was lost as Ernestine launched herself forward, swinging the stiletto heel down onto the twin's head.

The woman staggered backward but did not fall down. In one hand she held a wicked-looking syringe, the type doctors use to give painful injections. Turning her attention on Ernestine, her eyes narrowed. *"You."*

"And me." Leaping out from behind the door, Maya brought the flashlight crashing down onto the Swanson twin's head. This time, the other woman collapsed onto the floor. Her fingers went limp, and the syringe rolled out of them.

Ernestine and Maya looked down at the unconscious woman on the floor. She wore a zombie costume, though the sparkly stiletto heels on her feet somewhat ruined the effect.

"Do you think she's dead?" Ernestine asked.

Maya checked her pulse. "No, she's still alive. I'll keep an eye on her while you untie Charleston."

Ernestine did as her mother said. As Charleston spat out his gag and she removed the ropes around his hands and ankles, he said bitterly, "Bait! I can't believe you used me as bait!"

"If it's any comfort, you were very good bait," Ernestine reassured him.

"I was?"

"Sure." Ernestine gave him a hand getting up. "And in the zombie apocalypse, I bet you could make good money renting yourself out as bait."

Together, they went over to Maya and looked down at whichever Swanson twin had come to finish them off.

"What do you think is in the needle?" Charleston asked.

"Something horrible." Maya smashed it beneath her heel as the ceiling above them shook and the sound of something breaking tinkled down through the floorboards.

"Mrs. MacGillicuddie!" Ernestine cried and took off through the darkened basement, her mom and Charleston close behind. Bursting out into the foyer, they heard a faint scuffling sound inside Mrs. MacGillicuddie's half of the floor, followed by a muffled scream. The door to her apartment hung open, the latch broken.

"Go call the police!" Ernestine hissed, grabbing Charleston as he tried to follow Maya into the apartment. Ernestine had already put him in enough danger for one night and wanted him safely out of the path of murderers (and possibly—but not probably—zombies). She pushed him back toward the stairs. "And then bang on every door! Wake everybody up!"

"What are you going to do?" Charleston cried, clinging to the bannister as she tried to force him upward.

"Stop a murder, of course!" Letting go of her stepbrother, Ernestine ran into Mrs. MacGillicuddie's apartment. It was pitch black inside, the heavy velvet curtains blocking out the neighborhood lights.

"*Whoa!*" Almost immediately, Ernestine tripped over something large and squishy that should not be lying in the middle of the room like an animal-skin rug. Flicking the lights on, she saw that it was an unconscious Lyndon, a gun in his hand and gash in his forehead big enough to cause the world's worst headache once he woke up.

After checking his pulse to confirm that he would, in fact, wake up eventually, Ernestine vaulted over the settee, only to once again land on something *else* large and squishy.

As Ernestine's legs collapsed from beneath her, a very frightened Aurora Borealis jumped up, grabbed a Ming vase, and raised it threateningly.

"I'll bash your head in if you try to kill me!" she shrieked. Then, realizing it was just Ernestine blinking up at her, she lowered the vase in relief. "Oh, it's just you."

"It's just me," Ernestine agreed, getting up. "What are you doing here?"

"Almost getting murdered, that's what! By those crazy

Swanson twins!" Both her clothes and her hair were in wild disarray, and her Instagram followers would have been shocked by her lack of makeup. They might (or might not) have been even more shocked by the blood pouring down the side of her face. "Lyndon and I got an urgent text from Grammy saying she needed to see us about our inheritance. When I got here, I found them standing over Lyndon, putting a gun in his hand while he was lying there unconscious or dead or whatever. When they saw me, they shot me, too! Well, it hit that vase of flowers instead, but I pretended like the bullet hit me."

"You're bleeding." Ernestine thought she should probably point that out just in case Aurora Borealis hadn't noticed it.

"One of the vase shards got me." Aurora Borealis dug the chunk out of her hair and offered it to Ernestine as though she thought she might like a souvenir. Ernestine held up a hand to indicate that she would pass.

Before either one of them could say or do anything else, one of the interior doors burst open, allowing a wild melee to pour out of it. Both Mrs. MacGillicuddie and Eduardo struggled to pry a gun out of the hands of the remaining Swanson twin, while Maya tugged her backward. It was as though the three of them thought their assailant was the rope in a fun game of tug-of-war.

Aurora Borealis shrieked and threw the vase at them. However, rather than taking out the would-be murderer, she clonked Eduardo on the head just as he managed to get the gun out of the twin's hand. Both butler and gun clattered to the floor, leaving the firearm up for grabs.

"Eduardo!" Mrs. MacGillicuddie shrieked but didn't let go of the Swanson twin.

"Oh, *heck.*" Aurora Borealis peered down at the fallen manservant. "I missed."

With a shriek of her own and a mighty wrench, the Swanson twin shoved both Mrs. MacGillicuddie and Maya away from her. Ernestine's mother tripped over the piano bench and landed on the floor with a cry of pain as she clutched at her knee.

"Mom!" Ernestine leaped over the settee to get to her, bringing them both to the attention of the remaining Swanson twin. She wore the remains of a zombie costume, though Mrs. MacGillicuddie had torn most of it off.

"*You.* What have you done with Libby?" Wig half-hanging off her head, zombie sores dangling from her face and neck, she picked up the gun and turned to advance on Ernestine.

"Not let her murder me." Ernestine jutted her chin out defiantly and clenched her fists. Mora might shoot her, but she wasn't going to cower. "What did Mrs. MacGillicuddie ever do to you and Libby, anyhow? It isn't her fault that her husband's family was so awful to you."

That drew Mora up short. For a moment, she was struck as dumb as the zombie she was impersonating. Behind her, Mrs. MacGillicuddie got shakily to her feet. She had a green mud mask on her face and the glint in her eyes said that *somebody* might die tonight but it might not be who the Swanson twins had intended.

"So, you figured out who we really are." Mora cackled bitterly and yanked off the wig and wiped the remaining zombie makeup from her face. "It was that photo Sangfroid had, wasn't it?"

"That, and the halos you wore tonight. The way you both wanted to wear them on the same side of your heads." Behind Mora, Mrs. MacGillicuddie used a tea towel to wipe the goop off her face. Then she put a pair of giant, dangly diamond earrings in her ears, rather like a soldier donning armor for battle. "You still haven't answered my question: what did Mrs. MacGillicuddie ever do to you?"

"Why, took our inheritance, of course!" Mora waved the gun about as she spoke. Eduardo had started to get up, but the gun accidentally went off. The bullet passed through a taxidermied parrot inside a glass dome. As feathers and shards rained down upon him, Eduardo had the good sense to drop to the floor again. "Libby and I should have inherited part of the MacGillicuddie fortune when Mummy and Daddy died. Instead, they abandoned us at an orphanage in the mountains above Rio de Janeiro!"

"Why?" Maya gasped, clutching her knee. The lower half of her leg stuck out at a strange angle, and Ernestine worried that it was broken.

"Because..." Mora paused dramatically. Lowering the gun, she used her free hand to lift her shirt to reveal a long scar across her stomach and hip. "We were conjoined twins!"

Goodness. Her revelation had the intended effect: it brought everyone up short. Mrs. MacGillicuddie froze in surprise just as she had lifted up a vase of flowers to smash down onto Mora's head. Meanwhile, both Eduardo and Aurora Borealis sat upright to get a better look at the scar. Only Lyndon, still unconscious and therefore as oblivious as usual, missed out on this turn of events.

"In that picture, it looks like we're leaning against each other, but we weren't. We were *still connected together*. Our parents were horrified by it and ashamed of us. So they abandoned us and cut us out of their will! We wouldn't even have known the truth of who we are if one of our old nannies hadn't looked for us and told us everything."

"But—but—" Maya blinked in puzzlement. "But there's

nothing wrong with being a conjoined twin! That's like them abandoning you because you had freckles!"

"The MacGillicuddies were *awful* people, darling," Mrs. MacGillicuddie interjected, swinging the vase toward Mora, who just managed to duck out of the way in time. The vase shattered against the floor, but it at least knocked the pistol out of Mora's hand before it did so.

"Drat." Realizing she'd never be able to snatch it up again in time, Mora began to grapple hand-to-hand with Mrs. MacGillicuddie instead.

"You think *you* had a hard time of it?" Mrs. MacGillicuddie shrieked. "*I* had to live with my husband for nearly forty years before he had the decency to kick the bucket!"

"None of you deserve any of this money!" Libby burst into the room. Still wearing her zombie disguise and looking considerably the worse for wear for having been knocked out, she swayed from side to side as she advanced forward. "It should all be ours! We've had to work for a living all these years, dancing our way across six continents! All the while, you miserable lot have been living in the lap of luxury!"

"Oh, heck," Ernestine sighed to her mother. "We should have tied her up."

"Well, there was a lot going on." Maya said tensely. "Next time we'll know to do it."

Libby reached over to grab the pistol out of Lyndon's hand, but he chose that moment to regain consciousness. Sitting upright, he knocked her over without even meaning to. As she toppled over the ottoman, stiletto shoes up in the air, he looked about in confusion and asked, "What's going on?"

"What's going on? *What's going on?*" Mora repeated, her voice growing more shrill with each repetition.

"Yes, that's what I asked." Lyndon didn't seem to understand why she was so irate. Then he looked down and noticed the gun looped in his fingers. With a girlish shriek, he tossed it off to the side as though it were a spider he'd found crawling on his hand. As it landed, it went off, shooting a bullet into the fancy ceiling light dangling above.

"You fool! How we're related to you, I don't know!" Pushing herself up onto her hands and knees, Libby snatched up the fallen gun. Leaning across the ottoman like she was some sort of elderly sharpshooter, she pointed it straight at Mrs. MacGillicuddie. "We're framing you for your family's murder!"

Mrs. MacGillicuddie finally managed to get the upper hand against Mora and spun her about so that the other woman's body was blocking her own. "You'll have to shoot your own sister first!"

Libby's gun wavered, but she didn't put it down.

"Libby?" Mora gasped.

"I think the bullet would only nick your arm, Mora. Don't be such a baby!"

Mora gasped again. "You were always jealous that I was the nuns' favorite!"

"You were not! They just took pity on you because you were the less-pretty one!"

"*Was* I? Sangfroid only ever dated you after *I* turned him down!"

Maya, Ernestine, Eduardo, and Aurora Borealis all whipped their heads back and forth, watching this exchange and wondering if it made them all more or less likely to end up dead within the next few minutes. Then a new voice caught everyone's attention.

"Mom? Auntie Libby?" Dill walked into the room, a bag of groceries in his hands. Spotting his mom with Mrs. MacGillicuddie's arms wrapped around her and his aunt waving a gun about, he pulled up short, appalled. "What's going on?"

"*Mom?*" Maya and Mrs. MacGillicuddie repeated in astonishment, while Eduardo and Aurora Borealis gasped, "*Auntie Libby?*" Lyndon didn't seem either more surprised or confused than usual. Possibly because he always seemed surprised and confused by life.

"I told you not to call me that!" Mora snapped, still struggling to escape Mrs. MacGillicuddie's grasp. "And Mommy's busy right now, Dilly darling."

"But, um, I...got your text saying you'd found the money to help me open my restaurant." Hands shaking, Dill pulled out a bottle of organic carbonated apple cider. "I, uh, came over to celebrate. But, um, Auntie Libby, why are you pointing a gun at my mom?"

"They're trying to murder me!" Mrs. MacGillicuddie snapped, apparently annoyed at not being the center of attention.

"Oh, that can't be right." Dill clutched the bottle of cider to his chest, more appalled than ever as Charleston skidded into the room with Mr. Ellington.

Taking advantage of the distraction, Ernestine lunged forward as her mom cried out, "Ernestine, no!"

Before anyone else could react, Ernestine threw herself across the ottoman and on top of Libby Swanson. This time, the gun skidded underneath the settee, which should at least have made it a bit harder for anyone to retrieve it. In Ernestine's opinion, this was a huge improvement in their situation as she would much rather deal with a murderer who *didn't* have a gun than one who did.

Unfortunately, the force of her impact with Libby had

rolled them both over and over, with Libby ending up on top of her when they stopped next to a gold and ebony desk.

"You." Libby snatched a letter opener off a table and lifted it up like a dagger. Ernestine managed to dodge the first blow, but the second one tore through the winter coat she still wore. "You ruin everything!"

"I do *not!*" Ernestine shot back in outrage, trying to free her legs so she could kick at her attacker. "*I* make things more interesting!"

"Not for much longer, you don't." With a triumphant smile, Libby grabbed Ernestine's wrists with one hand and pinned them down. She held up the pointed letter opener so Ernestine could get a good look at it as she bent closer. Behind her, Mora threw off Mrs. MacGillicuddie and rushed to her sister's side, apparently pleased that they were *finally* going to be successful in murdering *somebody.*

Then, suddenly, a cane whizzed through the air, knocking Libby into Mora and the letter opener to the floor. On one good leg, Maya staggered toward them. She had grabbed up Mrs. MacGillicuddie's cane from where she had long ago lost it in the scuffle. Ernestine scrambled out of the way, taking refuge over by the umbrella stand. As Mr. Ellington and Charleston helped Aurora Borealis, Lyndon, and Eduardo out of the room, Libby shot a hand under the settee and yanked out the gun.

Well, so much for Ernestine's theory that no one would be able to get it.

"Stop right there, all of you!" Libby spat, Mora peering evilly over her shoulder.

Everyone in the room froze.

Everyone, except for Ernestine. Who suddenly remembered the shotgun she'd tucked into the umbrella stand the other day.

And who also remembered how this whole unfortunate business had started.

Wrenching the shotgun out of the umbrella stand, she aimed it up at the ceiling and blasted the light fixture Lyndon had only nicked.

For the second time in a week, a chandelier plunged to the ground in MacGillicuddie House.

This time, it did not miss its target.

In an explosion of crystal shards, Libby and Mora Swanson ended up trapped inside the metal frame, which had pinned them to the floor like a birdcage.

The gun spun away, only to be stopped by Eduardo's foot as he peered back into the room from around the doorframe.

Aurora Borealis rushed back in for her grandmother. For a moment, the two just looked at each other. Then, for the first time ever, Aurora Borealis took out her phone and proudly took a selfie with her grandmother.

Startled, Mrs. MacGillicuddie posed glamorously. For all their age difference, the two looked a great deal alike. As Ernestine sat, dazed, on the floor, she wondered for the first time if perhaps Aurora Borealis would be a great deal more likable when she was eighty.

Turning to Ernestine, Mrs. MacGillicuddie beamed. "I do love an exciting Valentine's Day, don't you?"

Chapter Fourteen
All's Well That Ends Well, Unless You're Dead or in Prison

SATURDAY, 10:38 PM

As it turned out, not only was no one murdered, but no one had forgotten Ernestine's birthday after all. They had just been planning the most amazing surprise party for her in the world.

True, it also doubled as a gallery opening, but that didn't bother Ernestine. And also true, neither a zombie apocalypse nor murder-most-foul occurred during it, which Ernestine normally would have found quite boring. However, for once she was more than happy to just sit back and enjoy the evening, leaving all of the details to other people.

The party had a "Cleopatra, Queen of the Nile" theme. Which meant fancy costumes for everyone, and the fanciest of them all for Ernestine, who loved her sleek black wig and gorgeous golden dress. She also loved the edible vegan pyramids made out of crostini Dill provided for his newfound great-aunt, as well as the nonvegan sphinx that Mr. Talmadge made out of various kinds of ham. She loved the Hep Cats dressed up as princes of Egypt as they wailed away on their instruments in the corner. She loved Mr. Theda, dressed up by Mr. Bara as Set, while Mr. Bara himself came as Ra. She loved that Mr. Price and Principal Langenderfer from school came in costume. She even loved grumpy Mr. Sangfroid, who'd finally been released from the hospital in time to get dressed up as a very wrinkly Marc Antony.

In other words, pretty much an ordinary, everyday party as far as Mrs. MacGillicuddie was concerned.

"I have to admit, this is the strangest case I've ever worked on," Detective Kim admitted as he sat next to Ernestine. Alone among the guests, he was dressed in a very boring suit and tie, having stopped by to wrap up some loose ends with Mrs. MacGillicuddie and gotten swept up into the party along the way. In fact, he was the one who had persuaded Mr. Sangfroid to wear the Marc Antony costume

Mrs. MacGillicuddie had picked out for him by pointing out that technically he could be charged with interfering with an investigation for holding back what he knew about the Swanson twins.

"It wasn't like I had any idea that they were going to try to murder us both!" Mr. Sangfroid snapped at Mrs. MacGillicuddie by way of apology. "I knew they were up to something the minute that old album fell out of the attic. When I saw that picture of Libitina and Morana, I recognized it right away. Libby had her own copy of it, given to her by the nuns at the orphanage. She kept it on the fireplace mantel back when we were seeing each other all those years ago. She and Mora hated their parents for abandoning them, but I didn't know who their family was until I saw that photo and put two and two together. I knew they must have been some sort of MacGillicuddie relation, so it seemed like enough to blackmail—er, *persuade*—Libby to go on one last date with me. For old times' sake."

"Instead, they decided to frame him for your murder," Detective Kim explained to Mrs. MacGillicuddie, helping himself to one of the thirteen different cakes Charleston had helped Mrs. Talmadge make for the occasion—one for every year of Ernestine's life. "They knocked him out in the garden before they broke into your apartment. When things went wrong in there, they still stuck to the rest of their plan. They shoved his head into the pond, making it look like he'd tripped as he escaped. Then, they planted the zombie clothes on him, though with you after them, Ernestine, they had to rush and left two right shoes next to him rather than a left and a right, along with the photo they'd meant to take off of him."

"Why not just shove him into the water before they broke in?" Ernestine asked, causing Mr. Sangfroid to shoot her an outraged look that she ignored. "Wouldn't it have been less risky to kill him first rather than risking he might wake up?"

"They didn't know how long they'd be in Mrs. MacGillicuddie's apartment and were worried that we would figure out that he died before she did. You can't murder someone if you're already dead," Detective Kim said cheerfully. He took a bite of his cake and looked astonished by its deliciousness.

"But if the plan was to get all of the other MacGillicuddie heirs out of the way, what were they going to do about Rodney, Aurora Borealis, and Lyndon?" Charleston asked, quite pleased by how much everyone was enjoying his cakes.

"After Mrs. MacGillicuddie was dead, they planned on making it look like Lyndon offed his uncle and cousin in a quarrel over his inheritance. Then, with all three of them out of the way, they planned to come forward to claim the MacGillicuddie fortune. The same nanny who found them in Brazil also brought them their birth certificates."

"So the Swanson twins used their acrobatic skills to climb up the side of the house and break into Mr. Theda and Mr. Bara's apartment and steal the zombie makeup," Ernestine surmised.

"They also used the crowbar to make it look like someone from outside the house had broken in through the laundry room window, in case anyone became suspicious about how the chandelier came to fall. At that point, they were planning on making it look like Rodney had killed his mother. But then they saw Mr. Sangfroid take the photo album at the Mardi Gras party, so they had themselves a new victim to frame."

"The very idea!" Rodney interjected, puffing out his chest beneath the bejeweled pharaoh's collar he wore. "We may fight all of the time, but she's still my mother!"

"They also snuck through your parents' apartment earlier in the day to loosen the screws holding the chandelier to the attic floor. If you recall, they were the ones who told Mr. Talmadge that Dill had commissioned one of your stepfather's sculptures. They did it knowing that Mr. Talmadge's competitiveness with Dill would drive him to commission one, too. Then they used the cover of all the noise Frank was making with his power tools to sneak through your apartment and get to the storage attic on the other side. Then, they used the bad blood between Dill and Mr. Talmadge to instigate the fight that got everyone out in the foyer and Mrs. MacGillicuddie beneath the booby-trapped chandelier," Detective Kim explained.

"What I don't understand is how they had time to make it out the back gate, back into the house, and up onto that tightrope from the time we saw them in the garden to the time we made it to the foyer," Ernestine said crossly, not at all liking that she hadn't been able to figure that part out.

"Oh, that wasn't them." Surprised, Detective Kim set his fork down. "They'd jimmied the laundry room window open earlier in the evening. That must have been someone else you saw go out the gate. One of the other partygoers, probably."

"Hm, maybe." Ernestine still didn't like it.

"They also said they didn't dig up the grave in the cemetery," the detective continued, dabbing his lips with a napkin.

Before Ernestine could open her mouth to ask him whether they'd found a body somewhere down in that grave, Dill cut in with an objection.

"But—but—the video from my grocery store showed that they walked up from the direction of the Palace

Theater a few minutes after Mrs. MacGillicuddie was attacked by the zombie!"

Understandably, he still seemed to be in a state of shock over discovering that not only were his mother and aunt would-be murderers, but he had a much larger family full of awful relatives than he'd realized. He was so upset that he'd even absentmindedly eaten a piece of ham, which he'd promptly spewed out again into a potted palm.

"I'm afraid that your mother and aunt planned that as well," Detective Kim said gently, laying a hand on Dill's shoulder as he got up to go. "After they planted the evidence on Mr. Sangfroid, they ran through the alleyway and went in the back door to the Palace Theater. Then, they came right out the front again, making it look like they'd been there the whole time and were just leaving. Mr. Talmadge just assumed that the reason they were sweaty and out of breath was because they'd been practicing their routine."

"I just can't believe my mother and Auntie Libby would do something like this." Dill said as the detective left. Charleston shoved a piece of vegan chocolate cake in his direction to cheer him up. He'd helped Mr. Talmadge make it as a peace offering for Dill, but the grocer looked down at it as though he couldn't figure out what on earth it was. Like the whole experience had zapped his brain.

"Oh, *darling*. I keep saying, the whole family is awful." Mrs. MacGillicuddie waved her carrot juice cocktail about dismissively. Eduardo lounged nearby, and, like Ernestine, he was letting other people do the work for once, having had a rough enough week himself. He lay on a dais as attendants surrounded him, waving peacock fans and offering him radish canapés shaped like lotus leaves. "Don't worry. You'll get used to it. Half of the MacGillicuddies tried to murder the other half at some point in their lives."

"They never would have tried to hurt the rest of you, if it wasn't for me." Dill hung his head miserably. "They knew I needed money to expand my grocery store into a proper restaurant."

"Now, now. It does no good to think like that." Mrs. MacGillicuddie patted his hand and then shoved a forkful of cake in his mouth. Immediately, Dill brightened a bit. "If they had just *asked,* I'd have been *more* than happy to just *hand* them wads of cash! As it is, I'll have to pay for an excellent lawyer to get them off. Can't have *family* sitting in jail. Things will be *much* more interesting if they're out and about, plotting awful things! Just imagine all of the jolly holidays we'll have together! Won't it be *thrilling?*"

"Mother!" Rodney protested, prompting Charleston to plunk a piece of cake down in front of him, too. "They tried to frame me for your murder!"

"You framed yourself, actually," Eduardo pointed out gently from his dais. "They were trying to frame Aurora Borealis when you confessed."

Rodney went bright red in the face but turned to his daughter, reaching over to give her hand a squeeze. "I didn't know if you did it, Aurora, but either way, I wasn't about to let you rot away in some prison."

"Oh, Daddy." For once, Aurora put down her phone and gave his hand a squeeze back. "If I was going to murder someone, I'd make sure to tell you first so you wouldn't worry. You've always been there for me, especially when I need a lawyer but even when I don't. I love you."

"I love you, too, Aurora." Beaming with pride, Rodney gave his daughter a hug. Well, as much of a hug as his naturally stiff nature and his uncomfortable costume allowed.

"You see, Rodney darling, I was right to let the nannies raise you," Mrs. MacGillicuddie said cheerfully. "They taught you much better parenting skills than I ever would have! I love you, too, you know."

"And yet you didn't hire a lawyer for *me*, Mother!" Letting go of his daughter so she could scoop up her phone again,

Rodney turned back to Mrs. MacGillicuddie, his moustache quivering with outrage. "*I* had to have my own come and bail me out! If that strange Montgomery family hadn't intervened, both you and Aurora Borealis would be dead, Lyndon and I would be locked up in prison, and those terrible aunts of ours would be able to contest Granddaddy's original will without anyone left to fight them!"

"My last name is Wheeler, actually," Charleston pointed out. "Not Montgomery."

"I was getting around to bailing you out, my darling boy, I swear! You'd only *just* been arrested, you know! You always were terribly impatient." Mrs. MacGillicuddie waved her hand dismissively. Then, seeing the continued hurt on her son's face, she softened just a bit. "Rodney, I do love you, but it's just how we MacGillicuddies are. We wouldn't *be* Mac-Gillicuddies if we didn't let each other stew in jail a bit from time to time. At least we *aren't* trying to murder each other. That's a bit of an improvement over previous generations, don't you think?"

She reached over and took her son's hand just like he had taken his daughter's a minute ago. They didn't squeeze them or hug, but for the first time since Ernestine had known them, they did look at each other with genuine affection.

Taking advantage of the calm, Charleston finally just

wheeled an entire cake over to their table and handed everyone in Mrs. MacGillicuddie's family forks. They all immediately dug in, Mrs. MacGillicuddie included.

It looked like things were pretty much back to normal
for Mrs. MacGillicuddie and her family. Well, *their* version of
normal, anyhow. At least the psychiatrist Rodney had hired
to prove that his mother was insane was happy as a clam,
having gathered enough research on the psychosis of the
MacGillicuddie family to write a book.

Much, much later that night, they all returned home
exhausted. Charleston fell right to sleep, and for once, her
parents didn't stay up creating weird stuff out of old dish-
washer springs and automobile fenders. Ernestine climbed
into bed in her pajamas, but just as her head hit the pillow, she realized she hadn't put out fresh hay for the goat.
Which now lived in the vintage Mustang convertible Mrs.
MacGillicuddie stored in the carriage house along with
her limo.

Getting out of bed with a resentful groan, she pulled
on her boots and winter coat and trudged sleepily out to
the carriage house. The swans, chickens, and peacocks
cooed at her in a rather charming sort of way as she raked
the old hay out of the backseat of the Mustang and added
in some clean hay. On the other hand, the goat tried to eat

her coat, her hair, her boots, *and* her hand, but that was a goat for you.

A clattering out in the alleyway made her freeze for a moment. Then, pitchfork in hand, Ernestine let herself out the back door into the alleyway beyond. Something shadowy rooted through the garbage cans. Under normal circumstances, Ernestine would have assumed it was a homeless person and offered to bring him or her out something fresher. Quite frankly, though, her nerves were shot, which is why she banged her pitchfork against the dumpster and shouted, "Hey! *Oi!* No trespassing!"

The figure looked up in terror. In equal terror, Ernestine fell backward against the brick wall. The face looking up at her was half-decayed, the skin around the eye sockets pulled back to show rather a lot of eyeball with a tooth or two showing through where the cheek should be. Leftover roses from Fluffy-Wuffy-Kins's funeral jutted out of its mouth, showering its tie-dye shirt with white petals.

Rather than attacking and sucking out her brain, the zombie squealed and shuffled off as fast as it could in the other direction.

The shadowy figure that had darted out the gate that first night. The open grave last night. The figure she had seen in the alleyway.

So they really hadn't been part of the Swanson twins' plan after all.

For a long time, Ernestine just slumped against the wall, heart pounding. Eventually, she pulled her notebook and pen out of her coat pocket. Carefully, she made a note: *They're as afraid of us as we are of them.*

It looked like the apocalypse was back on.

ACKNOWLEDGMENTS

Thank you to my husband, Sean, for his unfailing patience and support, as well as for continuing to send this book out to agents when my willingness to believe it would ever get published finally gave out. His insistence on believing in my dream even when I didn't led me to the next person I need to thank — my wonderful agent, Heather Flaherty. Heather's enthusiasm, support, and fine eye for detail were invaluable in ensuring that Ernestine get the attention she deserves. Thank you to the amazing team at Jimmy as well, from Jenny Bak to Sasha Henriques, for their many invaluable observations and suggestions. Thank you to Sara Yaklin for loving Ernestine long before anyone else did. Finally, thank you to whoever first combined chocolate with sugar. I couldn't have written this book without you!

MERRILL WYATT lives in Toledo, Ohio, with her husband, daughter, three cats, and a hamster who might possibly be an immortal magician. She spent far too much of her childhood wandering around cemeteries and old Victorian homes. She is dollphobic and donut-obsessed, and she owns too many pairs of shoes.